Dear Little Black Dress Reader,

Thanks for picking up this Little Black Dress book, one of the great new titles from our series of fun, page-turning romance novels. Lucky you — you're about to have a fantastic romantic read that we know you won't be able to put down!

Why don't you make your Little Black Dress experience even better by logging on to

www.littleblackdressbooks.com

where you can:

- ♥ Enter our **monthly competitions** to win **gorgeous** prizes
- ♥ Get **hot-off-the-press** news about our latest titles
- ♥ Read **exclusive** preview chapters both from your **favourite** authors and from brilliant new writing talent
- ♥ Buy **up-and-coming** books online
- ♥ Sign up for an essential slice of romance via our **fortnightly email** newsletter

We love nothing more than to curl up and indulge in an addictive romance, and so we're delighted to welcome into the Little Black Dress club!

With love from,

The *little black dress* team

1. Growing up, I didn't like to read. I liked to play tetherball and wanted to be a tetherball champion.

2. I have a deadly fear of grasshoppers.

3. I am a shoe-aholic. I think ugly shoes are an abomination of biblical proportion.

4. I love to read the tabloids. Especially the ones featuring stories such as Bat Boy and women having Big Foot's baby.

5. I write romance novels, but I hate overly sentimental movies and sappy love songs.

Lola Carlyle Reveals All

Rachel Gibson

little
black
dress

Published by arrangement with AVON
An imprint of HARPERCOLLINS PUBLISHERS, USA

First published in 2002
by AVON BOOKS
An imprint of HARPERCOLLINS PUBLISHERS, USA

First published in Great Britain in 2008
by LITTLE BLACK DRESS
An imprint of HEADLINE PUBLISHING GROUP

A LITTLE BLACK DRESS paperback

1

978 0 7553 3741 5

Typeset in Transit511BT by Avon DataSet Ltd,
Bidford-on-Avon, Warwickshire

Printed and bound in Great Britain by Clays Ltd, St Ives plc

HEADLINE PUBLISHING GROUP
An Hachette Livre UK Company
338 Euston Road
London NW1 3BH

www.littleblackdressbooks.com
www.headline.co.uk

With much thanks and appreciation
to the Thursday night girls:
Laura Lee Guhrke, Jill Hill, and Cathie Wilson.
You make me laugh
and keep me relatively sane.

Acknowledgments

I would like to express my thanks to the following people who helped during the writing of this book: Floyd and Gloria Skinner, for sharing their knowledge of yachting with me; Coast Guard Petty Officer Mike Brock, for taking my call and answering all my questions; and the many authors of the many research books that I pored through in the writing of this book.

Prologue

Of all the humiliations Lola Carlyle had suffered in her life – and the list was quite long and juicy – seeing her naked pictures on the Internet was without a doubt the worst. Anyone with a modem and a credit card could view fifteen different photos of her in the buff. Each one a bit more embarrassing than the last. Knowing that they were out there was a constant disgrace, a weight on her shoulders, an anvil on her head pressing into her skull.

The photographs had been taken of her several years ago by her ex-fiancé, Sam The Jerk. Sam, the guy who'd always professed his unending love, the guy who'd told her she could trust him with anything, had used her photographs to bail himself out of his financial problems. Four years after their breakup, he'd developed *www.lolarevealed.com* and had created the source of Lola's biggest shame.

In the past, Lola had posed for professional photographers – too many times to count. But Sam was an investment banker, and he'd shot the pictures with a disposable Kodak he'd picked up on a munchie run. In a moment she could only look back on and attribute to complete insanity, she'd allowed him to snap a series of butt-naked photos of her in his bed, riding his stationary bike, and sitting in the middle of his kitchen table chowing on candy bars and bags of Doritos.

The absolute worst photograph had been taken of her kissing a king-sized Tootsie Roll. At the time, the pictures had been meant to be funny, a silly joke on her career, for which she never ate anything that wasn't baked, broiled, or tossed in zero-calorie dressing. Never ate anything fattening that wasn't routinely purged from her body.

What the photographs hadn't shown was the sickness that had begun right after she'd binged on all that junk food. The vicious cycle of guilt that always began after her total loss of control. The panic that she might have gained an ounce, which always sent her straight to the treadmill or the toilet.

It was a compulsion she now controlled, but at one time it had almost taken her life. Even now, every time she looked at the old images of her five-foot-eleven, one-hundred-and-ten-pound body, it triggered the voice in her head that told her she should skip lunch, or it urged her to visit the Colonel and order a bucket of chicken, mashed potatoes and gravy, and a diet Coke.

Worse than the humiliation of those tacky pictures appearing on the Internet for the world to see was the knowledge that there wasn't anything she could do about them. And she'd tried. She'd begged Sam to give her the photos and to remove them from the net. She'd offered him money, but even after all this time, he was still so bitter about their breakup, he'd refused. She'd hired an attorney and was told what she basically already knew. Sam owned the photographs and he could publish them wherever he liked.

She'd taken him to court anyway, and she'd promptly lost.

Her only option now was to hire a hit man. A choice she might actually consider if she knew beforehand that she wouldn't get caught, humiliating herself and her family further. Because in a family filled with fairly prolific sinners, Lola had always been the biggest black sheep. Which was quite an accomplishment when one considered Uncle Jed's recent troubles. None of them had spent time in the penitentiary, though county jail, yes. Pen, no. And seeing her in prison orange just might finally do her poor mother in.

Lola reached for the tabloid she'd tucked in her suitcase and glanced at her face on the cover of the *National Enquirer*. Beneath her picture the headline read, HEAVYWEIGHT FORMER MODEL, LOLA CARLYLE, GOES INTO HIDING.

She tossed the magazine aside, and with her Miniature Pinscher, Baby Doll, tucked beneath one arm, she walked out of the tiny bungalow. It seemed her name was never mentioned any more without comment on the twenty-five pounds she'd gained since she'd turned her back on the modeling business. *Heavyweight* was one of the nicer descriptions used these days. Her least favorite was Large Lola. She tried not to let the names hurt or bother her. Deep down inside, they did.

She wasn't fat, and she wasn't in hiding, either. She was on a much-needed mental health *vacation*. On a private island in the Bahamas, *resting*. But after two days of rest, she was bored to tears and likely to go crazy as a bullbat. She had a life to live and a business to run. And now, thanks to the warm sun and fresh air, she had a nice tan, a clear head, and a new plan.

She figured all she needed to force Sam to pull the plug on

his site was a good private investigator and some fresh dirt. Sam hadn't always been up front in his business dealing, and she knew there had to be plenty she could use to blackmail him. It was so simple, she didn't know why she hadn't thought of it before.

As soon as she got home, Sam The Jerk was going down.

Max Zamora was getting too old to play Superman. Adrenaline rushed through his veins and raised the hair on the backs of his arms, but did little to dull the fiery ache shooting up his side, stealing air from his lungs. At the age of thirty-six, he felt the pain of saving the world much more than he used to.

He took steady breaths to control the pain and the nausea threatening just below the surface. Above the pounding in his head, he listened to the sounds of tourists and taxicabs, of island music and waves hitting the docks. He heard nothing out of the ordinary filling the humid night air, but Max knew they were out there. Somewhere. Looking for him. If they caught him, they wouldn't hesitate before they killed him, and this time they would succeed.

Light from the Atlantis Casino illuminated blurry patches of the marina, and for a split second his vision cleared, then doubled again, playing havoc with his balance as he moved from the shadows. The soles of his tactical boots made not a sound as he boarded the yacht tied to the end of the dock. Blood trickled from the cut in his bottom lip and dripped down his chin to his black T-shirt. When his adrenaline ran dry, he knew he'd be in a heap of hurt, but he planned to be halfway to Florida before that happened. Halfway from the hell he'd visited on Paradise Island.

Max made his way to the dark galley and rifled through the drawers. His hand fell on a fishing knife, and he pulled it from its scabbard and tested the wicked five-inch blade against his thumb. Moonlight poured in through the yacht's Plexiglas windows overhead and lit up patches of the inky black interior.

He didn't bother to search the yacht further. He couldn't see much anyway, and he'd be damned if he'd turn on the lights and illuminate his position.

Flatware rattled in the drawer as Max slammed it shut. He figured if the owners were still on board, he'd made enough noise to roust them by now.

And if someone did suddenly appear from out of the darkness he'd have to switch to contingency plan B. Problem was, he had no plan B. An hour ago, he'd run through the last of his backup strategies, and now he was running on pure instinct and survival. If this last ditch effort failed, he was a dead man. Max didn't fear death; he just didn't want to give anyone the pleasure of killing him.

When no one appeared, he made his way back outside and quickly cut the docklines. He moved up the stairs to the flying bridge. Max's vision cleared for a few brief seconds, allowing him to see the bridge had a canvas top and plastic wraparound windows. He knelt beside the captain's chair within the variegated shadows, and his vison blurred and doubled again.

A wave of nausea rushed at him, and he breathed through it as best he could. Mostly by touch, he used the knife to pop a section off the top of the helm. Perspiration stung a cut on his forehead and ran into his brow as he pulled out a tangle of wires. His vision wasn't getting any better and it took him longer than he would have liked to locate the back of the ignition switch. When he did, he sliced through the wires, then touched them together. The twin inboard engines kicked over, sputtering and churning the water as Max placed one hand on his side, one on the helm, and rose.

He put the yacht in gear, slid the throttle forward, and eased the craft away from the end of the dock. If he tilted his head just right, his double vision wasn't as bad, and he could keep the yacht in the center of the waterway and away from hazards.

He motored the vessel out of the marina and into Nassau Harbor, beneath the bridge that connected Paradise Island to the capital and past the cruise ships docked at Prince George Wharf. Nothing that night had come this easy, and at any moment, he expected a spray of automatic fire, shredding the canvas top and chewing up the deck. The minute he'd landed on the island that afternoon, his luck had gone from bad to worse, and he didn't trust that his bad luck was through with him yet.

'Excuse me, but what are you doing?'

At the sound of a female voice, Max spun around and gripped the arm of the captain's chair to keep from falling. He stared at the double image of a woman outlined by the fading lights of the harbor. A lighthouse at the end of the island sent a bright beam sliding across the floor and lighting up two identical pairs of feet with twenty red toenails. It made a leisurely journey up two red-and-blue skirts and bare flat bellies. Two white shirts were tied between two pairs of big breasts. Then it slipped across the corners of two full mouths and drifted through a tangle of blond curls. Her face remained hidden as the fuzzy image of two small dogs yapped from her arms, the shrill barking enough to make Max's ears bleed.

'Shit, I didn't need this,' he said, wondering where the hell she'd come from. The poor excuse for a dog jumped from her arms and bolted across the floor, stopping by Max's feet and barking so hard his rear legs rose from the deck. The woman moved forward, and her double image trailed slightly behind as she rushed to scoop up the mutt.

'Who are you? Do you work for the Thatches?' she demanded. He didn't have time for dogs or questions or bullshit in general. She had to go. The last thing he needed tonight was a barking mutt and a yapping woman. She and her dog were going to have to jump. The tip of Paradise Island was less than a hundred feet behind them now. They'd probably make it. If they didn't, it wasn't his problem.

'Shut that dog up or I'll drop-kick it overboard,' he said instead of forcing her and her mutt into the sea. Damn, he was getting soft in his old age.

'Where are you taking this yacht?'

He ignored her and glanced one last time at the fading lights of Nassau, at the fuzzy green buoy markers and flashing lighthouse, then he turned his attention to the controls. He had a few questions of his own, but he would have to wait to get the answers. At the moment, he had more important concerns. Like survival.

His hands shook from pain and adrenaline. Through the sheer force of his will and years of experience, he steadied them. He hadn't detected another vessel following him, but that didn't mean much.

'You can't just take this boat. You have to return to the marina.'

If his head hadn't ached like a bitch and his body hadn't been used for a punching bag, he might have found her damn funny. Turn back, after the hell he'd lived through? Take the yacht back, after he'd gone through the trouble of stealing it? Not freaking likely. It took a rare talent to hot-wire when a person couldn't even see straight. He'd been aboard just about every Navy vessel imaginable. Everything from an inflatable to an attack sub. He knew how to read a Global Positioning System, and in a pinch he could read chart maps and use a compass. Problem was, with his vision, the best he was capable of at the moment was to head west and haul balls to the walls.

'Who are you?'

He squinted at the golden blur of the controls in front of him and reached for the radio. He missed and tried again until he felt the knobs beneath his fingertips. Static filled the air around him, drowning out the woman's questions. He adjusted the squelch knob, cutting out the background noise, then he turned it slightly. The radio picked up the marine operator's transmission with a passenger ship, then he switched to a noncommercial channel. He heard nothing out of the ordinary and continued to switch. Each channel sounded normal. Again, nothing out of the ordinary, but he wasn't listening for normal or ordinary traffic.

'You have to take me back. I promise I won't tell anyone about you.'

Sure you won't, honey, he thought as he glanced over his shoulder, but he could see nothing out of his left eye and turned his attention back to the controls. If she'd shut the hell up, he could almost forget she was there.

He'd been out of communications with the Pentagon for twelve hours. In his last transmission, he'd informed them that there would be no need for a rescue, no need for further negotiations. The two DEA agents he'd been seeking were dead, and had been for a while. Obviously unused to torture, they'd succumbed at the hands of their captors.

'People will notice I'm gone, you know. If fact, I bet someone has missed me by now.'

Bullshit.

'I'm sure someone has already contacted the police.'

The Bahamian police were the least of his problems. He'd been forced to kill André Cosella's oldest son, José, and he'd barely managed to escape with his own life. When André found out, he was going to be one extremely pissed-off drug lord.

'Sit down and be quiet.' Through his double vision, he made out the lights of a sailboat heading toward them on his port side. He didn't think the Cosellas had found the body yet and doubted the sailboat was filled with drug smugglers, but he knew better than to rule anything out, and the last thing he needed was for the woman beside him to start screaming her head off.

He felt rather than saw her move, and before she could take a step, he reached out and grabbed her arm. 'Don't even think about doing anything stupid.'

She screamed and tried to pull out of his grasp. The dog

yapped, jumped to the deck, and locked his jaws on the leg of Max's pants.

'Get your hands off me,' she yelled, and swung at him, almost connecting with his already aching skull.

'Damn it!' Max swore as he spun her around and slammed her back into his chest. He set his jaws against the pain shooting along his ribs and grappled for her wrists. She fought to escape, but she was soft and very feminine and no match for Max. He easily forced her forearms to cross her breasts, pinning her to him and controlling her jabbing elbows. Her hair piled on the top of her head tickled his cheek as he clued her in on their untenable situation. 'Be a good girl, and who knows, you just might live to see the sunrise.'

She stilled instantly. 'Don't hurt me.'

She'd misunderstood him, but he didn't bother correcting her. It wasn't *him* she had to worry about. He wasn't going to hurt her, unless she took another swing at him. Then all bets were off.

The sailboat sliced through the calm waters, a blur to Max, and all too clearly reminding him of his weakened position. He couldn't see straight. At the moment, his vision was better in the dark than the light, which had just about as many advantages as disadvantages. He didn't need a doctor to tell him his ribs were cracked, and he was sure he'd be pissing blood for at least a week. Worse, Cosella's men had taken all of his toys – his weapons and his communications. They'd even taken his watch. He had nothing to fight back with, and if they found him, he was a sitting duck. Worse than a sitting duck. His bad luck had cursed him with a soft civilian woman and her irritating mutt. He shook his leg and the little yapper slid across the wooden floor.

'Let me go and I'll sit down like you said.'

He didn't believe her. He didn't believe she wouldn't try something, and in his present state, he wouldn't even see it coming. He'd lived through too much already tonight to let her finish the job. He narrowed his gaze and his double vision slid into one image. The stern light of the sailboat slid past without incident, and to his vast relief his double vision did not return.

'Who are you?' she asked.

'I'm one of the good guys.'

'Right,' she said, but she didn't sound convinced. More like she was trying to pacify him.

'I'm telling you the truth.'

'Good guys don't steal boats and kidnap women.'

She had a point, but she was just plain wrong. Sometimes the line between the good guys and the bad guys was as hazy as his sight. 'I didn't steal this vessel, I'm commandeering it. And I'm not kidnapping you.'

'Then take me back.'

'No.' Max had been trained by the best the military had to offer. Excluding tonight's fiasco, he could shoot and loot better than most. Scale just about any installation, get what he needed, and be out by dinner, but he knew from experience that one hysterical woman could make a solid situation as unstable as hell. 'I am not going to hurt you. I just need to put some distance between me and Nassau.'

'Who are you?'

He thought about giving her a fictitious name, but since she would probably find it out when she tried to have him arrested for kidnapping, he told her the truth. 'I'm Lieutenant Commander Max Zamora,' he answered, but he didn't give her the whole truth. He left out that he was retired from the military and that he currently worked for a part of the government that didn't exist on paper.

'Let go of me,' she demanded, and for the first time Max looked downward into the blurred image of his hands wrapped around her wrists. The backs of his fingers and knuckles pressed into the soft pillows of her breasts, and suddenly he felt every inch of her slim back crushed into his chest. Her rounded behind was shoved into his groin, and hunger mixed with the ache riding his ribs and thumping his skull. He was equally disgusted and surprised that he could feel anything beyond pain. Awareness of her spread across his skin, and he pushed it back, tamped it down, and forced it into the dark recesses where he buried all weakness.

'Are you going to take another swing at me?' he asked.

'No.'

He released her and she flew out of his grasp as if her clothes were on fire. Through the dark shadows of the cabin, he watched her disappear into the corner, then he turned to the controls once again.

'Come here, Baby.'

He looked over his shoulder at her, sure he hadn't heard her right. 'What?'

She scooped up her dog. 'Did he hurt you, Baby Doll?'

'Jeesuz,' he groaned as if he'd stepped in something foul. She'd named her dog Baby Doll. No wonder it was such a nasty little pain in the ass. He returned his attention to the

GPS and pressed the switch. The screen illuminated, a gray blur of lines and fuzzy numbers. He squinted and brought the screen a bit more into focus. On the port side of the screen, he could just make out the approaching lines of Andros Island and the chain of Berry Islands off his starboard side. He couldn't see well enough to read the increments of longitude and latitude, but he figured as long as he headed northwest for another hour before turning due west, he would land along the coast of Florida by morning.

'If you're really a lieutenant, then show me your identification.'

Even if every piece of identification hadn't been taken from him when he'd been captured, it wouldn't have told her anything anyway. He'd entered Nassau under the name of Eduardo Rodriguez, and everything from his passport and driver's license to his pocket litter had been falsified.

'Take a seat, lady. This will all be over before you know it,' he said, because there was nothing more he could tell her. Nothing she would believe anyway. The American public was better off not knowing about men like Max. Men who operated in the shadows. Men who performed untraceable missions for the U.S. government and were paid with untraceable money. Men who answered nonexistent calls from nonexistent phones in a nonexistent office in the Pentagon. Men who gathered intelligence, disrupted terrorist activity, and took out bad guys while allowing the government its deniability.

'Where are we going?'

'West,' he answered, figuring that was all the information she needed.

'Exactly where west?'

He didn't need to see her to know by the tone of her voice that she was the kind of woman who expected to be in charge. A real ball-buster. Under the best of circumstances, Max didn't let anyone bust his balls, and this wasn't the best of circumstances. And he'd be damned if he'd allow some woman to screw up his night even more than it had already been screwed.

'Exactly where I decide.'

'I deserve to know where I'm being taken.'

Normally, he didn't enjoy intimidating women, but just because he didn't enjoy it didn't mean it bothered him, either. He backed the engine off to a nice cruising speed of about twenty knots, punched up the cruise control, and stalked to where she stood with her dog, a shadowy figure in a dark corner of the bridge.

Light from the full moon slipped through the windshield and lit up the top of her shoulder and throat. She must have gotten a glimpse of his face, because she sucked in her breath and sank back even farther into the corner. Good. Let her be afraid of him.

'Listen real close,' he began, towering over her and placing his hands on his hips. 'I can make things easy for you, or I can make them real hard. You can sit back and enjoy the ride, or you can fight me. If you choose to fight me, I guaran-goddamn-tee you won't win. Now, what's it gonna be?'

She didn't say a word, but her dog propelled itself from her arms and sank its teeth into his shoulder like a rabid bat.

'Shit!' Max swore, and grabbed the mutt.

'Don't hurt him! Don't hurt Baby!'

Hurt him? Max was going stomp it into a grease spot. He pulled and the fabric of his shirt ripped. The snarling beast came off in his hands and he dropped him to the floor. The dog yelped and scampered away.

'You bastard!' she yelled. 'You hurt my dog.' Only after her fist connected with the side of his head did he realize she'd blindsided him. His ears rang, his vision blurred a little more, and he called her some very choice names.

She took another swing, but he was ready for her and grabbed her wrist in midaim. He swept her feet out from beneath her and she went down, hitting the deck hard. Max was through playing nice. He flipped her onto her stomach and planted his knee in her back. She flailed and fought and called him a few pathetic names of her own.

'Get off me!'

Get off her? Not likely. He was going to gag her, tie her up, and dump her overboard. *Sayonara*, sweetheart. Dim light from the GPS spread across the floor and reached her bare feet and calves. She kicked, and he grasped two fistfuls of her skirt and ripped a long piece from the bottom.

'Stop! What in the heck do you think you're doing?'

Instead of answering, he straddled her and squeezed her hips between his knees to keep her still. She tried to twist and turn, but he managed to grab one flailing ankle and tie a half hitch knot around it. Then he grabbed the other and wound the material in a locking cleat around them both. She yelled her lungs out while Max secured her feet. Then he grabbed the bottom of her skirt once more and ripped. This time the whole thing came off in his hands. The backs of her long legs were pale against the darker wooden deck. Her panties might be pink or maybe white. Max wasn't sure and he wasn't going to dwell on it.

She begged him to stop, but her pleas fell on his still ringing ears. He tore another long strip from the skirt, then placed his hand flat on her behind. Silk. Her panties were silk, he discovered as he held her down. He quickly reversed his position so that he faced the back of her head instead of her feet. He knelt over her, her waist squeezed between his thighs like a vise while he tied a half hitch knot, and she still fought him. She tucked her hands beneath her body, but he grabbed her arm and easily brought it to the small of her back. He tied her wrists together, then stood over her. Now that the rush of adrenaline was slowing to a trickle and it seemed as if he just might live after all, his neurotransmitters were running less interference, and the pain in his head and side made him more nauseous than before.

Breathing hard, he stepped over the woman on the floor and moved to the helm. He'd wasted precious time dealing with an unwanted passenger and her unwanted dog. He flipped off the cruise control and pushed the throttle to fifty-five knots.

The scratch of the little dog's nails reached his battered ears as it scurried from its hiding place to dart past him. Then silence filled the cabin, and he reached for a box of emergency signal flares stuck to the side of the helm. Over the next half an hour, his vision cleared enough for him to sort through the ten handheld flares. As far as making them into any sort of defense weapon went, he determined there wasn't enough magnesium to make a decent incendiary bomb.

He set the box of flares on the helm and glanced at the

Global Positioning System. He could now see the outline of
Andros and the Berry Islands to his stern. He changed the
heading a few degrees west and headed toward the coast of
Florida. Then, once he was fairly sure they wouldn't run
aground on one of the seven hundred islands and cays that
made up the Bahamian Commonwealth, he once again
lowered the speed of the boat and flipped on the cruise
control.

Max set his teeth against the pain in his side, and as he
walked from the bridge, he looked into the dark corner. The
woman had managed to pull herself into a sitting position.
Within the shadows, he could make out the white of her blouse
and a sliver of light from the window shone on her red
toenails. Her little dog lay curled up by her feet.

Without a backward glance, Max walked from the bridge,
slowly making his way down the stairs, holding his side against
the jolt of each step. His breathing became more labored, and
by the time he entered the lit galley, he saw spots in front of
his eyes. He found a first-aid kit beside the stove and a tray of
ice in the freezer.

In the refrigerator, he discovered bottles of wine, several
fifths of rum and tequila, and about a case of Dos Equis beer.
Under normal circumstances, Max only allowed himself a beer
or two. Tonight he needed more, something with a bigger kick,
and he reached for the rum. He unscrewed the top of the clear
bottle and brought it to his mouth. He winced at the pressure
against his split lip but took several big swallows anyway. He
wrapped the ice in a hand towel, then stuck it beneath one
arm.

Grabbing the first-aid kit, he headed through the salon and

flipped on the switch in the bathroom, coming face-to-face with his reflection in the mirror above the sink. He didn't know which was worse: the way he looked or the way he felt. The left side of his face was swollen and turning purple. Dried blood from his nose smeared his cheek, and the cut in the middle of his bottom lip had bled down his chin. He took a long drink of the rum as he studied the rip in his shirt and the small dog bite on the ball of his shoulder. It wasn't deep. Just a scratch, really, and, compared to the rest of his injuries, didn't even warrant inspection. He just hoped like hell the mutt had had all his shots.

With one hand, Max pulled his shirt from the waistband of his black jeans and lifted it up. Nasty red welts crisscrossed his torso, while a bruise in the shape of a bootheel marked his left side. At least he was alive. For the moment anyway.

He rummaged around in the first-aid kit until he found a bottle of Motrin. He emptied five tablets into his palm and chased them down with rum, then he wrapped an Ace bandage around his ribs. The elastic bandage didn't help all that much, but he pinned it in place anyway. He found some antiseptic soap, and as he washed the blood from his face and neck, he thought of what had happened to him tonight, and wondered how the mission could have gotten so messed up from the beginning.

The intelligence he'd been given had been wrong, his contingency plans had all failed, and he wanted to know why. The report had placed Cosella's men in one part of the church on the vast compound, when they'd clearly been in another. The DEA agents had been held in the front of the building instead of the back, but none of that really mattered. Terrorists weren't the most predictable people and intelligence was subject to change on a minute-by-minute basis. Max knew that, dealt with it often.

But he'd never had all his escape routes so unexpectedly and totally blocked before, and it occurred to him that perhaps someone on the inside hadn't meant for him to survive this one.

He washed away the traces of blood and closed the gash on his forehead with a few Steri-Strips. With the icy towel held to the side of his face and the fifth of rum in his other hand, he returned to the galley. There was only one person he completely trusted at the special ops command. Joint Chief of Staff General Richard Winter, a chain-smoking, foulmouthed straight shooter who'd served in Vietnam and Desert Storm and knew a thing or two about living in the trenches and fighting with your back against the wall.

The general was a real hard-ass, but fair. He understood about going clandestine, what it took, and what it involved. But Max couldn't risk contacting the general yet. Not on an unsecured line. Not when the transmission could be picked up by anyone within a thirty-mile radius. Not when he was such an easy target.

Once again, he rummaged through the yacht, looking for a weapon. He searched the closets in the stateroom and cupboards in the salon and galley, but found nothing more threatening than plastic cocktail swords and a set of dull steak knives.

He emptied the bottle of Motrin in his pocket and reached for a big purse sitting on the dinette table. He dumped out the contents, looking for prescription analgesics, like codeine or

Darvocet, but came up empty except for a travel-sized Tylenol. The purse contained cosmetics and dog treats. A toothbrush and hairbrush and casino chips. He flipped open the wallet and stared at a North Carolina driver's license. With one hand, he held the ice to his face, while with the other he brought the license closer to his good eye. For an instant he thought the face looked familiar, but it wasn't until he read the name that he recognized the woman.

Lola Carlyle. Lola Carlyle, famous underwear and bikini model. Maybe *the* most famous. Her name conjured up images of a near-naked woman, rolling about in the sand or on satin sheets. Of long legs, big breasts, and hot sex. Her *Sports Illustrated* pictures had always been a real favorite with the boys at Little Creek.

Max tossed the wallet on the table. Damn. The situation just got a bit more complicated. A bit less easy for the government to cover up. And if he was recaptured before he made it back to the States, the soft pampered woman on the bridge didn't stand a chance. A few minutes ago, he would have sworn that his luck couldn't get any worse, but it sure as shit had just gotten a lot worse.

A grim line sealed his lips as he grabbed the rum and the ice-filled towel and headed back up to the bridge. Maybe the woman upstairs wasn't Lola Carlyle. Just because Lola Carlyle's purse was in the galley didn't mean the tall blond woman he'd tied up was her. Yeah, maybe, and maybe he could just go ahead and sprout wings and fly home.

Climbing the stairs on the way up to the galley didn't hurt any less than on the way down. He paused twice and held his side against the sharp pain before continuing. In the past, Max had broken about every bone in his body, and ribs were by far the worst. Mostly because it hurt to even breathe.

Within the dark cabin, he picked out her white shirt. She was exactly where he'd left her, and he moved to the console and placed the bottle of rum and the towel next to the throttle.

'This will all be over soon,' he said in an effort to reassure her. Although, after she'd tried to knock his head off, he didn't know why he was bothering. Maybe because if he were in the same situation, he would have done the same thing. But, he thought as he pressed the ice against his left eye, he would have succeeded.

'Could you please untie me? I have to go to the bathroom.'

The only lethal weapon on board sat next to his rum on the console, so he considered her request. 'If I do, are you going to clock me again?'

'No.'

Max stared at her outline, looking for any detail that might identify her as the woman known throughout the world by her first name alone. He couldn't make a positive determination one way or the other. 'That's what you said last time.'

'Please. I really have to go.'

Max looked around. 'Where's your mutt?'

'Right here, asleep. He won't bite you again. I've talked to him about it, and he's really sorry.'

'Uh-huh.' He grabbed the fish knife and crossed the deck and, keeping his back as straight as possible, knelt beside her outline. Within the dark corner he felt for her feet, then easily slid the knife through the cotton strip. 'Turn around,' he said, and when she'd done as he'd told her, he sliced the material binding her hands. He grabbed his side, and with more difficulty than it had taken him to kneel, he rose to his feet. 'This could have been avoided in the first place,' he said through the pain, 'if you'd just done what I told you to do.'

'I know. I'm sorry.'

A warning bell sounded in his splitting head as he replaced the knife in its scabbard, then slid it in his waistband at the small of his back. He didn't trust her sudden passiveness, but perhaps she'd realized that she couldn't win and it was in her best interest not to fight with him any more. Yeah, maybe. Or maybe he really was getting soft in his old age.

She slipped past him with her dog in her arms and headed for the door. At the top of the stairs, the moon shone across her back and bottom, and in her hurry to get by him, she left the scent of her hair in her wake.

He moved to stand by the captain's chair and grabbed the bottle of rum. He took a drink and looked out the front windshield at the Caribbean moon. At the rolling waves before him and the vast emptiness of the ocean. Beside a folded-up newspaper, he spotted a pair of binoculars. He carefully raised them to his eyes, but saw nothing except black ocean. He relaxed a degree.

Max had always taken the worst that life could throw at him, and he'd always mastered it. He'd made it through six months of SEAL training, been in Desert Storm, taken out terrorists in Afghanistan, Yemen, and in the South China Sea, but tonight had been the worst. Because of José Cosella's desire to impress his father with his brutality, and a shoddy piece-of-shit handgun, Max was still alive. The same could not be said of José.

Still fresh in Max's mind, he recalled in precise detail the click of the jammed gun, José taking his eyes off him to examine it, and Max making his move. The chair splintering and coming apart within the ropes that bound his hands. Him using a piece of the wooden back to save his own life. Running to the docks, hiding in the shadows, and picking his opportunity.

Max set the bottle on top of the newspaper and caught a flash of white reflection in the windshield.

'Turn this boat around,' the woman behind him commanded in a slightly breathless, faintly southern voice. She flipped on the galley lights and the glare immediately stabbed Max's corneas. 'Turn it around or I'll shoot.'

Max squinted against the pain and light that suddenly flooded the bridge. He slowly turned and no longer had to wonder if he'd accidentally commandeered a famous underwear model along with the yacht.

Lola Carlyle was just as gorgeous in person as she was staring back from the cover of fashion magazines. She stood in the doorway, half her blond hair piled on top of her head, the other half curled about her shoulders as if she'd just gotten out of bed. Her deep brown eyes stared back at him from beneath the perfect arch of her brows. She'd untied the white shirt from between her breasts and had buttoned it all the way to her bottom. Her long smooth legs were every man's fantasy. She might have been his, too. If it weren't for the orange flare gun pointed right at his chest. Ms Carlyle had been busy.

Well, he'd wondered if his night could get any worse, and it sure as shit just had. He should have known. He should have followed her, but he'd rather face a dozen flare guns than a trip down those stairs again. 'What are you going to do with that thing?' he asked.

'Shoot you if you don't turn this boat around. Now.'

'Are you sure?' He really didn't believe she'd shoot him. Most people didn't have what it took to look a man right in the eyes and end his life. 'That'll leave a mighty big hole. Make a really big mess, too.'

'I don't care. Turn the yacht around.'

Maybe she had what it took. Maybe not, but there was no way in hell he was turning back to Nassau.

'Now!'

He shook his head. 'Not even for you, Miss July.' Her eyes narrowed, and he provoked her further, waiting for her to make a move so he could make his. 'What was the name of that magazine where you appeared on the cover wearing that red thong bikini? *Hustler*?'

'It was *Sports Illustrated*.'

He raised his hand to touch his split lip. 'Ah, yes.' He looked at the traces of blood on his fingers, then returned his gaze to her. 'I remember.' Her brows scrunched together even more. 'You were a real hit with the teams that year. I do believe Scooter McLafferty cuffed the carrot several times in your honor.'

'Charming.' Her frown told him she was neither flattered nor amused. 'The boat,' she reminded him, and waved the flare gun. 'Turn it around. I'm not kidding.'

'I told you I can't do that.' He folded his arms over his chest as if he were relaxed. But the fact was, he could have the knife out of its scabbard and in her right eye before she took another breath. Now, he didn't want to do that. He didn't want to kill a famous lingerie model. The government frowned on the killing of civilians, so maybe he'd just kick the gun out of her hand. That was going to hurt like a bitch and he wasn't looking forward to it. 'If you want this yacht headed back to Nassau, you'll have to come over here and turn it around yourself.'

'If you try anything . . .' She took two hesitant steps forward, her dog at her bare feet.

'You'll sic your vicious mutt on me again?'

'No, I'll shoot you.'

He even moved over for her and pointed to the wheel. 'It has a tendency to vibrate below about fifteen knots,' he provided.

She stopped and motioned with the gun for him to move completely away from the helm.

Max shook his head as he watched her. He waited until she took one more hesitant step, then his arm shot out and grabbed her wrist. She tried to yank away and the gun exploded. The twelve-gauge shotgun shell blew a ball of flaming red fire into the helm. It slammed into the GPS, smashed the bottle of rum, and sent sparks shooting in all directions. The ignited rum flowed like a flaming river across the controls and into the hole Max had created when he'd removed the panel to hot-wire the engine.

Both Max and Lola hit the deck as the fifteen-hundred-candela ball burned its way through the faux-wood panel and shot beneath the console, where it exploded with a loud pop, sending flames up through the hole. The red flares lit one by one, burning the helm like ten mini blowtorches. The wiring cracked and sizzled and the engine shut down. Like the dying throes of the *Titanic*, the lights blinked out completely. The only illumination in the pitch-black night, the dancing flames and orange glow of the burning helm.

'Oh, my Lord,' Ms Carlyle cried.

Max crawled to his knees and looked up at the blazing newspaper, the flames licking the windshield and igniting the custom-made canvas top. Apparently, his rotten luck wasn't through with him yet.

L ola shone the beam of a MiniMag on what was left of the helm. The canvas top covering the bridge had almost completely burned away, leaving nothing behind but a few yards of charred canvas and the blackened aluminum poles. A light salty breeze ruffled her hair and fluttered the tails of her shirt against the very tops of her thighs and the bottom of her butt. The sea air stirred the white potassium bicarbonate covering the floor and what was left of the captain's seat and helm.

This wasn't real. This wasn't happening to her. She was Lola Carlyle and this wasn't her life. She was on mental health vacation. In fact, she was leaving tomorrow to go home. She *had* to get home.

This was crazy and had to be a dream. Yes, that had to be it. Earlier, she'd boarded one last 'snack and swizzle' tour of Nassau and had fallen asleep in the yacht's stateroom, and now she was having a nightmare starring a demented madman. Any moment she would awake and thank God that it was all just a dream.

Through the darkness, the empty fire extinguisher sailed

through the air and hit the helm. It bounced, then got stuck in the burned hole.

'What's next? Napalm hidden in your underwear?' asked the all-too-real madman behind her, the anger in his voice slicing through the night air that separated them.

Lola looked over her shoulder at the moonlight touching his bruised and battered face. She'd expected to be murdered and turned into fish bait. When he'd tied her up, she'd been more afraid than she'd ever been in her life. Fear had sat on her chest and squeezed the breath from her lungs. She'd been so certain that he'd hurt her then kill her. Now she was too numb to feel anything at all.

'If I did have napalm, you'd be barbecue,' she said before she thought better of it. Then her self-preservation kicked in and she took a few steps back.

'Oh, I don't doubt that, sweetheart.' He moved toward her and reached behind his back. 'Here.' He pulled out a knife encased in a fawn leather scabbard and grabbed her free hand. She flinched when he slapped it in her palm. 'If you want to put me out of my misery,' he said, 'use this. It'll be quicker and less painful.' Slowly he moved to what until a few minutes ago had been the doorway, but now was just a metal frame and a bit of burned canvas flapping in the breeze. She heard him suck in a breath before he continued down the stairs.

At the first hint of flames, Baby had tucked his stubby tail between his stubby legs and headed for safer quarters. She'd run for cover too, or rather crawled across the floor and down the stairs. She'd stood on the aft deck below as the madman named Max had battled the flames. She'd watched, incredulous, as pieces of burning canvas floated away on the breeze.

The galley door slammed and echoed into the night. Then all was silent again, the soft lapping of waves against the side of the boat the only sound in the absolute stillness. She looked about her, out at the darkness. Out at nothing, feeling like one of those hurricane survivors she always saw on the news. Wild-haired, vacant-eyed, and numb. Her mind hardly grasping the reality of her situation, that she stood somewhere in the Atlantic Ocean, aboard a disabled boat, wearing nothing but her underwear and a white blouse, while a clearly deranged man slept below her feet.

Lola turned for the doorway and made her way down the stairs. The whole evening was surreal, like being trapped in a Salvador Dali painting. Warped and twisted and leaving her looking around and thinking, *What is this?* She shone her light on the aft deck, and her footsteps slowed as she moved into the galley.

'Baby,' she whispered, and found him on the bench seat behind the table, awake and frightened and curled up on the pashmina she'd discarded earlier that day. By degrees, as if she expected the bogeyman to jump out at her, she shone the small beam of light down the galley and salon. Through the doorway to the stateroom, the beam moved across the thick blue carpet to the edge of the striped bedspread. She shone the flashlight up the spread and stopped it on the soles of a pair of black boots. At the sight of them, the fear she'd felt all evening rushed across her flesh, and she snapped the light off.

'Baby,' she whispered once again, and leaning forward, she felt around on the bench seat. She switched the knife she held to the same hand gripping the flashlight. Her fingers brushed the pashmina, and she scooped it up, along with her dog wrapped inside. Through the black galley, she walked as silently as possible until she once again stood on the aft deck. She moved to the same spot where she'd sat hours before, sipping wine with the other passengers of the yacht and listening to the owner's pirate stories. The cool vinyl of the wrap-around seat chilled the backs of her thighs as she sat, and she tucked her feet beneath her.

Baby licked her cheek as she fought back tears and tried not to cry. Lola hated crying. She hated being afraid and feeling helpless, but the tears leaked from her eyes before she could stop them.

Baby hadn't been afraid. He'd been brave and fierce, but for the first time since she'd picked him up from the breeder's a year ago, she wished him to be a rottweiler. A big mean rottweiler that could tear off a man's arms. Or balls.

Lola brushed her tears away and thought of the box of aerial flares she'd found in the stateroom. They were useless now. The gun melted in the fire. But even if the gun hadn't melted, she wasn't brave enough to walk in that room and recover them. Not with Mad Max lying on the bed beside them.

He'd said he was a lieutenant commander, but she didn't really believe him. He could have made it up. More than likely he was one of those modern-day pirates the owner of the yacht, Mel Thatch, had told them all about.

Lola unfolded the pashmina and wrapped it around herself and her dog. She stared up at the burned remains of the bridge and the stars dotting the sky, so compact in some places they appeared crammed one on top of another.

Her hand tightened around the knife he'd given her. For a criminal, it seemed like a stupid thing to do, but he obviously didn't consider her a threat. He didn't think she'd use it on him, and he was probably right. It was one thing to shoot a man with a flare gun or defend yourself while in the heat of battle, quite another to sneak into his bed and cut his throat while he slept.

More than likely, he'd slapped the knife in her palm because he knew he could overpower her as he had all night. She could still almost feel his grasp on her wrists and the solid wall of him pressed against her back. The man was hard muscles and brute strength and she was no match for him. The second he'd grasped her wrists and held her against his chest, she'd known that he could do anything he wanted to her, and there was absolutely nothing she could do to stop him.

After he'd let her go the first time, she'd stood in the shadows, waiting for him to come after her. To subject her to every woman's nightmare. To come after her and tear at her clothes and hold her down and rape her. There had never been any question that she would fight him. Never a question that she would defend herself and protect Baby.

She hadn't gotten where she was in life by being passive. She hadn't survived a business that fed off the bodies of young starry-eyed girls by submitting to men. And she hadn't left that business to start her own mail order lingerie company by sitting on her hands. For most of her life, she'd battled demons of one sort or another, but when Max had held her down and tied her up with her own skirt, she'd thought for sure she would not survive this time. She'd been certain he would rape her and kill her and throw her and poor Baby overboard as he'd threatened. But he hadn't. She was still alive long after she'd expected to be dead. A sob passed her lips and she pressed shaky fingers to her mouth.

Her gaze lowered from the stars overhead to the burned-out bridge. She'd realized when he'd first grabbed her that if she were to survive the night, she needed a weapon. Preferably a .357 magnum, just like her granddaddy Milton's. She'd had to make do with the flare gun, and now that it was over, she wondered if she really would have shot him like Nicole Kidman had shot Billy Zane in the movie *Dead Calm*.

Now that the worst was over, her hands shook and images rushed at her. Pieces of this and slices of that. Of her and Baby boarding the yacht for one last 'snack and swizzle' and perhaps doing a bit too much swizzling and not enough snacking. Lying down and waking up a bit disoriented and then finding a crazy man at the captain's helm. The sight of him standing at the controls, Baby barking furiously at his feet. Being tied up with her own skirt. Finding the flare gun. The shock of his beaten face.

Lola stretched out on her side on the bench seat and hugged Baby to her chest. Her wineglass still rested on the deck where she'd set it earlier, before she'd slipped into the stateroom to rest. She wondered if the Thatches had yet discovered that their yacht was missing. She doubted it, because although this nightmare felt as if it had already lasted several lifetimes, it was probably only now approaching one A.M. The Thatches wouldn't even return to the harbor for another hour. She wondered how long it would take before they realized that she was missing, too. Before anyone started to look for her. Before her family was told she was missing.

If no one at her company – Lola Wear, Inc. – heard from her, they wouldn't really think much about it. They'd just think she was taking a longer-than-anticipated break. For a while, they'd just continue as usual with the business she'd started two years ago. They'd probably carry on just fine without her, but none of that mattered as the reality of her situation sank deeper into the pit of her stomach.

There was no way off the boat. At least not tonight. There was probably a life raft somewhere, but she wasn't so stupid or irrational that she would leave a forty-seven-foot yacht in the middle of the night in favor of a rubber dinghy. Even if the yacht did come with a crazy man. She was stuck, and there was absolutely nothing she could do about it. There was no way off the boat. No way out. For the first time that night, she was truly helpless.

She was at the mercy of the currents and a kidnapping pirate.

Lola woke with the sun warming her left cheek. For a moment she forgot where she was and almost rolled off the bench seat. She opened her eyes to the blinding Caribbean sun and rolled onto her back. Disoriented, she shut her eyes for a moment before everything came back to her in one horrifying blast. The fear and helplessness grabbed at her stomach, and she abruptly sat up. She looked down at her blouse twisted around her waist; her pashmina covered one of her bare legs before trailing to the deck. Lola glanced through the open door of the galley as she sat up and pulled the ends of the red cashmere wrap around her hips. Her flashlight lay on the seat, but the knife was gone. She glanced around for Baby and didn't see him. She didn't see Max, either, but she heard him.

'Goddamn!' he swore from the direction of the bridge. A mixture of Spanish and English cursing peppered the still morning air. Lola didn't speak Spanish, but she didn't need to. His tirade was followed by a series of whacks, as if he were hitting hardwood with a hammer.

Lola rose and slipped into the galley. Morning light poured in through the tinted windows, and she found her Louis Vuitton purse on the table just as it had been the night before when she'd come in here searching for a weapon – everything inside was dumped out.

The thumping continued, and she rolled her eyes toward the ceiling. Not only had the jerk kidnapped her, he'd gone through her things. Within the mess on the table, she found a safety pin and pinned her pashmina together above her left hip. She took down her hair from the night before, then snagged her brush before shoving everything back into her bag.

As she brushed the tangles from her hair, she walked through the salon and into the stateroom, quietly whistling for Baby. Patches of light landed on the rumpled bedspread and across the blue carpet. Lola looked inside the master bathroom, at the big spa tub and tarnished brass fixtures. She checked in the closet and found a few men's shirts printed with palm trees and flamingos hanging inside along with a few tropical print sundresses, but she didn't find her dog.

She tossed the hairbrush on the couch as she moved back through the salon. Since Baby wasn't inside the boat, he had to be outside, and if he wasn't outside . . . Her thoughts were interrupted by one final whack above her head, and she raced to the aft deck. If he hurt her dog, she'd kill him.

She climbed the stairs to the bridge two at a time, then came to a complete halt at the sight that greeted her eyes. The helm looked much worse in the light of day, black and melted, with a big hole in the center. Baby sat in the middle of the deck, so rigid he looked like he was stuffed, staring down the enemy, who sat with his back against the gunwale, his black boots spread wide, his forearms resting on his knees, and a wrench held loosely in one hand.

It was a sad fact of Baby Doll's life that he was compelled beyond his control to take on the biggest dog. No matter size or breed. He'd obviously decided to take on Max, and the two males were locked in a staring contest, neither moving. A light breeze didn't so much as muss Max's short black hair or ruffle Baby's brown fur.

'Your dog took a crap in the corner,' Max said, his voice as raspy as she remembered. He turned his attention to her, and for the first time she got a really good look at him. In the light of day, he didn't appear much better than he had last night. Some of the swelling in his face had gone down, but it was still puffy and very black and blue. He was only slightly less scary.

'I'm sure he couldn't help it,' she said, determined not to show her fear. She glanced about the bridge but didn't see a dog mess.

'I cleaned it up. But from now on, that's your job.'

She returned her gaze to his and noticed that his eyes were blue. The same light blue of the Carribean waves just before they hit the beach. Given his dark complexion and hair, not to mention his bruises, they were a startling contrast.

'I don't like worthless dogs,' he said. 'And yours is about as worthless as they come.'

'You're a thief and a kidnapper, and you're calling a little *dog* worthless?'

'I told you last night that I *commandeered* the yacht, and you aren't kidnapped.'

Lola shrugged. 'That's what you say, but here I am. Taken against my will on a boat that doesn't belong to you. I don't know where you're from, but I think in most countries around the world, that's against the law.'

He reached behind him and grabbed the top of the gunwale. As he struggled to his feet, Lola took a cautious step back. 'If you hadn't set the helm on fire, you'd be in Florida right now all safe and cozy, with nothing more to worry about than what to order for breakfast. Or you'd be on your way to Washington, where at least one general would be kissing your ass and apologizing on the behalf of the U.S. of A. Instead you had to get hysterical and fuck things up.'

'Me!'

'Now I'm stuck in the Bermuda Triangle during hurricane season with an underwear model and a wussy dog.'

He made it sound as if the whole situation was *her* fault. Anger replaced her fear and she pointed a finger at him. 'Now, just a minute. None of this is *my* fault. I was asleep when you snuck aboard and "commandeered" Baby and me.'

'Probably more like passed out. I made enough noise to wake the dead.' He made a sound, half grunt, half groan, and pressed a hand to his side.

'I wasn't passed out. I was very tired,' she defended herself, although she didn't know why she bothered, since she really didn't care what he thought.

'And *you* aren't commandeered. The yacht was commandeered. You weren't supposed to be here.' She opened her mouth to argue, but he interrupted her before she could speak. 'And you aren't kidnapped, either.'

'Than what am I?'

He shook his head. 'Offhand, I'd say you're a real pain in the ass.'

Baby, having finally given up on the stare-down, scrambled over to Lola and she picked him up. She didn't even bother with a reply, and instead turned on her heels and left him alone on the bridge. She had more important concerns than arguing with a deranged kidnapper.

There had to be a way to signal a rescue vessel, she thought as she entered the galley and dug around until she found a box of granola bars in one of the cabinets. She chose honey nut for herself, cinnamon crunch for Baby, and slid behind the dinette table. She would have killed for a cup of coffee, and once again thought of the knife in the buckskin-colored sheath. He must have taken it from her while she slept. She wanted it back. As she polished off her breakfast, Max entered the galley, seemingly filling the space with his broad shoulders and dark energy. 'Do you have my knife?' she asked.

'Yep.' He tore into the box of granola bars and added, 'I took it back.'

'I need it.'

He ripped open a honey nut and raisin and looked at her. 'Why?'

'I just do.'

'Are you going to stab me in the back while I'm not looking?'

'No.'

His blue eyes stared into hers as he reached behind him and pulled the knife from the waistband of his pants. 'Sure you won't,' he said, and took a step toward her. She sank back into the seat cushions as he set the knife on the table.

'You can stop that.'

'What?'

'Jumping like I'm going to attack you.'

'I'm not.' But she knew she was, he frightened her, no doubt about it. She estimated him to be at least six-five. The top of his head barely cleared the ceiling, and she knew from recent experience that he was solid muscle.

'If I wanted to hurt you, I would have already.'

She didn't say a word, just reached for the knife and slid it into her lap.

'And if I really wanted to hurt you now, that knife wouldn't stop me.'

She believed him but held on to it anyway.

'Did I hurt you last night?' It was a rhetorical question, but she answered anyway.

'Yes.'

He took a bite of his granola bar, then asked, 'Where?'

She held up her wrists and exposed the faint purple marks his fingers had left on her skin. He leaned forward for a better look, and Lola held her breath, steeling herself for what he might do. At the moment he was being perfectly amiable, but she didn't trust his mood.

'Those are so small, they don't even count.' He straightened and popped the rest of the granola bar into his mouth. He watched her as he chewed, his gaze serious, and then he shrugged. 'You're too soft.'

'Are you blaming me again?'

Instead of answering, he dug into the granola box and pulled out another bar. 'You can relax your grip on that knife. I'm not going to rape you.'

A criminal with scruples? She wasn't reassured and held the knife tight in her hand.

'I've never forced a woman to be with me.'

She didn't comment, but raised a brow as if she had her doubts.

He broke off a piece of a granola bar and tossed it toward Baby. The little dog caught it midair. 'Never had to,' he continued. 'You can strip naked and run around in the buff and I won't feel a thing. Not an itch, twitch, or semi-stiffy for good old Max.'

'Charming,' she said as Baby crunched away on his breakfast bar.

'I'm a charming guy.' He managed half a smile and looked down the galley to the salon.

Right, and she was a natural size two. 'Is the radio working?'

His quiet laughter was her answer, then he asked a question of his own. 'Does this yacht belong to you?' he wanted to know.

'No.'

'Boyfriend's?'

'No.'

He returned his gaze to her. 'Why don't you tell me who provided me with their yacht?'

'Why should I tell you anything?'

He folded his arms across his big chest and leaned his behind into the edge of the counter. 'If I know who holds the owner's papers, I can probably tell you how soon you're likely to be rescued.'

'Mel Thatch,' she answered without hesitation. 'He owns Dolphin Cay, the island where I've been vacationing.'

He studied her face. 'Never heard of him. Is he somebody famous?'

'No.'

'Anyone sitting on Dolphin Cay waiting for you? A Kennedy, Rockefeller, or crusty old billionaire?'

She'd never dated a crusty old billionaire. 'No. I'm not seeing anyone at the moment.'

He straightened and it was his turn to raise a dubious brow over his good eye. 'You're on vacation alone?'

'No, I'm with Baby,' she answered. 'How long before someone finds us?'

'Hard to say. I'm sure the yacht's been reported stolen by now, but the thing is, yachts are stolen all the time, or sunk for insurance money. The Coast Guard will search, but no one will get real worked up about it. Except the owner, of course, but he's probably already called his insurance company. And he won't feel real bad, since he's likely to get more for it than it's worth, especially since this boat has been neglected and seen better days.'

Her gaze narrowed. 'How long?'

He shrugged. 'I can't say.'

'You told me you could!'

'If you were dating a congressman or somebody with

connections, the search would be intensified and the chances of a quick rescue more likely. But the fact is, I'm sure they're trying to figure out your connection in this. Whether you were taken against your will or not. I can tell you that no one will rule out the latter just because you're a famous underwear model.' He took a bite of his granola bar and slowly chewed.

She wasn't a famous underwear model any longer, but she didn't bother to enlighten him. And no one in his right mind would believe she'd stolen a yacht. 'What about you? Won't someone be looking for you? A wife? Family?'

'I don't know,' was all he said before he stuck the box of granola bars under one arm and walked out of the galley.

Obviously, he didn't want her to know anything about him, and that was fine by Lola. She really didn't want to know any more about him than she already did. He was a thief and someone hated him enough to beat him up. That was enough info for her. She had more important concerns. Namely, finding a way home.

She scooted from behind the table and slid the knife and scabbard beneath her underwear at her hip. The elastic kept it in place. She grabbed her sunglasses with the light blue lenses and a ponytail holder from her purse. She went in search of a pair of binoculars and found them in a cabinet in the salon. In the emergency kit she'd discovered last night, she found a mirror, an orange flag, and a whistle. Of course, the aerial flares were still there but were useless to her now. She grabbed the three items from the box and headed outside. Max had lifted the hatch to the engine room, but she spared him only a glance as she headed down the foot-wide gunwale to the bow of the boat, Baby hurrying behind her.

Years ago, as part of her recovery from bulimia, she'd had to learn that she couldn't control everything all the time. She'd learned the difference between controlling her disorder and letting it control her. It had taken a long time to recognize the difference, but it was a lesson that she used in every aspect of her life.

Lola could not control the currents nor the direction of the wind, but she would not just sit around and wait to be rescued. She had a life waiting for her. A life she loved and had worked hard to achieve. She had a business to run and a private detective to hire. She'd be damned if she'd just sit around and twiddle her thumbs with 'good old Max.'

A stingy breeze touched Max's cheeks as he raised his head out of the engine room and glanced toward the bow of the boat. He leaned to the left and looked down the gunwale. She was still at it. Still sitting at the tip of the bow, her legs dangling over the side, staring through a pair of binoculars, searching for a rescue vessel with her signal mirror in one hand. Even though Max had no way of telling time, he figured she'd been at it for about three hours. He could have told her that using a signaling mirror in the ocean was futile and pretty much a waste of time and energy.

First off, if anyone was looking for them, they wouldn't know where to begin the search. Second, a mirror worked in the desert, not on the ocean. And third, most survivors reported seeing between seven and twenty vessels before they were actually rescued. If another vessel was out there, they'd think the reflection of the mirror came from the sun hitting the surface of the water. But he didn't bother telling her anything because he liked her on the opposite end of the yacht. Away from him. Busy with something pointless and safe.

It wasn't likely he and Lola would be rescued today. Probably not tomorrow, either. Which suited Max just fine. He needed time for his body to heal, and the last thing he wanted was a distress beacon or flare signaling his position to every Tom, Dick, or drug lord in the area.

The sun beat down on his shoulders and he grabbed a fistful of his black T-shirt and pulled it over his head. The humidity was so thick he could cut it with his hand, and using his shirt, he rubbed the moisture from his neck and chest, then he tossed the shirt onto the deck.

As he'd lain awake in bed last night, he'd gone over every exigency scenario in his mind. When he'd risen with the sun, he'd discovered that what he'd feared the night before was realized: they were dead in the water.

He'd found the circuit breakers that had tripped due to the fire, and he'd switched them back on. Until the diesel fuel ran out, the engines and generators were operable and would provide electricity throughout the yacht. But even though the engines were operable, without a way to navigate or control the speed and direction of the craft they were useless except to provide power inside the cabin. The water tanks were filled to half capacity, and Max figured that if they conserved fuel and water, they had enough to last about thirty days. After that, things would get dicey.

The navigational and communication systems had been destroyed beyond repair. That morning, he'd taken one look at the melted fiberglass and plastic and electrical components, and he'd known that there was nothing that he could do to get the systems up and running.

The ocean current was pushing them in a northwesterly direction at what Max estimated to be about two and a half knots, or a whopping three miles an hour. At their current rate of speed and direction, they would drift close enough to one of the Bimini Islands to be spotted by sports fishermen. Hopefully, in just a few days, nice friendly fishermen would see them and take them to the nearest harbor.

Unless, of course, the wind blew them south, in which case they might end up in Cuban waters. Max looked up at the clear sky, at the few straggling cumulus clouds. It had been a while since he'd enjoyed a Cohiba cigar.

He really wasn't worried about dying at sea. Barring a storm or accident – which, given what had taken place the night before, wasn't an unrealistic consideration – every floating vessel reached land or was discovered at sea. The only question was, how long would it take?

When he'd risen, he'd gone through every cupboard, cabinet, closet, and storage compartment. He'd found fishing equipment, nonperishable food, clothing, an electric razor, and a box of condoms – ultra-thin. Medium. What he hadn't found was a spare radio or any communications equipment. There were no weapons on board, either, which made him vulnerable and jumpy and reinforced his belief that lying low was his best option at the moment.

While Ms Carlyle had snoozed on the aft deck, one long leg exposed from hip to toe, he'd searched for the Emergency Positioning Radio Beacon. He'd needed to find it before she did. He'd planned to dismantle it until he felt the time was right to use it – if ever. The EPRB was bolted to the side of the yacht where it was supposed to be, but when he'd opened it, he'd discovered the batteries were not only old but corroded, rendering it useless.

He'd looked in the survival kit for fresh batteries, but they hadn't been changed since the kit had been purchased in 1989. Needless to say, they were all dead also.

He hadn't lied to Lola earlier when he'd told her he didn't know if anyone was looking for him. By now the Pentagon knew he was missing, and they would also know that a yacht was missing out of Nassau Harbor. Whether they connected the two would be conjecture on his part. And if they did suspect him of commandeering the yacht, they were more likely to wait for him to come in than to come looking for him. At least for now.

André Cosella was a different story. He would be looking. The big man wouldn't know where to search, but he'd be looking. That was the problem with drug lords, they weren't happy when you had to kill their son. If André found Max, it would get real nasty, and Lola was better off not knowing about that. She'd sleep better at night if her biggest concern was how to use the signal mirror.

The click-click-click of toenails on fiberglass drew his attention to the starboard gunwale. That pain-in-the-butt dog moved toward him, probably wanting a rematch of their staring contest. The sun caught on the silver spikes on his collar as he came to sit by the engine room hatch. They were on eye level with each other, and Max wondered if he could get the little rat to chase an imaginary stick off the side of the yacht. Splash. Good-bye.

Baby Doll Carlyle again assumed a position like he was freeze-dried, definitely spoiling for another pissing match. The dog had won the previous stare-down, and Max told himself it was only out of sheer boredom that he locked eyes with the poor excuse now.

A good ten minutes later, Max saw one of the dog's brows twitch, and he figured he was wearing him down. 'I crap bigger than you – boy,' he growled in his best impression of a SEAL instructor.

'Charming.'

Max glanced up at Lola standing above him, up past her feet and calves and the red wrap she'd pinned around her waist. Up the buttons of her white blouse, past her breasts to the hollow of her throat. The blue Caribbean sky framed her face and matched the blue-tinted lenses of her sunglasses. All traces of the makeup she'd worn the night before were gone. Her cheeks were flushed from the heat and sun, strands of her hair were stuck to the side of her neck, the rest pulled back in a limp ponytail. She was absolutely gorgeous, and the dip at the corners of her mouth told him she thought he was an idiot. Which was better than the way she'd looked at him that morning, like he was a rapist.

'I told you, I'm a charming guy.'

'So was Ted Bundy.'

He hadn't been far off in his assumption of her opinion of him. Not that he cared – not even a little. But the way she jumped when he did nothing more than look at her, the fact that she stepped back or sank deeper into her seat and her eyes got big as if she were waiting for him to attack her, did bug the hell out of him.

'The generators and engines are working,' he said, and climbed up out of the engine room. He ignored the pain in his side as he shut the hatch. 'We have to conserve fuel, so I'm only going to turn them on at night for a couple of hours, or during the day only if you have to use the head.'

She didn't say a word and he turned toward her. Her gaze was directed at the bandage around his ribs and the deep red and blue bruises the wrap didn't cover.

'Someone beat you up pretty good,' she said. 'What were you caught doing, raping and pillaging?'

'Nothing that much fun, I'm afraid. I just overstayed my welcome.' When she raised her gaze back to his, he added, 'A case of bad timing and lousy luck.'

'I know what you mean,' she uttered, and he figured she did. 'Where were you that you had such bad timing?'

He looked past the lenses of her blue sunglasses, into the sexy-as-hell tilt of her famous eyes. The rich brown color reminded him of a bottle of Macallan Scotch, smooth, slightly smoky, and very expensive. A taste to be savored all the way down, and old enough to warm him up inside.

Old enough to know what she was involved in, too, and looking at her, he changed his mind about keeping her in the dark. He decided to fill her in, not all of it, but enough. 'Have you ever heard of André Cosella?'

'No.'

'He's the head of the Cosella drug cartel and has been smuggling cocaine into the United States through the Bahamas.'

'Are you a member of a drug cartel?'

He studied her face, and damn if she wasn't serious. 'Hell, no.'

'Are these drug people looking for you?'

'It's likely.'

She folded her arms beneath her breasts and cocked her head to one side. 'Why?'

Max decided to give her the short version. 'Because I was caught on their compound without a party invitation.'

'And?'

'And they didn't appreciate my company.'

'I'm sure you're used to that.' She licked her lips and drew Max's attention to her full mouth. 'But there has to be more.'

Sunlight caught on the moisture of her bottom lip and glistened for a few brief seconds. Max wondered what she'd taste like, right there on that tender spot. If she'd taste as soft and as sexy as she looked. He forced his gaze up and his mind off kissing Lola Carlyle. 'André Cosella's oldest son was killed.'

She unfolded her arms, and he expected her to ask him if he'd been the one to kill José. 'Is there fresh water?' she asked instead. She was obviously smart enough to understand the situation without being told.

Either that or she was too dumb to catch on.

'I filled a pitcher earlier and put it in the refrigerator,' he told her. 'It should still be cool.'

She turned to leave, then stopped and looked back at him over her shoulder, her big brown eyes staring at him through those blue lenses. 'I suppose there isn't enough water for showers.'

'Nope. You'll have to bathe in the ocean.' He heard her long-suffering sigh and watched the sway of her hips as she moved into the galley, that red shawl brushing the backs of her knees.

Just like in all the magazines and billboards and television commercials he'd ever seen her in, everything from the top of her blond head to the polish on her toenails, teased and hinted of hot sweaty sex. As her dumb dog trailed after her, Max wondered if she'd be brave enough to strip off her clothes and jump in the ocean in front of him. It seemed the least she could do after starting the yacht on fire and stranding him in the Atlantic.

He sat on the bench seat where he'd seen Lola sleeping that morning and slowly leaned forward. He took as deep a breath as possible, then held it as he untied one boot and then the other. The night before, he'd wondered if there'd been some underhanded government plan to get rid of him. Now that he'd had time to think it over, he didn't believe that to be the case. With every job, there were always a dozen or so things that could go wrong at any given time. It was Murphy's Law, and last night, Murphy's Law had ruled from the very beginning.

Max had first recognized it when his flight to Nassau had been delayed an hour and he'd missed his contact within the local DEA. No problem, he still had fresh intel, less than twenty-four hours old, locked away in his brain.

From the moment he'd set foot on Nassau the assignment had gone straight to hell, and he should have aborted right then, but he couldn't. He was Max Zamora, and the one thing that made him so good at what he did was the one thing that had almost cost him his life this time. He hated failure. He'd only failed once in his life, and he took it personally.

That hatred was also the one thing that made him the perfect government operative. That and the fact that he had no family, and when he wasn't covert he lived a fairly normal life.

Lieutenant Commander Maximilian Javier Gunner Zamora was officially listed as retired from the United States Navy. He'd been a member of SEAL Team Six, and after the team had been disbanded in the mid-1990s, he'd been recruited by the Navy's Special Warfare Development Group.

Currently, he was self-employed as a security consultant. Max's firm, Z Security, was very much a legitimate company and was more than something he did when he wasn't covert. He'd built it from the ground up and employed retired SEALs to work for him. He and his men instructed major corporations on how to tighten their security against guys like them. Guys who found ways to walk into secure installations.

He unpinned the elastic bandage around his abdomen and took it off. He pressed his fingers against his sixth and seventh ribs and sucked in his breath. Pain was good, he reminded himself. Pain let him know he was alive. Today he was *very* much alive, but he'd certainly lived through worse. Freezing his balls off and getting shot at in the North Sea while clinging to an ice-covered oil rig came to mind. Now, that was Max's version of hell, and he was certain when he did eventually die, that was where he'd play out eternity. In comparison, sitting aboard a disabled forty-seven-foot yacht with a few cracked ribs, a pain-in-the-ass underwear model and her pain-in-the-ass dog wasn't so bad. In fact, a little Carribean vacation might be just what he needed.

Wearing nothing but her patented Cleavage Clicker bra, Lola stuck her head out of the bathroom and looked around. Her gaze moved from the locked stateroom door to the blue dress lying on the king-sized bed. She'd forgotten to bring the dress into the bathroom with her, and she glanced up at the tinted porthole. When she didn't see a set of black and blue eyes peering back at her, she rushed to the side of the bed and quickly threaded her arms through the short sleeves. The nightmare of a dress was covered with bunches of red cherries, yellow bananas, and green grapes. It looked like it had been hit by a fruit stand, or with ambrosia salad, the stuff her grandmother always took to the families of those whose loved ones had 'passed over'.

She pulled the front closed and buttoned the material over her breasts and her pink bra. The Cleavage Clicker had been one of her first designs, and at that time a revolution in comfort and support. First-year sales had beaten projection by twenty-six per cent, and it was still her biggest moneymaker. Embroidered lace over soft stretch satin, with delicately scalloped edges, it was not only comfortable, it gave the wearer three different cleavage-enhancing options. Of course, shortly after it had appeared in her first catalog, the bra had been copied by just about everyone.

At the moment, though, enhancing her cleavage was the absolute last thing she wanted, but with the dress so tight across her breasts, it couldn't be avoided. When she was through with the buttons, she reached into her purse and pulled out her brush. She carefully removed the tangles from her hair, then raised her arms and wove it into a single braid. It was coated with salty sea air and felt like straw. She would have killed for a bath. A real dunking with soap and water, but she didn't dare. Not with 'good old Max' aboard.

Using the water from the pitcher Max had told her about, she'd brushed her teeth, then filled the sink in the bathroom and had washed as much of her body as possible. Then she'd taken off her pink panties and washed them as well. Once she'd finished, she'd hung them over the shower stall to dry. She figured if she kept her arms down, no one would notice that she wasn't wearing panties. *No one* meaning Max.

Besides being a thief, the man might be a murderer, too. And why that didn't frighten the heck out of her, she didn't know. Maybe because, other than tying her up and bruising her wrists, he hadn't really hurt her. And she figured after she'd threatened him with the flare gun and accidentally shot the helm, he probably wasn't going to kill her at this late date.

He did scare her, though. Even with his bruised face and battered body, he had overpowered her with ease. With the fish knife, she felt slightly safer around him.

More than her fear of him was the impotent anger building inside her. The more she thought of it, *anger* didn't even begin to describe what she felt about him and the situation he'd forced on her, never mind that he probably hadn't meant to drag her into his problems. He had anyway, and now she was stranded and there was a real possibility that she and Baby would die in the middle of the Atlantic. After the conversation she'd had with him that morning, she not only had to wonder if she'd die either of hunger or of dehydration, but now she had the added worry that she might die at the hands of the drug lords who'd beaten Max to a pulp.

Now when she held the signaling mirror in her hand, she'd have to wonder if it would save her life or bring a fate worse than starving to death. Either way, she had to try. No doubt the Thatches had already reported the yacht stolen, and surely *someone* would have noticed her missing also. They had to be searching for her.

So she would take her chances, be it with a drug lord or Coast Guard. She would keep signaling for help until someone got her off the darn boat.

Lola searched the stateroom for sunscreen and found a tube of SPF15 in the bathroom. She rubbed it into her dry skin, giving her face and neck a double coating. Sometime last night, she'd lost her sandals, and she looked around the room for another pair. She found nothing but an old pair of canvas sneakers and decided to pass.

She tilted her head to one side and studied herself in the mirrored closet doors. Besides being god-awful ugly, the dress obviously belonged to Dora Thatch, a woman who was five inches shorter than Lola and thirty pounds heavier. It fit loose about her hips and tight across her chest. The buttons closing the front gaped, and even when Lola lowered her arms, the dress hit her about midthigh. But the most disturbing part was the bunch of cherries strategically placed like a big fig leaf over her crotch.

From outside, Baby let loose with a barrage of wild barking and her heart about leaped from her chest. She grabbed the binoculars and mirror and headed out through the galley.

It wasn't until she stood on the aft deck, staring at nothing but endless blue ocean and sky, that she realized she'd expected to see the Coast Guard speeding toward them. Hope shriveled in her chest and sank to the pit of her stomach.

Baby stood at the open door at the stern of the boat, staring down at the swimming platform. He barked so hard his back legs rose off the deck. Lola moved to the wraparound seat, glanced over the stern, and got an eyeful of good old Max's naked butt. Obviously, he didn't suffer from modesty and had no problem bathing in front of *her*.

He lowered a bucket tied to the end of a rope into the ocean, then raised it and dumped it over his head. Water ran through his black hair and splashed on his wide shoulders. It ran down the defined muscles of his back and the indent of his spine. Droplets slid down the cheeks of his behind, the backs of his thighs, and puddled at his feet. He shook his head and beads of water flew in all directions.

Lola turned away, feeling a bit guilty for staring. God only knew what he really did for a living and what sins he'd committed doing it, but he had the kind of body reserved for the pages of a men's fitness magazine or a stripper calendar.

Even with his bruised face and obvious criminal bent, he was the kind of guy who made weak and silly women stick out their chests and purposely ignore obvious warning signs, like hairy knuckles and prison tattoos.

Lola was neither weak nor silly, nor was she attracted to men who tied her up against her will and threatened her dog. She took a quick peek over her shoulder as he lathered up his armpits with a bar of soap. He didn't have tattoos, but she had to admit that he did have a great butt. For a criminal.

She sank down on the bench seat and turned her attention to the burned-out bridge. When she'd spoken to him earlier, she couldn't help but notice the hard definition of his chest and arms. Beneath the purple bruises and short black hair covering his chest, the corrugated muscles of his six-pack were hard to miss. For years Lola had worked with beautiful male models, and she knew from experience that kind of body took a lot of work and dedication.

After barking himself hoarse, Baby gave it up and jumped into Lola's lap. She adjusted his spiked collar, then ran her hand over his fur to his tail. He'd been such a good boy through this whole trying ordeal. Once they were rescued, she'd take him to his favorite retreat, Spas and Paws, where he'd be pampered and made to feel like a Great Dane. Once they were home, she'd pamper herself, too. Get a herbal body wrap and deep muscle massage.

She gathered her binoculars and mirror in one hand, and with her dog in the other, she walked up the stairs to the bridge and looked around for her sandals. She found one in the corner and half the other one beside the helm, the heel scorched and the toe completely burned off. She left them where they lay and raised the binoculars to her eyes.

Nothing but blue sky and blue water filled her vision. She

stared so long through the binoculars, Baby abandoned her. Perspiration rolled down her temples and neck, and she wiped at it with her hand. Lola hated to sweat, and she suspected that she smelled bad. Neither of these things improved her mood as she looked for a hint of land or the speck of a boat or ship. She saw nothing, and after a while she couldn't tell where the sky stopped and ocean began.

A woman of action, she was unused to sitting around staring at the horizon, waiting for something to happen. Yet she had no other choice. She felt restless and fidgety, but with nothing else to do, she stayed up on the bridge with her binoculars and mirror.

She'd been missing less than twenty-four hours. She had to have patience and faith that she would be rescued. The problem was, she'd never had much patience, and she didn't have faith in anything but her own abilities. Although there had been a few times in her life when a strong shoulder to lean on would have been nice. When it would have been wonderful to dump her problems in the lap of some capable man and let him take care of things. Lola had never found that man, and she doubted she'd let him take care of her anyway.

Lola didn't know how long she stayed up on the bridge, but only after her head began to ache and her stomach grumble did she abandon her post.

She found Max on the aft deck, his behind in a folding chair, a fishing pole stuck in the chair's arm, a Dos Equis beer in his hand. He looked like a man at ease, as if he had nothing more pressing than polishing off a few. His wet T-shirt and jeans hung over the back of the boat to dry, as well as a pair of boxer briefs, ribbed cotton, charcoal gray, with a kangaroo fly. She was afraid to see what he was or wasn't wearing, afraid she'd see more than a fishing rod. She looked anyway.

A pair of navy nylon shorts with an elastic waist fit him snug just below his navel. He'd wrapped the bandage around his middle again, thin strips of white around his big chest. A tin of smoked salmon rested on his thigh, and he shoveled a chunk on a cracker, then popped it into his mouth. He dipped his fingers into the tin and flipped a small piece of fish to the dog sitting at his left foot.

Baby opened his jaws and swallowed without chewing. If Max thought the way to Baby's heart was through his stomach, he was right, but only to a point. Baby was a slave to his appetite for forbidden treats, but he was an absolute prisoner to his Napoleon complex. He would not be swayed from his mission to conquer bigger dogs by a few bites of smoked salmon.

'I thought you hated my dog,' she said.

He raised the beer to his lips and took a long swallow. 'I do,' he answered without looking at her. 'Just trying to fatten him up in case I need to eat him later.'

She wasn't certain he was kidding. 'Come on, Baby.' She motioned for the dog to follow as she walked inside the boat, but Baby refused to obey, choosing instead to stay by the man feeding him.

Feeling a bit betrayed, Lola checked on her underwear in the bathroom, found them only slightly damp along the elastic, and slipped them on. In the galley she scrounged around for lunch, although since she didn't have a watch, she supposed it could be time for dinner. In a sealed container in the refrigerator, she found a wheel of Brie. She grabbed it along with a bunch of grapes and a banana. Since Baby had opted to stay outside, Lola was forced to join him to make sure he didn't eat too much greasy salmon and get sick.

She found a place to sit between Max's wet pants and T-shirt, then opened the container of cheese. She needed something to cut the Brie, and as if Max had read her mind, he handed her the fish knife sheathed in its scabbard.

'You keep forgetting this,' he said as she took it from him.

Lola opened her mouth to thank him but didn't. She wouldn't need a knife at all if it wasn't for him. She cut off a slice of cheese and ate it along with two grapes. Max shoved a box of crackers toward her, and she took a stack of Rye Crisps into her hand. 'Please don't feed Baby any more fish. He'll get sick.'

Max didn't respond, but he polished off the rest of the salmon himself. He didn't offer her any, which Lola thought was rude, but she really didn't expect polite behavior from him. She peeled her banana and glanced out at the ocean, looking anywhere but at him. She hated to admit it, but he still made her nervous with his battered face and hard muscles. She took a bite of her banana and spotted her toothbrush sticking up out of a holder in the stern. 'Why is my toothbrush in a fishing pole holder?'

'I used it.'

She did look at him then, straight at his bruised face and light blue eyes. She swallowed the banana. 'For what?'

'To brush my teeth.'

'Tell me you're kidding.'

'Nope.'

'You stole my toothbrush?'

He shook his head. 'Commandeered.'

'That's disgusting!'

'I soaked it in rum first to kill your germs.'

'*My* germs?' Her mouth fell open as she stared at him, at the slight swelling beneath his left eye, at his black and purple cheekbone, and the white Steri-Strips on his forehead. She was tired, hot, and sweaty, and a man she didn't know had used her toothbrush. 'That's just sick . . . and . . . and,' she sputtered as she rose, knife in one hand, banana in the other. The container of cheese fell to the deck and Baby pounced on it. Lola didn't care; she had another sort of pouncing in mind. 'And disgusting!'

His gaze lowered from her face to the knife in her hand. 'It's not like I brushed my ass with it.'

'Just about!'

'What are you so mad about?' he asked. He rose also and gestured with the beer bottle. 'I put it in the fish holder so the sun would sterilize it.'

She couldn't believe he was actually serious. 'You kidnap me, get me stranded in the middle of the Atlantic, use *my* toothbrush, and wonder why I'm mad? What's wrong with you? Did you eat paint chips as a child?'

He didn't answer her last question, but instead pointed out, 'Give it a rest. You *weren't* kidnapped, and *you* got us stranded.'

Lola was in no mood to even consider taking the blame for anything. 'What are you going to do next, steal my underwear?'

His gaze slid down the front of her dress, over her breasts, and down her abdomen. He took a slow drink of his beer as he contemplated the red cherries printed on the material over her crotch. 'I don't know,' he drawled, 'are they still hanging up in the bathroom or would I have to wrestle them off you?'

'They're no longer hanging in the bathroom,' she informed him through tight lips.

He looked back up into her face and smiled, with his nice, white, recently brushed teeth. 'Go ahead and keep them. Pink really isn't my color.'

With the realization that he'd probably touched her underwear, she discovered in that moment what she'd wondered the night before. No, she couldn't stick a knife into a man's throat, because if she was capable of it, she'd have killed good old Max. Gladly.

'I don't know what has you tight as a tick,' he said right before he polished off his beer. 'It's not like I have anything you can catch.'

'What? Am I supposed to take your word on that?' She took a step back and looked him up and down. 'I don't even know who or what you are.'

'I told you last night who and what I am.'

Moisture trickled down her neck, and she wiped it away with her shoulder. She had a headache, her eyes felt scratchy, and she wanted a bath. She was so darn miserable, she couldn't stand herself. All she really wanted was to slip between clean sheets and sleep until this nightmare was over. 'I know what you said, but you can't prove it.'

'True. You're just going to have to take my word for it.'

'Right.' Lola carefully resheathed the knife and desperately tried to control her emotions before she did something mortifying like break into a fit of crying hysterics in front of him. 'I'm supposed to take the word of a man who stole my private property and just threatened to eat my dog.'

He shrugged. 'You don't have a choice.'

'Oh, I always have a choice, and I choose not to believe a word that comes out of your mouth.'

'Suit yourself, but fighting with me over something so trivial as a toothbrush might not be in your best interest.'

'You don't scare me.'

'I should. I'm bigger than you and meaner than you ever thought of being.'

'You don't know how mean I've ever thought of being.' And at the moment, she was feeling mean. Real mean.

He tipped his head back and dismissed her with a deep laugh filled with amusement, which pushed her beyond her fear of him. She took a step closer and stuck her finger in his chest. 'Don't laugh at me.'

'What are you going to do about it? Poke holes in my chest with your fingernail?'

'Maybe I'll smack your good eye and give you a matching shiner.' The thought of it almost brought a smile to her face. Almost, but she was too mad at the moment.

He wrapped his hand around hers and removed her finger from him. 'I probably wouldn't let you take a jab at me.' She tugged, but he tightened his grasp, imprisoning her within his strong warm palm. 'Now that I can see it coming.'

'I could wait until you're asleep.'

'You could, but I wouldn't advise you to come anywhere near me when I'm in bed.' Again she pulled, and instead of letting go, he took a step closer, closing the slight gap between them.

'Or what? You'll tie me up again or something?'

His gaze dropped to their hands, his still wrapped around hers and the only thing separating her breasts from the dark hair on his chest. 'Or something,' he said just above a whisper, then raised his gaze as far as her mouth. 'Oh, I'd definitely come up with something. Something a little more fun than a poke in the eye.'

Lola recognized the suddenly rough texture in his voice. The flash of desire in his blue eyes. She'd heard and seen it a lot in her life. While she felt no answering spark, no reciprocating interest, neither did she feel a flicker of revulsion. Which really didn't surprise her, given her all-consuming anger.

'Well, don't tax your brain,' she told him, and finally pulled her hand free. The force of the motion carried her a few steps back. 'I will never be a willing participant in any of your warped fantasies.'

The light inside the galley poured over Max's head as he studied the map he'd spread out on the table. He'd started one of the generators as the sun had dipped below the horizon, and he had changed into his dry clothes, the material still stiff from the salt water. He'd plugged a Jimmy Buffet tape into the stereo, and 'Cheeseburger in Paradise' competed with the hum of the refrigerator. With the lights on, the *Dora Mae* would be a little easier to spot by passing vessels, but Max wasn't overly concerned. It wouldn't be that easy to spot and, since they weren't sending out any sort of distress signal, wouldn't attract much attention.

He circled his estimated position on the map, which he had

determined by using the position of the stars in the sky and a compass he'd found in the stateroom. He was certain they were between Andros and the Bimini Islands. How close to either one was the question. They were still drifting on a warm northwest current, but a southeasterly wind had picked up a little. He doubted they were traveling much more than two knots in any direction.

The click-click of toenails drew Max's attention to the doorway. Through the darkness, Baby Doll Carlyle entered the galley and jumped up onto the seat. He hopped onto the table, put his ears back, and stared at Max.

'Oh, Christ, not again,' Max groaned, and rose from behind the table. He grabbed his second beer of the day from the refrigerator and held it up in silent salute. Not only had the Thatches furnished him with a yacht, but they'd provided him with good beer, too. The galley was stocked with enough party food and booze to last a month.

Luckily, he'd also found more substantial staples in the pantry. Mostly it was filled with tomato juice, jars of green olives, and vermouth. He figured if he were a big drinker, there was enough alcohol aboard to keep himself good and drunk for weeks on end. But on a bottom shelf he'd also discovered white rice and cans of pears.

He thought of Lola, of seeing his hand wrapped around hers and her breasts threatening to pop the buttons on the front of that ugly dress. He pried off the top of the beer, and for about half a second the thought of getting shit-house drunk, to escape into a bottle for a few days, held a certain appeal. But Max knew the reality of that sort of existence. He'd watched it take his father, and he'd made up his mind long ago that it would never take him. He was stronger than that. Stronger than booze and stronger than his old man. He would never let anything control him the way rum had controlled Fidel Zamora.

The little dog on the table let out a yap, and Max slid him a glance. 'Where's your owner?' he asked, although he had a pretty good idea. The last he'd seen of her, she'd grabbed a chaise lounge from a storage compartment and dragged it to the bridge.

Max took a drink of the Dos Equis and headed outside. Lola hadn't said a word to him after their toothbrush confrontation. Maybe he should have asked her permission first, but he'd figured she'd say no, and he would have used it anyway. So he hadn't seen any point in asking and still didn't. And like he'd told her, it wasn't as if he had anything she could catch. God knows part of his annual physical consisted of every test known to the medical community, but if it made her feel better, he'd boil the damn thing.

His feet bare, he moved up the stairs to the bridge. He took a few steps and looked down at her through the deep shadows of night. The running lights from the port and starboard sides still worked and shone in Lola's hair. Her eyes were closed and her lips were slightly parted. Her breasts rose and fell on soft even breaths, the buttons on her dress still gapping and threatening to pop. One empty hand lay open across her abdomen, her other hung over the side of the chaise, the mirror clutched within her fingers.

The red shawl she'd worn earlier for a skirt was tangled about her legs. Max pulled it up over her, then reached for the binoculars on the floor. He looked out at the horizon, searching for buoys or any signs they might be nearing a coastline. He saw nothing but the reflection of the moon on the black surface of the ocean and the slight breaking of waves.

There was a real possibility that after Max was rescued, he would be arrested for theft and kidnapping. At the very least he would be detained, but he wasn't real worried about that. One phone call and any charges would disappear.

The only thing that had him worried was sitting in the middle of the Atlantic without his vest of lethal goodies, namely his 9mm sidearm, two mags of subsonic ammunition, and his K-Bar assault knife. Without them, he felt naked and at the mercy of any passing vessel. Max trusted no one and nothing, least of all unknown elements.

He glanced at Lola, and at the fish knife that had slipped from her hand to the deck. As a warrior, she sucked. She slept through his intrusion of her space, and she couldn't keep track of her weapon. He reached for the knife and slid it into the waistband of his jeans.

Moonlight caressed one side of her face and touched the bow of her top lip. No doubt about it, Lola was one beautiful woman. The kind of woman men fantasized about.

I will never be a willing participant in any of your warped fantasies, she'd told him as if she'd read his mind. Warped? His fantasies weren't warped. Well, not as warped as some guys' he knew.

He'd never been the kind of man to buy swimsuit calendars or flip through underwear ads, but he would have had to have lived on another planet not to know who she was, not have seen her on calendars, in bra commercials, on billboards and the covers of magazines. He would have to be dead below the waist not to have wondered what it would be like to have sex with her. To get all sweaty and mess up her hair and eat off her lipstick.

Max thought of the first time he remembered seeing her likeness. It had been in Times Square, probably about eight years ago. He'd been waiting for a cab outside the Hiatt when he'd looked up and seen her, staring back at him from a billboard, her blond hair scraped back from her face, her brown eyes heavy, as if she were gazing at her lover, her lush body clad in nothing but a pair of peekaboo lace panties and matching bra.

White. His favorite.

As he'd looked up at her that first time, he'd wondered who she was. And just like every other man looking up at her, picturing her naked, knowing he didn't stand a chance with a woman like that, he'd told himself she was probably a lousy lay anyway. Too skinny and afraid of smudging her lipstick to be any good. Probably the type of girl who expected the guy to do all the work. Yeah, that's what he told himself, only he'd never been a man opposed to work. Especially not that kind.

Looking at her now, he decided she didn't appear too thin. In fact, she was just the sort of woman Max liked to wrap his arms around. Full-breasted and enough behind to fill his big hands. When he held a woman, he liked to feel her soft, curvy body pressed against him. He didn't want to feel bones. He didn't want to worry she'd break.

He gazed at her softly parted lips, and unbidden, his thoughts turned to kissing Lola Carlyle. She wasn't wearing any lipstick now, and he wondered what it would be like to sink slowly into a kiss and taste her lips. To feel her hesitation, the uncertain hitch, right before he felt her sigh. The ahhh that let him know she wanted him, too. The moment she turned soft and willing beneath his mouth. Beneath him, Max Zamora. Fidel Zamora's boy. The dirty-faced kid whose father forgot about him whenever he fell into a bottle of rum. Which was most of the time.

Max hadn't been born into money, he wasn't a famous actor or rock star, the kind of guys women like Lola Carlyle usually went for, but that didn't keep him from wondering what it would be like to touch a woman like her. To feel her soft breasts pressed tight against his chest as he tangled his fingers in her sweet-smelling hair.

Max sucked in a breath of cool salty air and let it out slowly. All that wondering was quickly taking him to a place he was better off not going. Someplace that had his battered body reacting as if there were something he could or would do about it. Someplace that spiked his blood and shot a burning ache straight to his groin. Someplace he would never go with a woman like Lola. Someplace she would never go with a man like him. He wasn't rich and famous or a pretty-boy model. She wasn't the kind of woman who'd put up with a man who disappeared for days and weeks on end, never telling her when he'd be back or where he'd been. Hell, he'd never found any woman who'd put up with that for very long.

Max turned on his heels and walked from the bridge. It was best for them both if he didn't think about her at all. Taking a seat in the folding chair he'd sat in earlier, he reached for the fishing pole and reeled in the line. He concentrated on the empty line instead of the sleeping underwear model on the bridge.

He figured he'd have more luck catching a fish if he had a better idea of what he was doing. Over the past several years, he'd fished a few times in lakes and streams, but he'd never been a real angler. Hell, he'd done most of his 'fishing' in the front yard of the old house he and his father had rented in Galveston.

Thinking back on it, he figured he must have been about seven when the old man had bought him that Zebco reel mounted on a six-foot rod. He still had it hidden away in a closet, one of his few childhood possessions.

Even now, he could recall the weight of that rod and reel in his hands. His father had been on the wagon then, and he'd tied a sinker to the end of the line and had given Max casting lessons, the two of them side by side, standing in that yard as the sun set, aiming the sinkers at clumps of grass and talking about the fish they planned to catch someday. Max could still recall the touch of his father's hands and the sound of his Cuban accent on the soft humid breeze.

Unfortunately, the old man spent most of his time off the wagon and he'd never managed to take Max fishing, but that hadn't kept Max from waiting and practicing. After a few years, he'd become one hell of a caster. Overhead, sideways, and underhanded, he could hit any target dead on. He'd always figured all that practice had come in handy and was the reason he'd breezed through sniper training.

As he shifted positions in the chair, his ribs ached only slightly less sitting down than they did walking or standing. He raised the binoculars to his eyes and gazed out into the black ocean. The only complete relief he'd found from the pain in his side had been the few hours he'd managed to lie perfectly flat on his back the night before. He could use a few hours of sleep, but he wouldn't get it tonight. Not when anyone could catch him off guard.

But Max hadn't slept in over two days, and he drifted to sleep an hour before the sun rose above the eastern horizon.

4

Max wasn't sure how long he'd slept before his eyes snapped open, and he came instantly awake. The morning sun bounced off the waves and the chrome handholds on the yacht. Without turning, he was aware of movement behind him. He didn't have to look to know that it was Lola. Not just because she was the only other person on the boat, but by now he'd learned the unique sound of her light footsteps. She paused by the galley door before proceeding inside, her little dog following close behind.

Slowly Max rose and moved his head from side to side, working out the kinks. The yacht rocked within a foot-high chop, and the ache in his ribs felt worse than when he'd first been kicked; his muscles were stiff from the cramped position he'd slept in. Max was thirty-six and had spent the last fifteen years pushing the limits of his body. When he'd been younger, he'd been able to sleep on his head without so much as a twinge the next morning. Not now. Now the older he got, the more his body pushed back. He rolled his shoulders and heard Lola and her dog exit the galley. He cast a backward glance as they moved down the gunwale to the bow of the boat. The bottom of her fruity dress brushed the backs of her thighs, and she held her binoculars in one hand and a granola bar in the other.

Since she hadn't said one word to him, he figured she was still ticked off about the toothbrush. He looked up at the cloudless sky and stretched his arms over his head. She was obviously one of those women who liked to hang on to her anger, and he figured he'd let her. No need to disrupt the peace just to hear her bitch at him. And now that she was up and manning her post at the bow of the yacht, he figured he'd slip into the stateroom and catch a few.

An ear-piercing scream split the still Carribean morning, and he turned so fast, pain stabbed his ribs like a stiletto. He sucked air into the top of his lungs and moved toward the gunnel just in time to see Lola go over the side, her dress flying up past her butt. She hit the water, and quick as a cork, she popped back up within the waves, sputtering and sobbing almost incoherently.

'Baby!' she cried, and frantically looked about her in the water. 'Baby, where are you?'

The dog bobbed up once, then went down again, a brown spot of fur in the blue sea.

'Shit,' Max swore as he tore off his T-shirt. With his ribs throbbing and his muscles protesting, he dove into the Atlantic Ocean after Baby Doll Carlyle. The cool salt water hit his face and rushed over his chest. He dove just deep enough to come up under the dog, and he grabbed him in one hand. When his head cleared the water, he glanced around for Lola, but he didn't see her. The dog coughed and hacked and immediately started to shake. Max was just about to chuck the dog and dive for Lola when the back of her head surfaced.

'Baby!' she coughed on a mouthful of ocean.

'I have him,' Max called to her as he easily trod water.

She turned and splashed toward him. Not only was she a lousy warrior, she couldn't swim worth a damn, either. Her brown eyes were huge and she sucked in quick, shallow gasps of oxygen. If she wasn't careful, she'd hyperventilate, but it didn't look like she was going to be careful anytime soon. She grabbed Max's shoulder and nearly pushed him under. At the height of his SEAL team days, Max had been able to hold his breath for three minutes underwater, bob back up, and swim for hours. He wasn't worried that either of them, or the dumb dog, would drown. He was only concerned that she'd make getting to the back of the boat harder than need be.

'Is Baby o-okay?' she managed, and reached for her dog. A wave washed over their heads and she pulled them under this time. Down they went in a tangle of legs and arms. One of her knees smashed into his side, and he sucked in half a mouthful of salt water. The dog's toenails scratched Max's neck as Lola got him into a headlock, smashing the side of his face into the tops of her breasts, and clinging to him as if he were a buoy. He pried Lola's arm from around his head, kicked to the surface, and spit out the water in his mouth. 'Relax,' he said into her panic-stricken face so close to his own. Their noses touched and they shared the same breath. 'Relax or you'll drown.'

Her mouth opened and shut, working to get the words out, but only a sob came from her chest.

'I can get us all to the back of the boat, but you have to relax and let me do the work. No more grabbing me and pushing me under. And keep your knee out of my chest.' He thought a second, then added, 'If you knee my *cojones*, you're on your own.'

She nodded and he handed her the dog. She held Baby's head next to hers as Max wrapped his arm over her shoulder and across her breasts. He towed them toward the swimming platform, but she didn't make it easy for him. She kicked him twice in the shins when she should have done as he'd said and let him do all the work. She twisted her head around to see where they were going and the top of her head bumped his bruised cheek. He pulled her back tight against his chest as he scissor-kicked in the water. This was the absolute last time, Max vowed as he reached a hand for the swimming deck, that he would jump into the Atlantic to save an underwear model and her worthless dog.

He hoisted Baby onto the back of the yacht, grabbed the boarding ladder from the platform, and pulled it down into the water. Getting up those steps was going to hurt like a son of a bitch, which was why he'd rigged the bucket and rope to bathe the day before. Lola started up first, her muscles sluggish, her grasp on the rail weak as if her hands were numb, which Max figured they were because she was hyperventilating real bad now. Her dress clung to her thighs and water ran down her smooth legs and the backs of her knees. He placed one of his hands on the curve of her wet behind and pushed.

Max went up after her, and he'd been right. Climbing the ladder hurt like hellfire. He lay on the platform, his pants soggy, and concentrated on slowing his breathing and controlling the pain in his side.

Lola sat next to him, clutching Baby to her chest, crying and gasping for air. If she wasn't careful, she would pass out cold, which was one way to cure hyperventilation, he supposed. But there were other, less dramatic ways.

'Concentrate on taking slow easy breaths through your nose.' He wiped salt water from his face and he pushed himself to a sitting position. Other than a paper bag or passing out, taking slow breaths through your nose was the only way he knew to ease hyperventilation.

She looked at him as if he were speaking a mystery language, her brown eyes wide with fear. 'I ca-ca-can't catch my br-breath.'

'Lie down with your arms above your head,' he instructed, and moved to give her room. When she stretched out, he told her again, 'Close your mouth and breathe slowly through your nose.'

As her dog licked her face, she nodded and sucked a huge breath into her lungs through her mouth. Max had only hyperventilated once in his life, and he knew it wasn't all that easy to control your breathing when you felt like you couldn't get enough air. Ocean water lapped at the platform as he straddled her hips and shoved the wet dog out of his way. The buttons on her dress had popped open to her navel and droplets of water slid from the pink lace of her bra and pooled in her deep cleavage. Her breasts heaved with each breath, and Max placed his hands on both sides of her face. Ocean water clung to her lashes, and he stared deep into her eyes.

'Close your mouth,' he reminded her, and he had to give her credit for trying.

'I'm – I'm going to – to pass out,' she gasped.

'Concentrate on breathing only through your nose.'

'Ca-can't.'

He thought about putting his hand over her mouth, but he figured she'd accuse him of trying to kill her. 'Then concentrate on this instead,' he whispered, and, against his better judgment, lowered his face to hers. He told himself this wasn't a kiss. He was helping her, forcing her to breathe through her nose so she wouldn't pass out.

Beneath the pressure of his mouth, he felt her tense. She sucked in one last breath and held it as he lightly pressed his lips into hers. He brushed his thumbs across her smooth cheeks. 'Relax now,' he whispered against her mouth. She put her hands on his shoulders and he thought she would push him away, but she didn't. Her big brown eyes stared into his, and in a flash, the warmth of her palms spread across his bare skin. Pure lust sped like a wildfire through his blood and tightened his groin.

Whether it was for the taste of food or drugs or rum, Max hated weakness of any kind. He didn't like to admit to having any weakness at all, but if he did have one, this was it. He had a weakness for the taste of a woman's mouth and the feel of her face held within his hands. The catch in her voice, and the smell of her skin and hair.

Her lips parted as if she would speak.

'Breathe through your nose,' he reminded her, and his lips brushed against hers as he spoke. She tasted of sunshine and salt water and pure heaven. Women were such a mystery to him. They were illogical and often contrary to the point of being irrational, and yet there were times he craved the sound of their twisted logic. Just as there were times that he definitely craved the touch of their flesh beneath his hands and mouth and body. No doubt about it, a woman's satiny places and warm curves were an intoxicating weakness, but one he'd always managed to control. He would control it this time, too.

'Max?'

'Hmm.'

'You're not kissing me, are you?'

Max lifted his head and looked down into Lola's face. He saw confusion in the slant of her brow, and alarm in her clear brown eyes, but not a trace of the same lust that beat low in his belly and had turned him half hard.

'No,' he said as he sat back on his heels. 'If I were kissing you, you'd know it.'

'Good, because I don't want you to get any ideas about me and you.'

'What ideas are those?' he asked, even though he guessed he already knew.

She sat up and pulled her feet beneath her. An ocean breeze picked up several strands of her drying hair. 'I appreciate you saving Baby, but you and I will never become romantically involved.' She shook her head. 'Never.'

There it was. A cold slap that cooled the warmth in his blood. The reminder that good old Max was good enough to save her butt, but not good enough to kiss her lips. At least Lola was honest about it.

'Honey, don't flatter yourself,' he said as he put his hands on his thighs and stood. His ribs ached, and the cut on his forehead stung. 'I don't get romantically involved with anyone. Not even for you.'

*

Jumping in after Baby, Lola had lost her binoculars and signaling mirror in the Atlantic. And she wasn't sure, but she thought she may have hurt Max's feelings, too. She sat on the aft deck, huddled beneath a wool blanket he'd thrown at her. Waves slapped against the sides of the yacht as it rode the ocean current. The morning sun touched her cheeks and bounced off the white walls of the *Dora Mae*.

'I *am* grateful to you for saving Baby,' she said as she raised one hand to shield her eyes. Her dog's wet fur tickled her chest and she hugged his shaking little body.

Without acknowledging her in any way, Max unpinned the wet Ace bandages around his chest.

'And me, too.' She'd never been a strong swimmer. Though, under normal circumstances, she was certainly competent enough to have made it to the back of the boat, but the thought of Baby drowning, scared and helpless, of him sliding beneath the waves as his little lungs filled with water, had stolen her breath, and she wasn't so certain that she wouldn't have drowned right along with her dog. And even if she had managed to get back to the swimming platform, Baby would certainly be dead if Max hadn't dived in and saved him. She was pretty sure she'd insulted him, and after what he'd just done for her, she owed him more than that. 'I'm sorry I insinuated that you were using the situation to kiss me.'

Finally he glanced up and tossed the bandage on the seat next to her. 'The next time you hyperventilate, I'm just going to let you pass out.'

Yep, she'd insulted him and hurt his feelings. Or

rather, what passed for his feelings, because she wasn't certain he had normal human emotions. She lowered her hand and looked down at the wool blanket pooled in her lap. She didn't want to think of Max as having normal human emotions. She didn't want to think of him as a person. He was responsible for the current situation, and he was responsible for putting her and Baby into danger. If it wasn't for Max, Baby wouldn't be on the *Dora Mae*, and he wouldn't have fallen overboard.

The dog wiggled out of Lola's grasp and fought his way through the folds of the blanket. He jumped to the deck, shook once, then moved to stand by Max's left foot. For once, he didn't bark.

As she'd lain beneath Max on the swimming platform, trying to catch her breath, Lola had been so sure he'd been about to kiss her. She'd felt the heat of his lips and seen the desire in his eyes, and she was old enough, and had been around enough men, to know the signs.

Okay, maybe she'd been wrong this time. He'd obviously been trying to help her breathe, and she felt a little silly and embarrassed for misunderstanding him. She raised her gaze up Max's long legs to his fingers tugging at his button fly. He hooked his thumbs in the waistband of his pants and shoved them down his hips and thighs. 'I'm sorry I misunderstood what you were trying to do. I don't know what was—'

'Forget about it,' he interrupted, his wet boxer briefs clinging to him like a second skin. Lola turned her gaze away, but not before getting an eyeful. A *big* eyeful that almost had her doing a double-take. 'Tell me something. What were you doing vacationing all by yourself on Dolphin Cay?' he asked, and she got the feeling he wanted the subject changed as badly as she did.

'Why?'

He hung his wet pants over the side of the boat. 'Just curious.'

'I wanted to get away for a few days,' she said, which was basically the truth.

'To Dolphin Cay?'

She quickly looked up into his eyes and kept her gaze there, afraid to look below his shoulders. Afraid he'd whip off those boxers. 'Right.'

'I'd have thought a girl like you would rather spend time at Club Med, or . . .' He paused and ran his hands over his head from front to back, pushing water from his black hair. Clear droplets slid down the sides of his neck. 'What is that other swank place there on Nassau?'

'The Ocean Club,' she provided. She'd spent a few weeks there a couple of summers ago.

'Yeah, that's it. So what were you doing on a tiny island with just your dog for company?'

'I didn't want to be around people.'

'Why?'

'I didn't want people pointing and staring at me.'

'Aren't you used to that by now? A famous model like you, I bet you get stared at a lot.'

This was different. 'It's been different since those photographs appeared on the net.'

'What photographs?'

Was it possible that there was someone on the planet who hadn't seen those embarrassing photos of her on the Internet?

Hadn't heard about them? Beyond the tabloids, the court case had made national news.

'What photographs?' he asked again.

She didn't want to talk about it with Max. This morning she didn't hate him as she had the night before, and he'd probably say something to make her mad, like she'd been an idiot to let Sam take the pictures and she deserved what she got. Which might be true, but she'd been very much in love with Sam, and she'd trusted him. Or Max might say that she was only upset because *she* hadn't been paid for the photographs. The last opinion had been floated about by Sam's attorney and made her see red when she heard it.

Max grabbed the fishing chair and took a seat. He folded his arms across his chest and slouched a little as if he were prepared to wait all day for her answer.

Black stubble shadowed the lower half of his face where it wasn't bruised. The strips closing the cut on his forehead appeared very white against his tan skin, and he looked like such a disreputable pirate, she decided it didn't matter what she told him because he'd probably done a lot worse than trust someone with naked photos. 'Because of Sam's Internet site,' she said.

'Who's Sam?'

'My ex-fiancé.' She pushed the itchy blanket off her shoulders and it pooled at her hips. 'He set up an Internet site with some very embarrassing photographs of me.'

'Naked photos?'

'Yes.'

'Close-ups?'

'Close enough.' The ocean breeze ruffled the front of her

dress and brushed across her chest and stomach. She glanced down at the material, open to her navel, and began the work of buttoning it back up.

'What was so embarrassing?'

'Never mind.'

'Were you doing the mattress mambo?'

'The what?'

'Getting it on. Doing the nasty. Having sex.'

She glanced up into his blue eyes looking back into hers, then she returned her attention to the buttons. 'No.' Her fingers were cold and getting the buttons through the wet material was difficult.

'Were you flying solo?'

It took her a few seconds to figure out what he was asking. 'No,' she answered.

'Giving him—'

'No!' she interrupted before his one-track mind traveled any deeper into the gutter. 'I was riding a bike and kissing a Tootsie Roll.'

He was silent, and when he spoke, he sounded very disappointed. 'That's it?'

'Yes.' She glanced up into his face once more, and this time caught him watching the progress of her fingers as she pushed the last button through the last hole. She quickly dropped her hand to her side. Then as if he had all day, he raised his gaze up her throat, past her chin and mouth, to her eyes.

His voice dropped lower when he asked, 'Alone or with your fiancé?'

'Alone.' She reached for the ends of the blanket and wrapped it around her shoulders, shielding herself from his gaze. Again, she was surprised that his gaze didn't feel as creepy or repulsive as she thought it should have been. In fact, she didn't feel repulsed at all. More in the neighborhood of unnerved. Unnerved by the intense blue and the glimpse of hunger she saw in his eyes. Unnerved that it tightened her chest a little. Then he blinked, and the desire was gone as if it had never been there at all.

'That doesn't sound so terrible,' he said as if he hadn't been caught staring at her breasts.

He acted so nonchalant, she wondered why she suddenly felt a little flustered. It wasn't as if this were the first time a man had seen her bra, for goodness' sakes. At one time, she'd had the most photographed cleavage in the world. 'It was a king-sized Tootsie Roll,' she explained.

He raised a brow as if to say, *So what?*

'And I wasn't really kissing it.'

'What were you really doing?'

She told him because, while it was embarrassing, it wasn't exactly a secret. And if he was dying to know, he could pay twenty-five bucks like the rest of the world and see it on the Internet, anyway. Once they were rescued, that is. 'My Linda Lovelace impression.'

The corners of his mouth slid into a purely masculine smile that reached his blue eyes. 'You do a Linda Lovelace impression?'

'Don't tell me. You want the details?'

'God, yes,' he said on a rush of air.

She laughed. 'Forget it.'

'What if I ask real nice?'

'No.'

'You're no fun, Lolita,' he said, using the Spanish form of her name.

Baby jumped up on the seat next to her, and she took his soaked collar from around his neck.

'What's the name of this website?'

'Why, are you going to pay twenty-five bucks to see those pictures?'

'You've got me curious about the Tootsie Roll.' He shrugged. 'Would it bother you if I did?'

'Of course.'

'Why?'

She couldn't believe he was asking such an obvious question. 'Well, duh. I'm naked.'

'You've posed naked before.'

'Not completely.' The closest she'd come was during her days working for a major line of cosmetics. She'd been hired to endorse their skin-care products. In the straight-on shot, she'd worn nothing but scented body oil. She'd posed against a red background, her ankles crossed and her knees raised just enough to hide her pubic area. From behind, a pair of male hands covered her breasts. She'd starved herself for a week before that shoot. When it had wrapped, she'd hit the Wendy's drive-through window and ordered a number two Biggie-sized.

'I'd say getting photographed in lacy bras and panties is pretty damn close.'

It wasn't the same thing, and she didn't know why she should explain it to him, but she tried anyway. 'Whenever I agreed to do any shoot, I had control of my image. It was always my choice. *Lolarevealed.com* was not my choice. It is a violation not only of my body, but of my trust. I never would have chosen to have those pictures published anywhere, especially on a porno site on the Internet. My parents were mortified.' And she never would have chosen to see her image at the height of her sickness. When she'd been out of control, and every single waking and sleeping moment had been consumed with thoughts of food and guilt. Of obsessively clipping recipes she never tried and buying cookbooks she never used. 'I wouldn't expect you to understand.'

He grasped his side, took a deep breath, and stood. 'I understand a little about having no control.' He grabbed the fishing pole he'd used yesterday. 'No control over what happens in your life or how others see you. And I also know a bit about broken trust and getting screwed.'

'By who?' Perhaps he did understand, but it was hard to see the overpowering man standing at such ease in front of her in his boxer briefs upset by anything. Looking at him, with his big neck and broad shoulders, she couldn't imagine anyone brave enough to cross him. 'Who, Max?' she prompted.

'Not a who.' He glanced at her out of the corner of his eyes, then returned his gaze to the tangled line in his hands. 'A what.'

She could have told him he had the wrong kind of tackle for drift fishing, but at the moment she was more interested in what he had to say than in what he was doing. When he didn't provide anything further, she asked, 'Then *what*?' When he still didn't expand, she sighed. 'Come on, Max. I told you about the Tootsie Roll incident.'

He glanced at her, then returned his gaze to his lure. 'Several years ago I was "retired" from the Navy,' he began as he untangled line from the barbed hooks. 'During my career, I'd pissed off a few high-ranking officials, and when one of them was appointed secretary of the Navy, he wanted me gone. So it was *sayonara*, Max.'

'What did you do?'

He shrugged his bare shoulders. 'I didn't always play by the rules,' he said, which told her nothing. 'I did what it took to complete a mission, and for that I had a choice of retirement or federal prison.'

Okay, not exactly nothing. 'Prison? What was the charge?'

'Conspiracy. At that time, I was part of the Navy's Special Warfare Development Group.' He paused and looked at her as if she might have a clue what that meant. She didn't. 'DEVGRU is a counterterrorism, intelligence, and national security unit. We also created and tested weapons, and it seems I conspired with a private contractor to defraud the United States government out of thirty-five thousand dollars.'

'How?'

'By charging them for bogus assault weapons.'

Since she was dying to know, she decided there was no harm in asking, 'Did you do it?'

'Right,' he snorted, and dropped the lure in his hands. 'If I wanted to hang my ass out there for the government to chew on, I'd make sure it was for a hell of a lot more money than thirty-five grand.' He moved to the side of the yacht, brought the tip of the pole behind him, and snapped it forward. He cast so far out, Lola lost sight of the lure before it dropped into the Atlantic. 'All thirty-five grand will get you these days is a decent car, and a decent car isn't worth prison time.'

'What would be worth prison time? A Ferrari?'

He thought about it for a moment, then shook his head. 'Nah.'

She smiled. 'What took you so long to answer?'

'A Ferrari deserves some serious consideration.'

'That's true,' she laughed. 'Did you get a lawyer and fight it?'

'Yes, but when the evidence the government has against you is classified and you and your lawyer don't have the proper clearance to view the material, you're screwed, blued, and tattooed.'

Standing with his profile to her, his eyelids lowered against the bright Caribbean sunlight, the carved line of his jaw and chin softened with black stubble, he almost seemed like a real person with real problems. And it almost felt as if they were having a real conversation, too, and since they seemed to be communicating with each other like real people, she figured he'd want to know he was fishing with the wrong lure. 'You're not going to catch anything with that tackle,' she told him.

He glanced across his shoulder at her, the breeze drying the ends of his hair. 'I think I will.'

The blanket itched the backs of her thighs and she stood. 'Whoever used that pole before you rigged it with a spinner. You'll need a jig. Something that will attract deepwater fish. You might get lucky, but I don't think you will.'

He stared at her for several seconds before he said, 'Is that right?'

Okay, maybe he didn't want to know. Or perhaps he was like a lot of men when it came to taking any sort of advice from a woman. 'Yes.'

His black brows lowered over his eyes and he shoved the

end of the pole into the holder on the arm of the chair. 'Maybe you should stick to what you know. Modeling undies.'

Yep, he was like a lot of men. So much for conversing like real people. 'You'd be surprised at all the things I know. Before my grandfather died, he owned a fishing charter business in Charleston, and when I went to see him in the summers, I'd go out with him sometimes.' She tossed the blanket onto the seat. 'And I don't model any more. I design lingerie. Have you ever heard of Lola Wear, Inc.?'

'Nope,' he said as he sat.

'It's my company,' she informed him with no small measure of pride. His gaze was perfectly bland and so she elaborated a bit. 'I started it with a few bras I designed myself, and now I employ hundreds of people.'

'So now you make undies instead of modeling them?'

'That's right. I'm surprised you haven't heard of my business.'

He laced his hands behind his head and yawned. The muscles of his shoulders and arms bunched, and dark hair shadowed his armpits. 'You make anything edible?'

'No!'

'Then it's not so surprising,' he said. 'I wouldn't know a designer label unless I choked on it.'

5

Max let his gaze wander up the backs of Lola's calves to the red shawl she'd once again pinned around her waist. She'd changed out of the wet dress and into the white blouse again. Her damp bra made two very distinct marks on the front of the shirt and created a stripe across the back. Max wondered if she'd hung her panties in the bathroom like she had the day before.

She'd pulled her hair through the back of a baseball cap she'd found somewhere, and in her hands she held a fishing pole. On the end of the sturdy line, she tied two jigs several feet apart, then she cast them over the side of the yacht. She let the line play out about ten seconds before she flipped a lever on the side of the reel and stopped it.

He looked up into her profile, her narrowed eyes behind the blue lenses of her sunglasses, and the pinched determination at the corners of her mouth. Obviously, she was thinking of outfishing him, and Max would rather bite off his own tongue than admit that it might not take much to succeed. Lola pulled the end of her pole back, then let it drop down again, and he imagined that somewhere in the water below, her jig bobbed up and down, attracting the attention of unsuspecting cod or snapper or whatever was down there.

Without appearing too obvious, he reeled in his line. Slow and easy, until the lure hit the side of the yacht and popped up over the gunwale.

'Catch anything?' she asked, although it was pretty damn obvious he hadn't.

'Just a few nibbles.' He rose from his chair and moved to the tackle box.

She raised the end of her pole, then lowered it again, and gave him an all-knowing, 'Ahh.' Followed by, 'Need some pointers?'

'Nope.' He cut the lure from the end of his line and dug around for something that looked like one of those jigs she'd tied on the end of hers. 'But if I need some tips on how to make a bra, I'll keep you in mind.' Despite being one hell of a caster, Max had caught exactly two lake trout in his life. Twenty minutes ago, he hadn't been real worried about catching anything. The yacht was stocked with enough provisions to last a while yet, but she'd just issued an unspoken challenge and there was absolutely no way Max would be outfished by a girl. Especially such a girly girl.

He was a man. A meat eater. She used to model bikinis and had a little yapper dog. He'd been a member of SEAL Team Six when they'd secured Manuel Noriega, Pablo Escobar, and another half dozen dictators and drug lords. He'd been in on the planning and recovery of Haitian President Jean Bertrand Aristide, and when Six had been disbanded, he'd been recruited by the Navy's Special Warfare Development Group to head a counterterrorist assault team. She designed panties.

How hard could it be to catch a bigger fish than Lola Carlyle?

Max cast the jig over the side of the yacht and stopped it once he figured he'd let out enough line. His skivvies were just about dry, and he stuck the end of the pole into the holder. He moved through the galley to the stateroom, where he tucked himself into the shorts he'd worn the day before. For breakfast he grabbed some grapes and what was left of the granola bars, then headed back outside.

At the sound of his approach, both Lola and her dog glanced back at him. The breeze picked up the end of her ponytail and played with the hem of that shawl she was wearing as a skirt. While she continued to man her post, bobbing the end of her pole up and down, her dog hopped off the bench seat. Baby followed Max to his chair, and when he sat, the dog jumped up into his lap.

'Hey, now,' he said, and moved the dog to his left thigh. He dug out a few granola bars and tossed one to Lola. Then he unwrapped a honey and oat and fed a piece to her dog. He hated to see anything starve. Even the poor excuse sitting on his thigh.

'Didn't you tell me yesterday that you were in Nassau on government business?'

He looked up as Lola took a bite of her breakfast. 'Yep,' he answered.

With the blue Atlantic rolling beyond her, lightly rocking the yacht, she continued her inquisition. 'But today you said you were forced to retire from the Navy.'

'That's right.' Baby crunched and chewed and yipped for more. 'The Navy retired me four years ago.'

She shoved the butt end of her pole into a holder, then

turned to face him. 'How is that possible? If the Navy gave you a choice of retirement or prison. How is it that you still work for them?'

Max set the dog on the deck and gave him a big chunk of granola. Baby quickly chomped it down, then jumped up on the bench seat and prepared for a nice nap. His morning excursion in the ocean had finally taken its toll. 'Your dog has a garbage gut.'

'My dog has a name.'

'Yeah, and it's an embarrassment to him, too,' he said, even though the little mutt was kind of growing on him. Still, the name was downright stupid, and there was no way he was going to say it out loud. Not even if someone threatened another beating or another round of torture.

'You're avoiding my question.'

'Not avoiding, just not answering.'

'Are you some sort of spy?'

'No. I don't work for the CIA.'

The brim of her cap cast a shadow across the top half of her sunglasses. 'Are you one of those covert guys?'

'You watch too much television.'

'And you change the subject every time I ask you a question.'

'Not every time. Just when you ask a question I can't answer.'

'You mean won't.'

'Can't and won't.'

She polished off her granola bar before she continued, 'Are you married?'

'No.'

'Divorced?'

'No.'

'Trick some woman into being your girlfriend?'

'I already told you, I don't get romantically involved.'

'That's right. Why?'

'What's with all the questions?'

She moved a few steps closer and motioned for him to pass her some grapes. 'I lost my binoculars and mirror in the ocean, and now there's nothing to do but fish. I'm bored, and since you kidnapped me, the least you can do is give me something to think about besides how I'm likely to die out here.'

Max placed a bunch of grapes in her outstretched hand and ran his gaze up her smooth wrist to where she'd rolled up the sleeves of her blouse to just below her elbow. 'I didn't kidnap you, and there is enough food and power to last awhile yet, so you aren't likely to die anytime soon.'

'Maybe of boredom. I'm used to staying busy, and I need a diversion.'

Max watched her place a grape between her lips and suck it into her mouth. 'What did you have in mind?' he asked, although he was sure he could come up with a few good diversions himself. Ways of 'staying busy' that had nothing to do with talking and everything to do with the way she sucked grapes. He wished she'd never told him she was a Linda Lovelace impersonator.

'Tell me about yourself,' she said, then sucked one more into her mouth before she turned her attention back to her fishing pole.

Max rose from the chair a little too fast and set his teeth against the pain in his side. He grabbed his fishing pole and turned his back on Lola, the sudden bulge in his tight shorts plainly advertising the fact that he'd tucked to the left. She'd probably accuse him of wanting to get *romantically* involved again. Romance had nothing to do with the direction of his thoughts, but that particular direction needed changing. Fast. 'What do you want to know?'

'Have you ever been married?'

'No.'

'Ever close?'

'Never.'

'Why?'

'Never found a woman who made me want to think long-term.'

She was silent a moment before she said, 'Maybe you have a commitment phobia.'

Max would have loved to have been given a dollar for every time he'd heard that. It seemed to be a universal subject among women, as if they were born with it imprinted in their brains. 'Maybe I like my life the way it is.' Lack of commitment was not one of his favorite topics, but it did cool his desire. 'How many times have you been engaged?'

'Twice.'

'Maybe *you* have a commitment phobia.'

'No, I'm a jerk magnet.'

Max looked back at her, at her full lips and high cheekbones, her big breasts and long legs. Lola Carlyle was a magnet, all right. She definitely pulled dirty little thoughts to the forefront of his brain.

'Where are you from, Max?'

He returned his gaze to the rolling Atlantic. 'I was born

in Miami and have lived all over the South. But mostly in Texas.'

'Where in Texas?'

'You name it, I lived there.'

By the direction of her voice, he could tell she'd turned toward him. 'You don't have an accent. I dated a *bawl* player from Texas once, and his was real thick.'

Other than a few scars, Max had no traceable marks or tattoos, and he'd removed any trace of an accent that would distinguish him in any way. But the South was in his blood, and sometimes, when he was tired or real relaxed, it slipped back into his speech. 'I worked hard to get rid of it, and my father was Cuban, so I really didn't grow up with it in my home. If anything, I had to work hardest to get rid of the Spanish accent I picked up from him.'

'What about your mother?'

'She died when I was three.'

She was silent a moment, then said, 'I'm sorry. That must have been terrible for you.'

'Not really.' He kept his gaze on the chop of the waves, pinning it to the point where his line disappeared. 'I never knew her, so I never knew what I was missing. My dad missed her every day of his life, though,' he said, and wondered why he was all of a sudden spilling his guts. Max wasn't a man who talked very much about himself to anyone. Especially to women. Women tended to pat his head, analyze him down to his shorts, then want to sign him up for therapy. That he was talking about himself to Lola Carlyle was clearly an indication of the level of *his* boredom.

'What was her name?'

He turned and looked at her. 'Why?'

'I want to know.'

'Eva Johansson Zamora. She was Swedish.' And talking to her was better than thinking about Lola sucking grapes into her mouth. 'My father used to say that made me Cubish.'

She smiled and bobbed the end of her pole up and down. 'Unusual, that's for sure. How did she die?'

'She and my father were crossing Eighth Street in Little Havana, and she was hit by a car. He said her hand was ripped from his.'

Her smile died and the pole stopped. 'That's horrible, Max. Where were you?'

Since she didn't gush, look at him with pity, and wasn't rushing over to give him a warm fuzzy hug, he told her. 'In my father's other arm. Neither of us was hurt. She was dead before she reached the hospital.'

'Do you remember it?'

'Not really. I have a vague memory of flashing lights, but that's about it.'

'Man, and I thought I had a rough childhood.'

Glad for the change of subject, he asked, 'What made yours so rough?'

'Well, it wasn't really rough, but I used to think it was.' She looked out at the ocean, and the salty breeze ruffled the sleeve of her blouse. 'My mother's brother Jed was a Baptist preacher, and not the lax kind either. The kind where you can't drink alcohol, wear lipstick, or dance 'cause someone might get excited. Those things were "worldly and sinful." The only time you could dance was in church when the spirit moved you. In my family, having an uncle who was a preacher was like having the Pope for an uncle if you're Catholic. We always had to sit in the amen corner and shout, "Praise the Lord." And because we had a preacher in our family, all my relatives just assumed we were one step closer to God's knee than everybody else on earth.

'So, when I was three and wanted Santa to bring me lipstick, eye shadow, and a see-through bra, no one was amused. When I was fifteen and got caught drinking and making out with T. J. Vandegraft, my family was beyond mortified.' The end of her pole bobbed up and down and she continued, 'My mama was convinced I'd inherited deviant genes from my daddy's side. He's got some branch water cousins who drink beer from the bottle and breed like sailors on a weekend pass.'

Max laughed deep in his chest. 'I imagine modeling undies didn't go over real well.'

'Not at first, but then Uncle Jed was caught begetting behind the podium with one of the Lyle girls – Millicent, I believe was her name.' She shrugged. 'He did the whole "I have sinned" Jimmy Swaggart thing, and cried and carried on, but since Millicent was barely legal and pregnant to boot, his own wife left the church. After that, it was like rats jumping from a sinking ship, and suddenly what I did for a living wasn't so bad.' She looked over her shoulder and smiled at him. 'I was just glad that I wasn't the biggest sinner any more.'

He looked at her standing there, bare feet, long legs, with her hat pulled low on her forehead, and for the first time since he'd looked in her wallet and seen her driver's license, he saw more than just a pain-in-the-ass underwear model staring back at him. More than a beautiful woman with a killer body silhouetted against the blue of the Atlantic and lighter blue of the midmorning sky. He saw a woman with problems just like everyone else. A woman with a self-deprecating sense of humor and a smile that had him watching her lips.

'Any brothers or sisters?' he asked her.

'One older sister, Natalie. She was always perfect growing up. Never cared for lipstick or drinking. She has five perfect children and is the perfect housewife. She's married to a perfect husband, Jerry, who actually is a very nice guy.'

Max wasn't sure, but it sounded to him as if Lola actually envied her sister. Lola Carlyle, *Sports Illustrated* swimsuit model, envying a housewife? Impossible. 'Don't tell me you want five kids.'

'No, just two, but first I have to find a husband. Unfortunately, that means I have to start dating again. And I seem to attract controlling men. *Or*, worse, men who are incredibly needy, and I end up taking care of them.' She paused to take a breath before she asked, 'Do you want kids?'

Children were the very last thing he wanted. 'No.'

She studied him a moment. 'You look like I asked if you wanted a root canal. Don't you like children?'

He liked kids just fine. Other people's kids. 'Do you really want me to believe you don't date?' he asked instead of answering her question.

She sighed at his obvious attempt to change the subject, but she let it go. 'There's a difference between going out to dinner with a guy and wanting him to be the father of your children. I don't have the greatest track record with men.' Her pole suddenly bent into an arch and was almost pulled from her hands. 'I think I caught something!'

Max watched the end bend a bit more and he shoved his

own pole into the holder on the chair. 'Do you need help reeling it in?'

'No. Just find the net,' she instructed as she opened the door to the swimming platform. She moved down the steps and reeled as she spoke. 'And there should be some sort of hook puller, too.'

He found a fishing net in the fender storage where he'd discovered the fishing poles and tackle, and something that resembled a pair of pliers.

Damn if she hadn't outfished him.

'Hurry,' she called up to him as he made his way down the stairs. The chop had risen about another half a foot, and now seawater splashed over the platform and Lola's bare feet.

The first fish cleared the surface of the water, a small brilliant blue with a bright yellow tail and eyes. Max had no idea what kind of fish it was, but the second was obviously a variety of grouper. Its skin was a slick beige with brown stripes and gray spots. It made up for its less-than-impressive coloring with a weight Max guessed to be around fifteen pounds. He scooped the fish up into the net, the little blue flipping its yellow tail.

They headed toward the aft deck once again, and Lola fired instructions over her shoulder while Max carried the net and fish up the stairs. 'You need to take the hooks out, and then we need to find an ice chest or something cold to put them in. You can gut them right now if you want.'

No problem, but they weren't his fish. 'I thought you said you fished with your grandfather on his charter boat.'

'I did, but he took the hooks out and gutted them for me.'

Her brows lowered over her brown eyes as she looked up at him. 'Those are men's jobs.'

'So, your only job is to reel them in?'

'Of course,' she answered as if he were dense.

But Max hadn't been born that dense and knew she was making up the rules as she went along. He pulled the little blue from the net and removed the hook from its mouth. He set it on the deck, where it flipped itself onto its other side.

'Aren't they just beautiful?' Lola gushed, extremely proud, as if she'd created them herself.

'They're okay.' He hauled the grouper from the net and removed the hook. So, she'd caught two fish. Big deal. 'During a training mission in Malaysia, I shot the head off a cobra and ate it for breakfast.'

She looked at him out of the corner of her eye. 'And you're telling me this . . . why?'

He laid the fish side by side but didn't answer. He didn't know why he'd told that stupid story. Other than maybe he wanted to impress her, which was embarrassing to admit, even to himself.

'Do you feel threatened?'

He looked up at her. 'By what?'

'By me. Does my catching fish threaten your masculinity?'

Max chuckled as he stood. He didn't feel threatened, just ridiculous. 'Honey, my masculinity is just fine. It would take more than your tiny ol' fish to make me feel like less of a man.'

'You sound jealous.'

Maybe a little, but he'd never cop to it. Never. 'Of these little things? Not in this lifetime.'

Baby hopped off the bench and wandered over to the fish. The grouper slapped its tail against the deck and the little dog jumped back. 'Keep your eye on Baby while I find an ice chest,' she instructed, then walked into the galley.

The dog put his ears back and inched closer. He licked the grouper's tail and got smacked on the nose. Once again he backed off.

Max glanced at the galley door, then lowered his voice. 'Quit being such a pussy dog and get over there. Come on.' He couldn't bring himself to call the dog by its pansy name, so he settled on, 'Get over there, B. D., and show that fish who's boss.'

Buoyed by other male encouragement, Baby moved to the head of the fish, sniffed it twice, then licked its eye. 'Yeah, that's a good boy.'

'Baby!' Lola walked from the galley and hit the lid of a Styrofoam cooler with her hand. 'Get away from those fish.' She set it on the deck, then looked up at Max. 'I thought you were going to watch him.'

Max didn't recall making any such commitment. 'Your dog doesn't listen real well.'

Inside the chest, Lola had placed two frozen reusable gel packs. 'The ice in the freezer is pretty melted, but these are still solid,' she said. Then she glanced up at him and added, 'Go ahead and put them in.'

He also didn't remember signing on as her toady. 'That honor belongs to you.'

'That's okay. Your hands already smell like fish.' She looked down at herself. 'And I'm wearing white.'

'Uh-huh.' He knelt beside the cooler and placed the

fish inside. His fishing chair scooted a few inches across the deck and he glanced over at his own pole almost bent in half.

'Christ,' he swore, and quickly rose, hardly feeling the pain in his side as adrenaline shot through him. He grabbed the pole and reeled in line as he moved to the platform. 'Bring the net,' he hollered at Lola. The platform rolled with the waves and ocean water rushed over his feet. He pulled the tip of the pole up and reeled like mad. Compared to the two lake trout he'd caught, this fish felt like a Buick.

He caught his first glimpse of red just below the light blue surface. Lola scooped it into the net, and he immediately lifted it from her. With his pole in one hand, he studied the brilliant red snapper. It had to weigh at least twenty-five pounds.

Once again, he followed Lola to the aft deck and removed the hook. 'Would ya look at that,' he said as he knelt and laid it on the deck. It was the most beautiful thing he'd seen in a long time, with its pretty red scales and spiny fins.

'It's just a fish.'

He stood and took a step back to admire his catch. 'It's huge.'

Lola folded her arms beneath her breasts. 'Well, I caught more than you did.'

'Both your fish don't weigh as much as mine.'

'Haven't you heard? Size doesn't matter.'

He looked over at her. 'Bull.' A pout pinched her full lips and he smiled. 'Only a guy with a small package believes that crap.'

Her brows drew together and a frown creased her forehead. 'I just know it's true.'

Max shook his head and laughed. 'I could prove you wrong.'

'Thanks, but I'll take a rain check.'

'Anytime, Lolita.'

Lola set white rice on the back burner to boil, then mixed oregano, thyme, cayenne pepper, a dose of paprika, and a dash of salt into a bowl.

Anytime, Lolita, Max had practically whispered into her ear. Well, maybe not whispered, and not into her ear, he'd been standing too far away for that. But it had *felt* as if he'd whispered into her ear. He'd lowered his voice like an intimate caress that lifted the hair on the back of her neck. A not-altogether unpleasant experience. Which was bad. Really bad. And dangerous.

The first night she'd seen Max, she'd known he was dangerous, she just hadn't known the danger was in seeing him as a man, not as a thief and a pirate. She didn't want to look into his battered face and see the stunning contrasts beneath the bruises. The light blue of his eyes and his dark skin and hair. The hard set of his jaw and chin conflicting with the fullness of a mouth that might appear soft on any other man, but not Max. His blood was made up of ninety-nine per cent pure testosterone, leaving no doubt that he was one hundred per cent heterosexual male.

She did not want to see Max the man. A man to slay dragons. A man who rescued damsels and drowning dogs, then caught and gutted the biggest fish.

Only after he'd admired his catch from every angle and bragged about its size as if it were the biggest fish ever taken alive did he finally gut all three fish. He'd flayed them like a pro, and since they'd caught more than they could eat at one meal, they'd packed half the snapper fillets and the grouper in baggies and placed them in the back of the freezer.

While Lola had searched the galley for spices, Max had left to start the engines and clean up. In the pantry, she'd found fresh olive oil, five lemons, and the rice. While the rice cooked, she coated four fillets with the spices and added a dash of black pepper. When the olive oil was heated to the right temperature, she placed the fillets in the pan and cooked them for about seven minutes on each side.

She didn't consider herself a gourmet cook, but part of her recovery from bulimia had been learning how to have a healthy relationship with food. Learning how to eat again. And learning how to eat meant learning how to cook more than one microwavable Lean Cuisine a day. She'd taken a few classes, but mostly she'd learned by reading the many cookbooks she'd collected from all over the world.

She owned a hundred and twelve of them, and some she couldn't even read because they were written in French, Italian, or Spanish. She'd purchased them all during the last few years of her modeling career when her sickness had been out of control. When every thought had been of how many grams of fat in a chicken breast. Of pocket calorie counters and calculating how many minutes on the treadmill and stair-stepper to burn off a cup of yogurt. And then, ultimately, her total loss of control and her insane binges that always resulted in self-disgust and a trip to the bathroom.

Not a very glamorous picture, but Lola had been one of the lucky ones. She'd never picked up a needle or downed amphetamines, the price many paid for the glamorous life. The price for an unrealistic body image that the industry and the weight-conscious public demanded. Now, three years later, Lola still watched what she ate, but she watched to make sure she didn't *lose* weight. Her personal trigger that could potentially start another downward spiral.

The galley door opened and Max entered, bringing a slice of the afternoon sun at his back and Baby at his bare heels. The top of his head only cleared the cabin ceiling by two inches, and it seemed he filled the space with his wide shoulders. He'd cleaned up and changed into a jeans shirt he'd found in the stateroom. It didn't fit him, of course, and he'd had to slice off the short sleeves to accommodate his biceps. He'd left the front unbuttoned across his big chest.

'Smells like my favorite little restaurant in New Orleans,' he said as he moved to the dinette and poured two glasses of white wine she'd raided from the Thatches' wine rack.

Lola arranged the blackened snapper and rice on a celadon platter and wished she had some yellow zucchini and butternut squash to go with it. She'd set the table with matching celadon plates and stainless flatware and placed the platter in the center of the table.

For Baby, she cooked what was left of the pretty blue fish, which, after cleaning, was just the right amount for her dog.

Then the three of them sat down to lunch, Baby eating off a little plate on the floor.

Max dug into his meal with the enthusiasm of a man who clearly enjoyed food. He didn't place his elbow on the table, chew with his mouth open, or lunge at his fork, but he was definitely a hearty eater. 'This beats granola bars and crackers all to hell,' he said between bites.

Lola raised her glass and took a big swallow. His compliment pleased her more than it should have, and she had to remind herself to keep her guard up. This wasn't some sort of social occasion, and he wasn't her boyfriend or even her friend. She'd cooked lunch for him because she'd had to cook lunch for herself. It was survival. Nothing more.

As Lola took a bite of her fish, she looked into Max's face. He still wore the white strips on his forehead and his left eye was badly bruised, but most of the swelling was gone. Sunlight from the windows lit up the table and shone on the chrome and wood of the appliances. The natural light cast an ethereal glow from the outside in, and none of it seemed real. Not him. Not her. Not the *Dora Mae*.

He glanced up, and beneath his dark brows and spiky black lashes his blue eyes stared directly into hers. Then he smiled and she had to force herself to swallow. She needed to go home. Not only did she have to find a private detective and get her life back, the longer she was around Max, the more she had to fight not to see him as a man. A man who, beneath the bruises, made a woman want to check her mirror and pop an Altoid. A man who could easily fold her to his big chest and make her believe everything would be okay. That he could take care of all of her problems.

Only he was the person responsible for her problems.

She believed that he hadn't meant to drag her into his life and into his flight from Nassau, that she'd been in the wrong place at the wrong time. That he'd needed to get off the island in a hurry, and he hadn't known she was on the yacht. Knowing and believing him shouldn't have changed anything, but somehow it did. Since he'd saved Baby, she couldn't make herself hate him any more. On the contrary. The more he held back, the more he intrigued her.

Lola had never been accused of being patient or subtle and was dying to know more about him. 'So,' she began, 'if you aren't CIA, are you one of those black operations guys?'

'Are we back to that?'

'Yes. If you're retired from the Navy like you say, what sort of work do you do for the government?' She took several bites of rice and fish, then washed it down with her wine.

He polished off his snapper. 'I could tell you,' he said as he reached across the table and stabbed another piece, the smooth play of his muscles drawing Lola's attention. 'But then I'd have to kill you.'

'Funny.' She set her glass on the table. 'Why don't you tell me the stuff that won't get me killed?'

He laughed, and she was surprised when he actually told her. 'Let's just say that, hypothetically, some of the things the government might want done, can't be done through regular channels. In those cases, they might want to contract out.'

'For example, what?'

'Maybe breaking into key installations or disrupting a convoy of illegal arms in Afghanistan.' He took a few more bites and chewed thoughtfully, as if he were weighing exactly what to tell her. 'It's no secret that the U.S. government has rules and guidelines for everything, and those rules deem certain things unacceptable as national policy. Hostile targets like chemical war plants can only be hit during bona fide military strikes. But by the time the military plans a strike and the President signs the order, the bad guys know about it and have moved their chemicals, or nuclear warheads, or whatever. One way for the U.S. to strike back and still retain deniability might be to subcontract one or two or even five people for covert hits.'

'And one of those people is you.'

'Maybe.'

'So, you are sort of a James Bond meets Jean-Claude Van Damme?'

He just smiled and continued to eat.

Lola ate also, but she was by no means through with her questions. 'What's the development group stuff you mentioned yesterday?'

'Naval Special Warfare Development Group.'

'Yeah, is that like a SEAL team?'

'Somewhat,' he informed her between bites. 'Most of what DEVGRU does is classified and is a component of JSOC.'

'What's a J-sock?'

'Joint Special Operations Command.'

She shook her head and raised her brows. 'So, what did you *do*?'

He took a bite of rice and washed it down with his wine. 'DEVGRU is a counterterrorist unit.'

'And?'

'And does exactly as the name implies, although the

government will deny it. We also spent a lot of time and taxpayer money creating, testing, and evaluating tactics, weapons, and equipment. Which is how the government was able to make its bogus case against me.'

'Wait.' She held up one hand. 'You tested equipment? Electrical equipment?'

'All kinds.'

A tiny burst of hope made her sit up straight. 'Then you can make a new radio, right?'

He raised his gaze from his plate, and his brows were pulled together. 'Lola, you melted the radio, the navigational system, and even the depth finder.'

She'd had help, but she didn't bother pointing out his part in the destruction of the bridge. 'Isn't there something else you can use to make a new one?'

'What, my shoe?'

'I don't know. I don't know anything about electronics.'

He leaned back in his seat. 'Then take my word for it, there is no way to make radio contact with anything out there.'

Her burst of hope doused, she drained her wine and reached for the bottle to refill her glass. When she moved to refill his also, he placed his hand over the top.

'There is a bottle of red if you'd prefer it.' As Lola set the bottle back on the table, she felt the wine kick into her bloodstream, warming her from the inside out. Usually she wasn't such a lightweight, but she figured because she'd lived off nothing more substantial than hors d'oeuvres, she was feeling it more than normal.

'No, thanks. Like your daddy's cousins, I prefer beer from the bottle.'

He'd remembered what she'd said about her family. He'd been paying attention. In her experience, that was rare. More often than not, men paid more attention to how she looked than what she said. 'And do you prefer to breed like a sailor on a weekend pass?' she asked before she thought better of it.

His fork stopped and he glanced up at her. 'That's a subject we definitely shouldn't get into.'

Probably he was right. 'Why not?'

'Because you don't want to hear about horny sailors.'

No, she didn't want to hear about sailors. Sitting in the sunlit galley where nothing seemed real anyway, she wanted to hear about Max Zamora. The guy who ate cobra for breakfast. 'Did you have a girlfriend in every port?'

'Girlfriend?'

Baby jumped up onto the seat and curled up beside Lola. 'Was there more than one?'

'You really want to know?'

Did she? Lola had traveled to just about every country in the world, and she'd seen a lot. Experienced some of it, too, but she'd bet she hadn't seen or experienced anything like what Max had seen and experienced. 'Why not?'

'Okay, but just remember you asked.' He leaned forward and placed his forearms on the table. 'If you're a young guy and are deprived of pu—' he stopped, seemed to reform his thoughts, then continued, 'deprived of ass for months on end, pretty soon that's all you think about. Once you reach port, you tend to go a bit crazy and hump anything with a pair of tits.' Once again he paused before he said, 'Sorry about that, I meant breasts.'

Lola bit the inside of her lip to keep from laughing. She had to give him credit for at least trying to clean up his language for her, but if he thought he'd shocked her, he hadn't. She'd been around too many bad-mouthed photographers, sleazy agents, and groping playboys to be shocked by what he'd said. Just because she didn't use that sort of language herself didn't mean she hadn't heard it all before. Or that she hadn't heard worse from men who thought that because they'd seen her in an underwear ad, she'd enjoy nasty bedroom talk whispered in her ear. 'What about old guys?' she asked. 'Do old guys tend to go crazy?'

He sat back. 'Yes, but we know how to pace ourselves.' His gaze dropped to her mouth. 'Do you want the juicy details?'

Her lips parted on a breath, and a vision of him popped into her head. A vision of his wide muscular chest, the short black hair that grew across his defined pecs and abdomen, and the dark treasure trove trailing down his flat belly and disappearing beneath the waistband of his wet boxer briefs. The gray cotton clinging to him and outlining his impressive goods. *I could prove you wrong*, he'd assured her earlier when they'd been discussing size. At the moment, she believed him.

He raised his gaze to hers, and sexual awareness charged the humid air, hot and vibrant and zipping through her bloodstream along with the wine. Vibrant and totally her fault. She'd been playing with fire.

One brow rose up his forehead, silently asking if she'd like to continue to play. She knew without a doubt that with a guy like Max, she'd definitely lose. He'd burn her alive. He was a win-at-all-costs kind of guy. All or nothing. And while Lola was by no means a prude, neither did she have sex with men she'd just met.

At the age of seventeen, she'd lost her virginity to a guy named Rusty, and she'd never been sorry. Unlike other women she knew, she'd never had a truly bad sexual experience, just different degrees of fair to fabulous. She had a feeling Max would fall in the latter category, but she'd only laid eyes on him two nights ago, and for most of the time, she hadn't even liked him. She really didn't want to like him now, although she couldn't seem to help herself.

It was time to pull back. Time to change the subject. 'So, where did you say you live?' she asked.

A smile tugged at one corner of his mouth. 'Alexandria, Virginia,' he answered, and the subject changed to the two-hundred-year-old townhouse he was in the process of renovating.

She told him about starting her business, and about how she'd decided to base it in North Carolina because it was her home. He told her about his security company and how he'd started it because he needed a real job. The awareness between them cooled, fought back to a proper distance. But not completely gone. Once let out, it was there. Hanging between them, and like the humidity, she could almost touch it.

The air in the engine room was thick as tar and just as black. Max shone his flashlight on the four-hundred-and-forty-horsepower engine, then cut the power. Sweat trickled down his chest, and he grabbed a fistful of the front of the denim shirt and wiped his face. He swung the beam of light past the generators and freshwater tank, to the rudder and steering cylinder.

Maybe there was something he'd missed. Some way to navigate from the engine room. Another bead of sweat ran down his nose, and he moved to the hatch door. The sound of Baby's yipping and Lola's smooth reply to her dog reached his ears as he climbed from the belly of the yacht.

After lunch, she'd informed Max that she was going to bathe, and it was understood without her saying a word that he should busy himself elsewhere. She'd gathered up shampoo and soap and had taken her toothbrush from the glass of rum he'd placed it in earlier to soak. She hadn't asked how it had gotten there, and he hadn't enlightened her.

Max shut the hatch after him and couldn't help but notice Lola's red shawl and white shirt thrown in the fishing chair on deck. The ocean had calmed within the past hour, and Lola and her dog sat on the swimming platform below. Her bare legs dangled over the side. She'd washed her hair and it lay down her back in four big hunks. A pair of silky pink panties covered her butt, and she wore a pink lacy bra. With her back to him, he could just see the side of one of her breasts, but he didn't need to see all of her to feel the impact like a kick to the groin. He'd tried to ignore the insistent ache since he'd almost kissed her that morning, but it had gotten much worse over the course of the day. Especially during lunch.

Turning on his heels, Max walked into the yacht. He pulled in a breath and let it out slowly. He was trapped. Yesterday he'd been content to ride the current for a few days and slowly drift toward Bimini. Now he wasn't so sure he shouldn't send up a signal and take his chances with the Cosellas. Lola was driving him crazy. He almost wished she'd go back to calling him names and looking at him as if he were going to assault her, not looking at him through her big brown eyes and asking about his sex life. Making him think about how long it had been since he'd been with a woman. Making him wonder what she'd do if he tossed up the red shawl she wore as a skirt and got busy, right there on top of the dinette. Just looking at her had him thinking about running his hands up her long legs and wrapping them around his waist.

Lola Carlyle was a threat to his sanity. A relentless attack on his senses, and there was nowhere he could go to get away from her. Nowhere to get away from the sight of her looking at him over the top of her sunglasses, or bathing in the ocean. Nowhere that the breeze didn't carry the sound of her voice or the scent of her hair. And with each passing hour, it was getting more difficult to keep his hands to himself. More difficult to remember exactly why he should try.

Grabbing the binoculars, Max left the cabin and headed for the bridge, dragging the fishing chair with him. Lola had yet to return from the swimming platform, but Baby joined him. The little dog sat by Max's foot as he looked through the binoculars, out at the vast rolling Atlantic, and saw nothing. Baby leaned into Max's ankle and he lowered the binoculars and looked down at the little dog.

'What do you need?' he asked, but Baby seemed content just to sit beside him. To the left of the dog's stubby tail lay the partially melted flare gun that had started the whole mess. Max picked it up and turned it over in his hands.

No, he wouldn't use it to signal another vessel, no matter how insane Lola was making him. But it might come in handy when they drifted close to Bimini.

*

Stockholm syndrome. Baby had Stockholm syndrome, Lola decided. Ever since Max had pulled the dog from the ocean, he'd developed some sort of hero worship. He'd bonded with Max whether Max wanted to be bonded or not. And from where Lola sat on the sofa in the salon, it didn't appear to be totally one-sided.

She peeked over the top of the *Saltwater Fishing* magazine she was trying to read without success, and into the galley. Max had spread maps out across the table, and he had to constantly scoot Baby out of his way.

'Get off that, B. D.,' he said as he drew a line on the map. He fiddled with the sextant a bit, then drew another line. The sun had set about an hour ago, and he'd once again started the engines. Overhead light poured over him and Baby, catching in his hair and the tips of Baby's ears.

Lola didn't know what to feel about Baby's new attachment to Max. She'd never had to share him before, and she admitted feeling a bit jealous. But at the same time, she was glad her dog had finally found male companionship, no matter how temporary. Baby needed male influence in his life, and she was glad Max wasn't threatening to throw him overboard or eat him any longer.

Lola rose and moved to the galley. 'Have you figured out where we are?' she asked as she came to stand by the table.

He glanced up briefly. 'Here,' was all he said, and pointed to the map.

She couldn't believe she was back to pulling simple information out of him. 'Where's here?'

'About sixty miles southeast of Bimini.'

'How long before we reach it?'

'Can't say. We didn't make much progress today.' He picked up the melted flare gun, a fingernail file, and a tube of Super Glue.

'Now what are you doing?'

This time he didn't even bother glancing up. 'Making a radio, like you asked.' Then, without a word, he picked up the binoculars and shoved them toward her. 'Do something useful.'

Okay, something had made him very cranky, and Lola thought it best to just leave the area. She grabbed the binoculars, moved outside away from the patches of light falling across the aft deck, and was swallowed by the darkness. Millions of stars crammed the skies, and she turned in a circle until she found the Big Dipper. Strong wind blew her hair across her face, and she tucked several strands beneath the collar of her blouse.

She raised the binoculars to her eyes and gazed out at the black Atlantic Ocean. Not only was Max cranky, but she was fairly certain he was avoiding her. Which was ironic. Yesterday she'd tried to avoid him, and today he was avoiding her.

It seemed to her that if she were at one end of the yacht, he stayed at the opposite end. At first she thought it was because he knew she was bathing and he wanted to give her privacy, but even after she'd dressed and found him on the bow of the boat, he'd simply handed her a new pair of binoculars he'd found somewhere and walked away without a word.

With the sun pouring though his black hair, he'd moved to the swimming platform, stripped to his underwear, and dived into the Atlantic. She'd sat at the bow with her legs dangling over the side. Binoculars in one hand, she'd watched him swim laps around the *Dora Mae*. Occasionally he would look up at her, but he never broke form and didn't stop until he'd been at it for about an hour. No doubt about it, Max had been trying to avoid her since lunch.

The breeze ruffled the edge of her pashmina against her knees and gooseflesh rose on her bare legs. She gazed through the binoculars over the port side, out at the white tips of the waves several miles away. The yacht dipped and rose, and for a split second she thought she saw the blink of a light. Her heart leaped to her throat and pounded in her ears as she waited for it again. Long seconds passed and then she saw it once more.

'Max! Max, come out here. I think I see something,' she hollered. She didn't want to go in and get him, fearing that if she lowered the binoculars, she'd lose sight of the light. When he didn't appear, she screamed even louder. 'Max, come out here now!'

'Jesus,' he swore as he walked from the galley. 'What do you want?'

The light blinked again. 'I see something. I see a light.'

'Are you sure?'

'I'm sure.'

Max came up behind her, and his chest brushed her back. He reached for the binoculars and raised them to his eyes. 'Where?'

No longer able to see it, Lola pointed. 'Right out there. Do you see it?'

'No.'

'Look harder. It's there.'

The sound of the waves hitting the sides of the yacht filled the air, and then, 'Oh, yeah. There it is.'

'What is it?'

'I'm not sure. It's too far away. It could be a vessel, or it could be a buoy.' He was silent for so long, Lola felt like screaming. Finally, he said, 'It's moving, so it's not a buoy.'

'What should we do?'

'Nothing.'

'You can't mean that. We have to do something!'

He lowered the binoculars, and through the darkness he looked into her eyes, but he remained silent.

'Please Max. Please do something.'

He continued to stare at her, and she was just about to plead again, when he finally said, 'Get the remaining flares in the emergency kit. The gun is sitting on the table,' he continued, his deep voice cool and calm. 'And turn on every light you find.'

If Max was calm and cool, Lola was the opposite. She rushed to the closet and grabbed the three remaining flares. She flipped on the light switches in the stateroom and both bathrooms. On her way back out, she snatched the gun off the table. 'Is it still there?' she asked, out of breath as if she'd just done an hour on a treadmill.

'Yes, but it needs to move closer.'

'How close?'

'As close as possible.'

Her mouth was dry and she licked her lips.

'Lola?'

'Yes.'

'Take deep even breaths.'

Yeah right. 'Okay.'

'If you hyperventilate again, you're on your own.'

She placed a hand on her chest and pulled air deep into her lungs. She did not want to hyperventilate, pass out, and miss being rescued. 'Is it moving closer?'

'Yes.' It seemed to Lola as if five minutes passed before he handed her the binoculars and she gave him the flare gun. 'Stand back. I don't know if this thing will work.'

Lola moved to the starboard side and watched through the darkness as Max loaded the gun.

'Call your dog,' he said, and once she held Baby close, Max raised his arm and fired. Nothing happened. 'Fuck.' He pulled the hammer back once more and fired. This time a red ball shot from the barrel, the blast of the twelve-gauge shell louder than she remembered. The flare traveled at a ninety-degree angle for thirteen hundred feet before erupting like the Fourth of July. It lasted for six brilliant seconds, then burned itself out.

'It worked!' Too excited to stand still, Lola crossed the deck and looked out at where she knew the other vessel to be. 'How long before they get here?'

'Not long, if they saw the flare.'

'How can they miss it?'

He took the binoculars from her, and she looked up into his face. Light from the interior spilled out onto the deck, and she noticed the grim line of his mouth. For a man who was about to be rescued he didn't appear excited. 'If they're not looking for it, quite easily.' He raised the binoculars to his face and stared out at the Atlantic.

'Are they coming this way?' she asked, although she refused to believe that the other vessel hadn't spotted the flare.

Without a word, he moved to the starboard side.

'Are they coming this way, Max?' she repeated as Baby jumped from her arms.

'It doesn't look like it.' He lowered the binoculars and loaded the gun. The second flare fired on the first try and lit up the sky.

Lola took the binoculars and raised them to her eyes, but no matter how hard she looked, she saw no distant light hiding among the waves. 'Where is it?'

'It's traveling east, probably to Andros or Nassau.'

'I don't see it.'

'That's because it's moving away from us now.'

'Fire another flare.'

'We should save the last one for when we drift closer to an island.'

'No!' She reached for the gun. Max wouldn't release it. 'They'll see it this time and come back,' she protested. 'Please, Max.'

Within the deep shadows and slices of light, Max looked down at her. Then, without a word, he loaded the gun and raised his arm. Like the other two, the third flare traveled at a ninety-degree angle and exploded in a red ball of fire.

'They had to see that one.' Lola closed her eyes and said a quick prayer. She promised God a lot of different things. She promised to pray more often – even when she didn't need anything – and she ended by promising to attend Uncle Jed's new church, a real Pentecostal bible-banger, complete with tent and miraculous healings.

When she looked through the binoculars again, she half expected to see the distant light once more. She saw nothing but the black pitch and roll of the Atlantic. 'How could anyone with legal vision miss seeing those flares?'

'It's late and everyone is probably inside. Unless someone is standing on the deck looking up, they would miss it quite easily.'

She strained her eyes looking for anything. A dim light, a shadow on the water.

'Lola, they're gone now.'

'Maybe we just can't see them turning around.' She heard Max and Baby move into the galley and return a few moments later. Her arms began to tire, but she refused to give up. She refused to think that she'd been so close to a rescue, only to have it slip away.

Max peeled one of her hands off the side of the binoculars and wrapped her fingers around a cool glass.

'Take a drink of water, Lola. You're about to hyperventilate again.'

She wasn't, but she finally lowered the binoculars and took a drink anyway. The cool liquid wet her dry tongue and throat and she downed it all at once.

'There will be other vessels,' he told her as he took the glass from her.

Lola looked into his face and burst into tears. Appalled, she pressed her hand to her mouth, but she could not stop the pent-up emotion and crushing disappointment from escaping. The more she tried, the harder it became to control until she was caught somewhere between uncontrolled sobs and hiccups. 'I want that one, Max.'

He reached for her and pulled her into his broad chest. 'Shhh, now. It'll be okay.'

'No, it won't,' she cried into the denim material covering his shoulder, finally giving in. 'I want to go home. My family must be crazy with worry.' She shook her head and looked up into his dark face. 'My daddy has high blood pressure and this will kill him for su-sure.' She curled her fists into the front of his shirt. 'I want to go home, Max.'

He stared down into her face and brushed his warm palm up her spine. 'I'll make sure you get home,' he said. Then, for the second time in less than twenty-four hours, he lowered his mouth to hers.

'How?' she asked against the soft brush of his lips.

'I'll think of something.' Then he kissed her. This time there was no question of his intent. The firm press of his lips to hers made his intentions perfectly clear. He wasn't helping her breathe, and he wasn't asking permission. His finger plowed through the sides of her hair, brushing it back from her face and lifting it from her shoulders. He held her face in his palms, tilted her head back, and took advantage of her parted lips. His tongue swept into her mouth, warm and slick, instantly possessive and consuming. Lola wanted to be consumed. She wanted to forget about the rescue vessel slipping farther away, her family, her career, the humiliation of Sam's porno site, and whether she would die out here. She wanted Max to take away the disappointment and fear that were so real they griped her throat. Within his embrace, she wanted him to make her believe everything would be okay.

The binoculars fell from Lola's grasp, and she ran her hands down his shirt, then back up again, feeling beneath her palms the solid wall of his chest, the bunch and flex of his ripped muscles responding to her touch, the overwhelming strength of him. She wrapped her arms around his neck and rose onto the balls of her bare feet. One of his hands slid to the small of her back and brought her closer. The ridge of his erection pressed into the crease of her thigh and pelvis, and the kiss immediately turned hotter, wetter. With their mouths and tongues, both of them fed the desire running through their veins and threatening to consume them.

Like the flare Max had shot into the night sky, the kiss burned hot and intense and raised the tiny hairs on her arms and the back of her neck. It spread to the places her body touched his, her belly, breasts, and hands. To the places untouched, her behind, down the backs of her legs, her toes.

The yacht rode the waves of the ocean, pitching the deck starboard before righting once again. Max spread his feet wide and let the natural rise and fall of the yacht grind his hard penis against her. The erotic rhythm drew a deep groan from his chest and left her aching for more.

He slid his moist mouth to the side of her throat, and Lola leaned her head to one side to give him better access. The tip of his tongue touched her ear, then he whispered her name, a warm caress filled with rough longing. He worked his way to the base of her throat and paused to suck the sensitive flesh in the hollow as one of his hands unbuttoned her shirt. Before Lola could decide if she wanted her blouse removed, he peeled it from her shoulders, down her arms, to her elbows.

A fleeting thought about quick hands flitted through her head as he kissed a warm path across her collarbone. Then one of those fast hands found her breast through her bra. She sucked in her breath as her nipple instantly hardened in his hot palm, and she knew she'd better stop him before they went too far.

'Lola,' he whispered against her neck, and instead of stopping him, she raised his head and brought his mouth back to hers. His hand tightened possessively on her breast, then relaxed. Through the lace of her bra, he brushed his palm across her nipple. Perhaps she did not want to stop. Maybe she wanted to go wherever Max would take her. There was something about him. Some elusive thing she chased with her tongue. Something hot and vibrant and bigger than her. Something that turned the pit of her stomach hot and hungry. Something dangerous that made her want to shed her morals along with her clothes. She moved her hands to the front of his shirt and pushed the denim apart. In the grip of a wild hunger she hadn't felt in a very long time, she combed her fingers through the short fine hair on his chest, her other palm skimming the hard muscles of his stomach. Max Zamora was intriguing and frightening. Brute strength and supreme confidence. He was physical perfection.

Max stepped back from the kiss and looked into her eyes as he took her hand in his. 'Come inside,' he said, and turned toward the door.

The thought of getting naked in front of Max gave her just enough pause to stop her from eagerly following him. She was no longer the thin perfect model who posed in magazines and on bulletin boards. Her hips were rounder. Her butt bigger. Would he compare her to her former self? Everyone did. Would he be disappointed that she was no longer fashion's image of perfection?

While a part of Lola urged her to follow Max wherever he

wanted to take her, her sanity and reason returned just enough to allow her to pull her hand from his. 'We can't do this, Max,' she said on a deep, shuddering breath, and pulled her shirt back up her arms. No matter how much she might want to, no matter that her body ached for him to run his hand all over her, she couldn't make love to Max.

His chest rose and fell as he drew air into his lungs. 'We can do anything we want, Lola,' he said, his voice raw with desire. 'There is no one around to stop us.' He reached for her again, but she stepped back and he only grasped air.

'Making love right now is a very bad idea.' She couldn't look at him as she buttoned her blouse, afraid she'd see the hunger in his eyes. Afraid she'd give in to the hungry throb low in her belly.

'There are things we can do besides making love, Lola. We can start off by rolling around and getting sweaty, see where that takes us.'

'No, I'm not going to the stateroom with you.'

'Great, we'll do it here. On the deck, against the gunwale, in the fishing chair. At this point, I am not choosy.'

'Max, that's not funny.' She folded her arms beneath her breasts.

'Damn right it's not.' Frustration seeped into his voice and cut through the darkness. 'Until two seconds ago, you acted like we were interested in the same thing.'

He was right. She had been interested, but then sanity had intervened at the last minute. 'We don't know each other, and sex would be a mistake.'

'I don't see it that way.'

She finally looked up, into his dark face, and saw the clench of his jaw and the grim line of his mouth. 'Until I cooked you lunch, you didn't even like me.'

'I liked you.'

'You didn't act as if you did.'

'I liked you just fine.' He let out a breath then added, 'You've grown on me.'

She didn't think she could take such high praise. 'You make me sound like mold.'

He folded his arms across his chest. 'Not now, Lola.'

She wasn't a child, to be dismissed so easily. 'What is that supposed to mean?'

'It means I'm not up for one of those irrational conversations women insist on having before, during, and after sex, where everything gets turned around and I become the bastard.'

'Because I won't have sex with you, that makes me irrational?'

'No, that makes you a—'

'Don't say it, Max,' she interrupted.

He did anyway. 'Cock tease,' he finished.

Lola's gaze narrowed. 'That was crude.'

'Yeah, well, I'm in a crude mood. And if you stay out here, I'm liable to get a lot cruder.' He blew out a breath and dropped his hands. 'So, do me a favor and go in the cabin. Unless, of course, you want to come over here, stick your hand down my pants, and finish what we started.'

Lola had been born blond, but she hadn't been born stupid. She turned on her bare heels and walked into the galley.

Lola slid between the sheets of the king-sized bed and turned onto her side. She wasn't a tease. He'd kissed her, and she'd responded, kissing him back. He was the one with the fast hands. He was so slick, she'd hardly felt him work the buttons on her blouse. She hadn't even known what he was doing until he'd shoved it down her arms. No, she wasn't a tease. She was sensible.

She hadn't exactly kept her hands to herself, though. *But*, she told herself, his shirt had already been unbuttoned. She'd had no other place to rest her hands but on the hard muscles of his chest . . . and stomach. Okay, she'd let her fingers do a little walking, but that didn't make her a tease. Max was delusional.

She rolled onto her back and placed her arm over her eyes. After the previous two nights, a regular bed with clean sheets was pure heaven. She forced the thought of Max from her head, and lulled by the constant rocking of the yacht, within a very short time she was pulled into a deep sleep. But even in sleep, she could not escape Max completely. She dreamed of him, of his mouth and hands sending her on a wild roller coaster of sensation.

'Lola.'

She opened her eyes within the dark stateroom, saw nothing, and shut them again.

'Wake up, Lola.'

'What?' she groaned. Light from the salon flowed through the open door and lit up the corner of the bed and the bottom half of Max from the knees down. He'd changed into his black jeans and boots and his feet were spread wide.

'You have to get up.'

'What time is it?' she asked, then realized he would have no way of knowing.

'You've been asleep for a few hours.'

Lola sat up and immediately noticed the deep pitch and roll of the yacht.

'We're being hit by a storm,' he explained. 'You need to put on a life jacket.'

'Is it bad?'

'If it wasn't, I wouldn't have woken you up.'

'Where's Baby?'

Max leaned forward and set the dog on the bed. Baby jumped into her arms as the *Dora Mae*'s bow dipped and water smashed against the portholes. Lola glanced at the small round windows but could see nothing. Alarm shot up her spine to the top of her head. 'Is the yacht going to sink?'

He didn't answer and she threw back the covers. 'Max?'

From the other side of the room, he flipped the light switch. His hair was wet and plastered to his head and he wore a yellow slicker. 'Do you want the truth?'

Not really, but she guessed she'd rather know the worst than speculate. 'Yes.'

'The seas are at about seven to ten feet, and I estimate the winds at about fifty knots. If I had a way to steer the yacht, it wouldn't be so bad, but we're getting tossed about like a cork.' As if to prove his point, a wave slammed into the port side. The *Dora Mae* rolled starboard and the lights flickered. Max grabbed hold of the doorjamb and Lola and Baby slid to the edge of the bed.

'If water floods the engine room, we'll lose power,' he added to the already grim news.

When the yacht righted itself, Lola stood. 'What are we going to do?'

'Nothing to do but ride it out.' He moved toward her and held out a life jacket. 'Put this on.'

She took it from him and threaded one arm, then the other through the red and yellow jacket. 'What about you?'

He opened his slicker and showed his bottle-green preserver. She handed Max her dog and snapped the straps across her abdomen and stomach. Across her breasts, the straps didn't quite reach, so she left them hanging open.

'What about Baby? He needs a life jacket.'

'There isn't one small enough for the little rat,' he said, and moved from the stateroom.

She followed close behind. Droplets of water slid from the ends of his hair and down the back of his neck. 'You checked?' Except for a few sofa pillows that lay on the floor next to the magazine Lola had been reading earlier, the interior of the yacht was battened down tight.

'Yep.'

The *Dora Mae* dipped to the left, and Lola felt her stomach weave right. 'He might drown.' She grabbed the back of Max's slicker. 'Max, we have to do something.'

Max felt the tug on the back of the coat and looked over his shoulder into Lola's frightened brown eyes. She expected him to do something to save her dog. It was all there in her beautiful face. She expected him to save her, too. The burden of it felt like a noose around his neck. He was nobody's savior. The work he did for the government was never personal. Other than information from a brief, he didn't know the parties involved. He didn't know whom he helped, or whom he helped eliminate. He didn't want to know.

Lola grasped hold of his arm as the yacht tilted starboard. She was starting to look a bit green. He knew the feeling. He'd already lost his dinner over the side an hour ago. 'Sit down on the couch before you fall down.'

Instead, she wove her way to the bathroom as fast as she could. The pounding rain and the ocean's fury covered up any sounds from the head. Max didn't need to hear it to know she was sick. During a storm, everyone got sick.

With Baby in one arm, he moved to the galley, where he'd gathered the survival kit, life buoy, and folded self-inflating raft. Given the 1989 inspection date of the raft, he doubted the thing would even inflate. The survival kit, like the other emergency equipment on board, sucked. There was a small fishing tackle box and two waterproof lamps – complete with dead batteries.

Max set the dog on the bench seat in the galley, tossed his slicker on the table, then reached for the fishing knife he'd stuck in the top of his boot. He cut off two four-inch chunks of Styrofoam from the life buoy, then dug around in a duffel bag he'd filled with provisions they would need if they had to abandon the *Dora Mae*. He pulled out a roll of the silver duct tape he'd used earlier around the door of the cabin to help keep out the seawater. As the bow rose, he reached for Lola's dog. Max raised his gaze to the windows that ran the length of the galley and salon, but he could see nothing of the chaos outside. What he did see was his reflection holding Lola's dog against his chest, as if he had the answers to all their problems. Only he didn't have the answers. During his naval career, he'd been through rough seas and tropical storms, but he'd been aboard destroyers. In 1998, he'd ridden out Hurricane Mitch aboard a Seawolf-class attack submarine. Safe and sound below the surface.

Baby licked Max's chin and he looked down into the dog's beady black eyes. Even Lola's dog looked at him as if he were capable of providing a miracle. As if he could pull it out of thin air and save them all, adding to his burden. Tightening the noose.

He placed the Styrofoam on both of the dog's sides. Then he wound the tape around Baby's belly and back and the hunks of foam. When he was finished, the little dog looked like a silver tray with legs. It probably wouldn't save Baby's life, but it would keep him afloat.

The door to the head opened and Lola staggered out. Her face was as white as paper, and her lips were almost without color. She glanced toward the galley as she moved to the couch. The yacht swung hard to port, and she dropped down on her knees and crawled the rest of the way. From outside, unseen rain and sea smashed against the windows.

Max held on to the dinette and waited for a break in the

turbulence before he walked to the couch. 'This is the best I could come up with,' he said, and set the dog in her lap.

'Thank you, Max.' She lay down on her side and held Baby close to her chest. 'I knew, deep down in your heart, you liked Baby.'

'Yeah, he's grown on me.'

'Like moss?'

'Yeah, like moss.'

A weak smile touched the corners of her mouth. 'Me and Baby and moss.'

'Maybe I've decided I like you a little bit more than moss.'

'Yes, I know.'

'How's that?'

'You kissed me like you like me better than moss.'

A wave hit the *Dora Mae* starboard aft with enough force to knock Max to his knees. He hit hard and slid across the floor. The lights flickered and popped, then the engines shut down, pitching the cabin into darkness so complete, Max couldn't see an inch in front of his face.

'Max!' Lola's panicked cry filled the inky blackness.

'Are you okay?' he asked. 'Are you still over there on the couch?'

'I don't know where I am. Where's Baby?' A few tense moments passed before she spoke again. 'Here he is,' she said a few inches from Max's feet. 'Will the lights come back on?'

The emergency generator hadn't kicked on the first night, and he doubted it would tonight. 'Not unless I restart the engines.'

'Don't go outside.'

'Honey, I wasn't planning on it.' Through the darkness, he

crawled toward the galley and found the duffel bag on the floor. As he pulled the bag toward the couch, his eyes adjusted somewhat, taking in the varying degrees of black and gray. 'Are you hurt anywhere?'

'Just my elbow. I think I'll live.' She was quiet a moment, then asked, 'Max, do you think . . .' She didn't finish, but he figured he knew what she was going to ask.

'Do I think what?'

He could barely hear the sound of her voice over the howling wind from outside. 'Do you think we're going to make it?'

Lola and Baby crawled back up onto the sofa, and Max sat on the floor, resting his back against the arm. 'There's a chance.' He told her the truth. Too many times in his life he'd thought he was a goner, but he was still here. Still alive and still breathing.

She grasped the sleeve of his T-shirt and twisted it within her long fingers. 'Have you ever been close to dying, Max?'

More times than he could count. 'A time or two.'

A few moments passed, then she spoke just above the sound of the angry sea. 'I almost died once. It was scary and I don't want to go through that again.' Her head was close to his right shoulder, and he could almost feel the warmth of her breath on his arm.

'What happened?' He unzipped the duffel and pulled out a flashlight.

'My heart stopped in the bathroom at Tavern on the Green.'

He shone the light on her shoulder and it illuminated her mouth and the top of Baby's head. The little dog had a bad case of the shakes. Max looked down into the shadows cast across her face, and he wondered if she had some pre-existing heart condition, or if she'd taken too many drugs. Again he asked, 'What happened?'

'I'd gorged myself on lobster and mashed potatoes with extra drawn butter, then I did my usual fingers-down-the-throat thing,' she said as if she were talking about something she'd done quite often. 'My electrolytes went all haywire and zapped my heart. It wasn't the first time I'd passed out, but it was the first time I stopped my heart.'

'You almost died from puking?'

'Yes.'

Max had such an aversion to vomiting, he couldn't imagine anyone doing it on purpose. 'You were sticking your fingers down your throat? What the hell for?'

He watched her mouth as she spoke in a matter-of-fact tone. 'To stay thin, of course. The waif look was in, and I am not a natural waif.' The bow of the yacht rose and plummeted, and her grasp on his shirt tightened. She stopped talking until the *Dora Mae* leveled out once more. When she continued, he could hear the fear in her voice. 'Once I saw a girl overdose at a party at the Nepenthe in Milan. Heroin. A lot of girls do heroin to stay thin. Not me. I starved myself or barfed.'

'Jesus,' he whispered into the dark cabin. 'Why didn't you find something else to do for a living?'

'Like what? I have a high school education. Where else could I make several million a year without a day of college?' She chuckled, but it sounded dry and without humor. 'Not all of it was bad, Max. There were parts of it that I loved. Parts that were amazing. I met some wonderful people who are still my friends. Saw some incredible places. I was given the chance to be a spokesperson for great causes, and it opened doors for my lingerie business.' The wind outside howled and Lola leaned her forehead into his shoulder. She continued to talk as if talking would keep them afloat. 'Other parts of the business were addictive. The money. The travel. The clothes. The attention. That's hard to give up, Max. Going from a somebody to a nobody.'

As the yacht was tossed about, she told him a bit about recovering from bulimia and how her disorder hadn't been about something missing in her life or an abusive childhood, but rather her desire for perfection.

'Aren't you afraid it will come back?' he asked.

'Sometimes, but I can't obsess about that, either. I just have to eat like a normal person and make sure I don't have any erratic weight gains or losses.' Baby wiggled and she raised a hand and scratched his head. 'I have to remind myself that control and perfection are illusions, and that I am okay with my body,' she said. 'I don't have to be perfect.'

'Lola, you are perfect.'

'No, but I'm learning to live with my thighs.'

'Your thighs are perfect.' He couldn't believe he was having this conversation with Lola Carlyle, of all women. And under any other circumstances, he wouldn't waste his breath. 'When I met you, one of the first things I thought was that you're more beautiful in person than in the magazines.'

'You're sweet, Max.'

He didn't think a woman had ever accused him of being sweet before. He thought about it a moment and decided he didn't mind Lola Carlyle calling him sweet. And if they weren't in the middle of a storm, he wouldn't mind showing her just how sweet he could get. 'I don't like bony girls,' he said. 'I like women. Women with breasts and hips and a butt that fits in my hands.'

'You have big hands.' She laughed, but her laughter died as the yacht took a hit to the port side. Max braced his feet, and Lola let go of his shirt to grasp the couch. When the *Dora Mae* righted, she grabbed his shirt once more and finally confessed, 'Max, I'm really scared.'

'I know.' He covered her hand with his and squeezed.

'Talk to me. As long as I can hear your voice, I know I'm alive and I'm not so afraid.'

Under most high-stress situations, Max preferred silence, but if talking helped her, he would talk himself blue. He owed her that much. 'What's the first thing you're going to do when we're rescued?' he asked.

'Call my mama and daddy. I know they're just out of their minds worrying about me,' she said. 'Then I'm going to get my naked pictures off the Internet.'

'How are you going to do that?'

'I'm going to hire someone to blackmail Sam into closing down that site.'

Max thought there were probably more direct ways to go about it, but he didn't offer any suggestions because once they were off the *Dora Mae*, Lola was no longer his concern.

'What about you?' she asked. 'What is the first thing you're going to do?'

'Eat prime rib.'

'Before you call your father?'

'My father died when I was twenty-one.'

She was silent a moment as the rain pounded against the

door and windows. 'I'm sorry, Max. How did he die?'

'He was an alcoholic. Believe me, it's not a very nice way to go.' His father had been the one person Max had tried his hardest to save. Tried and failed, and he didn't need a psychiatrist to get inside his head and tell him the reason why he lived his life the way he did. Why he risked his own life for people he didn't know and a government that used him for its own needs. He knew.

'I've seen what alcohol and drugs can do to people,' Lola said, breaking into his thoughts. 'I know that sometimes there is nothing anyone can do to help.'

Max laughed, more bitter than he intended. 'God knows I tried, but nothing I did changed the outcome. When I was growing up, he was drunk most of the time. That sort of life is tough on a kid.'

'What did you do when he was drinking?'

'Now, those are some pathetic memories,' he said. Memories he wasn't going to talk about. Not with her. Not with anyone. He took her hand from his shirt and brought it in front of him. He shone the light on her smaller hand cupped in his, and he ran his thumb across her palm. The yacht rocked toward the starboard bow, and he turned her hand in his and squeezed. 'I played a lot with neighborhood kids,' he added. 'When I was old enough, I joined the Navy.'

'Why the Navy?'

Max grinned into the darkness. 'I liked the uniform. Thought I could probably get laid if I was in a uniform.' But once he'd joined, he'd set his sights on Little Creek and the SEAL program. He'd fit right in. While in the Navy, he'd earned a degree in political science and business, and he'd been selected to attend the National War College at McNair and was on his way to making commander when he'd been forced to retire.

'Did it work?'

'Yep.' He raised her hand to his lips and kissed her knuckles. Then he looked into her eyes, the light casting shadows in her hair and across her nose. 'I told you I'm a charming guy.'

She managed a weak smile. 'Probably not as charming as you think you are, though.'

The tip of his tongue touched the crease of her fingers. 'You're just lucky I can't show you how charming I can be,' he said against her moist skin.

Her response was cut short by the rise and fall of the ocean and the impact of a wave hitting them amidships. It pounded the windows and rocked the yacht hard on its port side. Max dug his heels into the carpeting and let go of Lola's hand. He slid a few feet across the floor. Either the bilge pumps weren't working or they couldn't keep up. The *Dora Mae* took longer than before to right herself. The creak and groan of the vessel was more frightening than the howl of the wind. It was time to get serious. Time to let Lola know what they might be in for at any moment. He couldn't put it off any longer. He crawled to where she and Baby lay on the floor and shone the light close to her face. Her wide terrified eyes watched him. 'Lola,' he began as he knelt beside her, 'how long can you hold your breath?'

'Why?'

'How long?'

'Maybe a minute.'

'If the yacht capsizes, it won't sink right away. Find a pocket of air and look for a way out. The galley door will blow in and the windows might break out – go out whichever way is easiest. You have your life jacket on, so once you clear the yacht, you should pop right up.'

'Are we going to capsize?'

'It's a possibility. The problem is that the yacht is orienting herself perpendicular to the wind and seas. Waves are mainly hitting us port with a few hitting starboard. The thing you have to remember is not to panic.'

'Too late.'

'I mean it, now. When water rushes in at you, it's going to be the hardest thing you've ever done, but you can't give in to your fear. You have to save yourself. And you can't save yourself if you panic.'

Her chest rose and fell. 'What about you?'

'I'll be right behind you. When I get to the surface, I'll deploy the raft and we'll get inside.' He kept his misgivings about the raft to himself.

'What about Baby? He'll never make it.' She held her dog tight in one arm and her free hand covered her face.

What she said was likely true, and as if he understood, Baby wiggled out of Lola's grasp and came to stand by Max's knee. His little pink tongue licked Max's pants, then his bare arm. 'I'll make sure your dog gets out alive.' He heard himself utter the ridiculous statement before he could stop it.

Lola raised into a sitting position, and, obviously tired of getting tossed on the floor, scooted to the couch and sat with her back against it. 'Thanks, Max.'

Her 'thanks' stuck in his chest as if it were the fishing knife he'd returned to his boot, and he had to look away. If it wasn't for him, she and her dog would not be in danger of losing their lives. She'd be at home. Safe in her warm bed. Maybe designing bras in her dreams. 'Lola, I'm sorry I got you into this,' he said.

'Me, too. And I'm sorry I burned down the bridge. I'm *really* sorry I did that.'

The sound of her self-deprecating humor twisted the knife in his chest. It was one of the things he liked about her, and with Lola, there was a whole lot to like. More than he'd ever let her know. He picked up Baby and moved next to her. 'For a pain-in-the-ass woman, you're okay.'

'Is that a compliment?'

He glanced across his shoulder at her, at the light shining across her chin and generous mouth. 'It was just a statement of fact.'

'Good, because it didn't sound like that charm you keep warning me about.' The bow rose and Lola scooted closer. 'And for an overbearing Steven Segal wanna-be, you're okay, too.'

He forced a dry 'Ha, ha' from his chest. 'Steven Segal's a pussy.'

'How did I know you were going to say that?' She grabbed his hand again and held tight. And when she laid her head on his shoulder, he lowered his face to the snarled part in her hair. She smelled like flowers and the ocean, like a garden growing near the beach.

Lola Carlyle wasn't at all what he'd expected that first night when he'd seen her driver's license. She wasn't flighty or hysterical. She wasn't a pampered model whose only worth came from how she looked in a thong. She was so much more than that. She was a person who faced her fears head-on and was braver than some men he'd known. She was a survivor – all wrapped up in soft sweet-smelling skin. A fighter.

She was horribly afraid, he could feel it in the death grip she had on his hand, but she controlled her fear. He'd been around too many people who didn't, not to appreciate and admire her strength.

The Atlantic continued to pound the *Dora Mae*. Within the dark cabin, Max held Lola's hand and just listened to the sound of her voice skipping from one subject to the next. She talked about her business, her family, and Baby's expulsion from dog school. And with each hour that passed, the knife in Max's chest twisted a bit more. With each minute, he had to fight the urge to take her into his arms and bury his face in her neck. No matter how he tried to ignore it, with every touch and sound and sigh, she carved out his heart.

The yacht listed portside, and there were a few times Max did not think it would recover. He held Lola's hand as the wind continued to howl. That was it. Just her hand in his, but the touch of her slim fingers and warm palm felt more intimate to him than some of the countless times he'd made love to other women. He continued to hold her hand until the winds died and the sea calmed. Then he held her while she fell asleep against his aching ribs.

When the first rays of morning sun finally touched the windows, he laid her on the floor and placed a couch cushion beneath her head.

Then he went out to survey the damage.

*

For the second time since she'd stepped foot on the *Dora Mae*, Lola awoke after a night of hell in which she'd fully expected to die. She heard the galley door open and pushed herself to her elbows. The first thing she noticed was the complete lack of motion. The yacht leaned to the left but was utterly still. Sunlight poured through the windows and over Max's shoulders where he stood in the doorway. He'd taken off his life jacket.

Lola rose to her feet and checked on Baby, asleep on the sofa. She tossed her life preserver on the floor, then followed Max outside. Raising one hand to her brow, she squinted against the morning sun. A hundred or so yards in front of her, blond sand and towering palms, jagged cliffs and thick vegetation filled her vision. Several palm trees and a Caribbean pine had been blown down by the storm and lay half in the water. The *Dora Mae* had run aground in a shallow bay of turquoise water.

'Where are we?'

'Don't know.'

'Do you think we're on an island?' she wondered out loud. 'Or maybe the tip of Florida?' she added hopefully.

Max pointed toward the jagged cliffs and rocks to the left. 'That doesn't look like Florida.' He, too, shielded his eyes with a hand to his brow. 'There are supposed to be some seven hundred islands in the Bahamas. I think we've landed on one.'

'Do you think there's a Club Med on the other side? Or maybe this is one of those secluded islands owned by the rich and famous.'

He dropped his hand to his side. 'Maybe one of your friends.'

She didn't have friends who owned islands. 'There's only one way to find out.'

Max moved to the swimming platform, tied a line from the lifeboat to the back of the yacht, then he tossed it onto the surface of the water. A length of nylon rope was attached to the raft, and Max pulled it. Within a matter of seconds the little rubber boat inflated. Just as quickly, it hissed in several places, and air bubbled to the surface from beneath.

'Shit.' Max folded his arms over his chest and scowled at the rapidly sinking raft.

'Well, I guess it's a good thing we didn't have to abandon ship last night.'

'We'll have to swim.' He glanced at her, and he asked, 'Do you think you can make it?'

'Yes.' Since she did not plan to panic and hyperventilate, she was sure she could swim to the beach.

Together they rounded up the food and supplies they would need to explore the island. Lola changed into the fruit dress and found a pair of old canvas sneakers without laces that wouldn't stay on her feet. Max grabbed the duct tape and knelt in front of her.

'What happens if I turn into a princess?' she asked as he took her ankle in one hand, then wrapped tape around her sneaker.

His gaze slid up her shin, past her knee, to the hem of her dress. 'What?'

'Like Cinderella.'

He looked up into her face, then reached for her other foot. 'Then I guess that makes me Prince Charming.'

Prince Charming? No, but he was growing on her. After the

shoes were securely on her feet, she brushed her hair and teeth, then she handed him the glass with her toothbrush. Without an exchange of words, he used it. When he was through, he tossed both Lola's purse and the duffel bag stuffed with goods into a garbage bag and blew it up with air. He tied the end as tight as possible, then they all went off the back of the yacht into the water. Max, Lola, and Baby. The Styrofoam taped to the dog's sides provided the buoyancy he needed.

The warm untroubled water with its sparkling shards of blue was nothing like the angry tempest of the previous night. So deceptively calm that it was hard to believe it belonged to the same ocean that had come close to taking all of their lives.

Twenty feet from the beach, Lola stood and walked through the waves to the shore. The gentle swells splashed the backs of her thighs and she plucked up Baby and carried him the rest of the way. The sand was still saturated from the storm, and when she set him down, he ran off to investigate a downed palm tree.

Lola didn't know if the island was inhabited or if she was simply trading one disaster for another, but it felt so good to finally be standing on solid ground that at the moment she didn't care.

She was cold and wet, and she felt like falling to the earth and kissing the beach. Instead, she sank to her knees on the moist sand and lifted her face to the sun. Last night she'd prayed for a rescue ship, and it hadn't come. Maybe this was God giving her another way off the *Dora Mae*. Another chance at being rescued.

With the sun touching her face and cool morning air in her lungs, a rush of emotion squeezed her chest. She was alive.

Several times last night she thought she would not live to see morning. Several times she would have become hysterical and lost it completely if not for Max. If not for the touch of his hand in hers and the reassuring sound of his voice within the dark cabin.

After everything, she and Baby were still alive when they could have easily drowned. She took a deep breath and let it out slowly. Now that it was all over, she sent God a quick thank-you and felt warm inside, like she might be having a religious experience. Not that she'd ever had one, but growing up she'd seen plenty. If not a religious experience, then just a wonderful moment to appreciate being alive. Of feeling her wet dress cling to her skin, and the gritty sand in her shoes and between her toes.

Max ripped open the plastic bag and dropped her purse by her side. 'Let's go, Lola,' he ordered, ruining her moment.

'Can't we just sit for a while and appreciate being on land again?'

'Nope.' He opened the duffel and handed her the pashmina. 'We're burnin' daylight.'

'Who are you? John Wayne?' She squeezed as much water from her dress as she could, then wrapped herself in the cashmere shawl. 'And you have to cut off Baby's water wings before we go anywhere,' she added, rising to her feet.

'His what?'

'The Styrofoam.'

'Come here, B. D.,' Max called to the little dog hiking his leg on the palm tree. At the sound of Max's voice, Baby hurried to stand at his boots.

'How did you do that?' She reached for her dog and held

him while Max cut the Styrofoam from his sides. 'He never comes when I first call him.'

'He knows I'm alpha dog,' Max answered. The top of his bent head almost touched her nose. His thick black hair was finger-combed and smelled of him, a combination of soap and sea and Max. He glanced up as far as her mouth and his hands stilled. For one brief moment, she saw the yearning in his beautiful blue eyes. She thought he would lean forward and kiss her, and she raised her hand to run her fingers through his hair. Instead, he looked away and she returned her hand to her side. She was left feeling disappointed and a bit confused. After everything they'd gone through together the night before, her feelings for him had deepened. She respected his strength, not only his physical ability that made her feel as if he could take care of her and Baby, but his strength of character. There was a core of honor in Max. He would never abandon his responsibility or betray a trust. He would never use her to boost his own ego or sell naked photographs of her.

She didn't love him, but there were many admirable qualities in him. No, she didn't love him, but when he looked at her as if he wanted to consume her for lunch, her stomach got a bit squishy and her mind wandered to the shape of his butt in his jeans.

Baby yelped and Lola turned her attention to her dog. 'Be a good boy, now,' she said as Max pulled off the rest of the tape. 'You are a very brave dog,' she congratulated Baby once the wings were gone.

Max muttered something in Spanish as he shoved the plastic bag and Styrofoam into the duffel. By the tone of his voice, Lola thought it best not to ask him to translate, and the three of them set out toward the dense tree line.

'Which way are we headed?' she asked as she shifted Baby to one arm and hung her purse on her shoulder.

'Up,' was his informative answer, and she followed him in between two palms. Within a few moments they were swallowed by the vegetation and were forced to walk single file. Thick ferns brushed Lola's ankles, and Max stopped several times, his hand outstretched to her.

Baby jumped from her arms and chased after a hissing iguana. They called at him to come back, but for once he didn't listen to the alpha dog, and Max was forced to chase after him. When he finally caught Baby and brought him back, he opened Lola's bag and shoved him inside.

'I thought he knew you were alpha dog,' she reminded him as he zipped it halfway.

Max's brows smashed together over his blue eyes and he gave Baby a very hard stare. 'Your dog has a real bad hearing problem.'

Lola didn't even try to hide her smile. 'Or maybe you're not top dog.'

'Honey, there is no question about who is top dog around here.'

'Uh-huh. Maybe I'm top dog.'

He rocked back on his heels and wiped the sweat from his brow with the back of his hand. 'I know you'd like to think you are, but you don't have the right equipment to be top dog.'

She didn't suppose he was talking about the equipment in the duffel bag. He was so delusional and male, she laughed. 'What equipment is that?'

'I think we both know.' His gaze slipped down the buttons of her dress, over her breasts, to the bunch of cherries covering her crotch. 'Or maybe you need me to show you,' he said, and lines appeared in the corners of his teasing blue eyes.

'I'll pass.'

He shrugged as if to say, *Suit yourself*, then they climbed upward, past bushy lignum vitae trees with their tiny purple flowers, and Lola wondered what he would do if she placed her hand in the back pocket of his jeans and let him pull her along. Tropical birds sang and called to each other overhead, and when they came to a small stream, he crossed first.

'Stay there,' he said, and set the duffel bag on the other side. Then he came back for Lola and straddled the stream, with a foot on each side of the bank. She could have crossed the stream on her own, but when he reached for her hand, she took it as she had last night and all morning. Their palms touched and little tingles traveled up her wrist. As she stepped over the stream, she looked up into his eyes. And there it was again. The heated flicker of desire. The dark hunger in his light-blue eyes that he couldn't hide. The craving that stirred passion deep in her stomach.

He dropped his gaze as he dropped her hand. 'Is your dog getting heavy?'

Baby weighed somewhere between five and six pounds, but after a while, he made her shoulder ache. 'A little.'

Max took the purse from her and placed the strap over his head and one shoulder. He reached for the duffel and started out again. Lola wished she had a camera to take a picture of Max carrying a purse with Baby's head sticking out of it, the dog's spiked collar making him look very tough. Max Zamora, carrying the dog he'd once threatened to drop-kick into the Atlantic. Somewhere beneath that hard, well-developed exterior, Max was a pussycat.

Baby chose that moment to let out a bark. He struggled to jump out of the purse.

Max placed a restraining hand on the dog. 'If you make me chase you again, B. D., I'm going let that iguana eat you.'

Well, maybe not a pussycat, but he wasn't quite the bad guy he wanted everyone to believe he was.

It took them another ten minutes or so to reach the highest part of the island, a breathtaking plateau heavy with Caribbean pines and rich foliage. They moved toward its edge and gazed over the side. The back of the island was less hospitable than the front, with jagged cliffs and vertical slopes. Pines and palms, but no Club Med. No reclusive rock star taking a break on his private island, just miles of ocean and endless sky.

They fought their way through low bushes to the middle of the plateau and discovered a blue hole. The freshwater spring was surrounded by pines and tall grasses. The hole was approximately fifty feet across, and a slight breeze rippled the water.

Max set the purse and duffel bag on the ground and Baby crawled out to stretch his legs. Then Max knelt on a rock jutting out from the shore, cupped his hands, and drank. 'Damn, that's cold,' he said as Lola sat beside him. She reached in the duffel bag and pulled out a canteen they'd filled earlier with drinking water from the tap.

'Any thoughts on what to do now?' she asked him. The back of her dress and the bodice was still damp, and she let the pashmina fall to her waist, hoping the slight breeze might help it to dry.

'Explore a bit more, then build a huge bonfire. After the storm last night, there should be rescue planes in the air.'

'What about a beacon?' Lola asked. 'I saw it on that movie with Anne Heche and Harrison Ford. They were stranded on an island and looked for some sort of beacon so they could break it. Then, supposedly, someone would come to fix it and they'd be rescued.'

'A navigation beacon?'

'Yeah, I think that was it.' She slipped off her shoes and stared down at her dirty feet. She took a thin bar of soap from her purse and scooted to the edge of the rock.

'It would have to be on the highest point and free of vegetation.' He stood and looked around, his hands on his hips. His spread fingers pointed to his crotch. 'Over there, maybe,' he said, and pointed to the west.

She removed her gaze from him and stuck her feet into the cold water. 'You go. Baby and I will stay here and wait for you.'

'Are you sure?'

She nodded and lathered her feet with the soap. 'Baby needs a rest.'

Max chuckled and once again knelt beside her. He placed his hand beneath her chin and raised her face to his. 'Okay, if Baby needs a rest,' he said against her lips, and she wasn't so certain he was talking about the dog. As naturally as if she'd known him forever, she leaned into him and opened her mouth beneath his. His tongue gently made love to hers, and the kiss was soft and sweet and turned her insides all warm. She dropped the soap to the ground and raised her hand to the stubble on his cheek. She ran her fingers through his thick short hair, but he pulled back, and the kiss ended before she was ready.

'Behave,' he said, and stood.

He took the canteen, a box of Chex Party Mix, an apple, and a bag of Ritz crackers. Lola was left with a wheel of Camembert, an apple, a box of wafer-thin crackers, and a hunger that suddenly had nothing to do with food.

The sun overhead had yet to reach midday, but it warmed Lola's back and arms. She finished washing her feet and legs, then she dug around in her Louis Vuitton bag and pulled out a small compact. She stared into the small mirror and gazed at her reflection, one-quarter of her face at a time. She looked like hell and searched in her bag again until she found her essentials. A pair of tweezers, a small bottle of Estée Lauder face lotion, mascara, blusher, and a tube of pink lip gloss. As she plucked several stray hairs from the perfect arch of her brows, she told herself that she wasn't primping for Max.

That's what she told herself, but she wasn't very convincing. Not when just the simple thought of his kisses sent tingles down her spine and brought warmth to her cheeks, as if she were sixteen again and had a crush on Taylor Joe McGraw, captain of the basketball team.

Taylor Joe hadn't known she was alive, but Max did. He let her know each time he looked at her.

From about the age of fourteen she'd noticed boys and, as she got older, men, looking at her. But Max was different. What she saw in his eyes was deeper. Darker, like the pull of something sinful and forbidden, and Lola had always had a weakness for sinful things.

She brushed mascara on her lashes until they looked long and feathery, then applied her blusher and lip gloss. Once she finished with her cosmetics, she put them away and looked out across the blue hole at the pines and tall grasses. A bug flew in front of her face and she swiped it away. She was certain today was Tuesday, but so much had happened since Saturday night, it felt as if a month had passed.

Baby barked at two dragonflies and would have fallen in the water if she hadn't grabbed him. She quickly glanced up at the sun overhead. It seemed to her that an hour had passed, and still no Max. She got up and moved their things from the buggy shore and found a nice place behind dense shrubbery and directly beneath a scrub pine. She spread her pashmina on the ground and she and Baby sat and ate crackers and cheese.

For the first time in several days, she was alone with only her dog. And without Max by her side, promising he'd make sure she returned home, she began to envision a life stuck on this island. A steady diet of reptiles and fish. The three of them growing old and crazy, Max looking as bad as Tom Hanks in *Cast Away*. Her looking like Ginger on *Gilligan's Island*.

Her heart fluttered in her chest, and she had to battle back the panic that threatened to pull her under. She hadn't even been missing a week yet. If anyone was looking for her, and she was sure her family was, she figured she had at least a few more days before a search would be scaled back. She took a deep breath and let it out slowly. Forcing the panic to the recesses of her mind.

When her nerves somewhat settled, she wondered what

was taking Max so long. Her mind raced from one distressing scenario to another. She worried that he'd broken his leg or fallen off a cliff. She should have gone with him. What if he needed her?

Wait, she thought to herself, this was Max. A man who could take care of himself and anyone else he'd happened to commandeer. If he broke his leg, he'd just whittle himself a splint and get on with things.

She picked up Baby and scratched his chest. She'd known Max for such a short period of time, how had she come to know him so well? How had he become so important to her life? She'd never needed a man before. Wanted, yes. Needed, no.

If for some reason Max weren't on the island, she and Baby could figure out how to build a fire and roast an iguana. So why did the thought of losing him give her palpitations? Why did it feel as if he were so important to her existence?

She looked down into her dog's watery eyes and the answer shone back at her. Stockholm syndrome. Both she and Baby suffered from a bad case of it.

The brush behind her rustled and she looked over her shoulder. Baby let out three barks, then Max appeared through the foliage. 'That's not much of a watchdog,' he said as he stepped from the brush and moved to stand in front of her. A strange little glow warmed her next to her heart and traveled to the pit of her stomach.

As she looked up at him, she was almost embarrassed at how glad she was to see him. He reached for the bottom of his shirt and pulled it over his head, and the little glow spread across her flesh and tightened her breasts. He wiped the perspiration from his temples and rubbed the T-shirt across his chest. The fine black hair curled, and she stared, fascinated by a bead of sweat that slid down his belly to the waistband of his jeans.

'Did you find a beacon?' she asked, and looked away. She did not believe in love at first sight. Or second sight, or even after a few days. Especially if two of those days had been spent in fear of the object of her infatuation. Her sudden attraction to Max was illogical. It made no sense at all. But she supposed Stockholm syndrome did not make sense.

'No.'

That one word brought her gaze back to his. 'What do we do now?'

'We build a huge fire. Somebody ought to see the smoke,' he answered. 'On the west side there are quite a few birds' nests,' he said, and let his eyes travel to her lips. 'A few hundred probably.'

'What?' While she'd been worried sick about him, envisioning disaster, he'd been bird-watching? 'While Baby and I have been sitting here, you were off counting birds?'

He lifted his gaze once more. 'That's not what I said.'

'Don't you think that's just a little bit inconsiderate?'

One brow lifted up his forehead. 'What?'

She set Baby on the ground and crossed her arms beneath her breasts. 'Did it even occur to you that Baby and I might be worried that something bad had happened to you?'

'No.' He tossed his shirt on the duffel bag, then knelt in front of her, one thick forearm resting across his thigh. The tree overhead shaded his face and bare shoulders. He wasn't wearing a bandage around his ribs today, and the fading black and blue bruises were visible on his tan skin. 'I don't think your dog worries about much beyond his next meal.'

'That's not true,' she defended Baby as he hopped up on the duffel, made three tight circles on Max's shirt, then settled in for a nap. 'He's sensitive.'

Max shook his head. 'You know what I think?'

'No.'

'I don't think Baby was worried one little bit.'

'He was.'

'I think *you* were worried.'

She shrugged. 'Well, there are a lot of bad things that could have happened to you.'

Smile lines appeared in the corners of his eyes. 'Like what?'

'You could have tripped and broken your leg or fallen off a cliff.'

'Now, why would I do that?'

'You wouldn't mean to,' she sighed, 'but it could happen.'

'No, it couldn't.' He brushed a lock of hair from her cheek and pushed it behind her ear. 'Do you know what else I think? I think I like the idea of Lola Carlyle worrying about me.' He slid his knuckle along her jaw to her chin and she held her breath. 'You look real pretty.'

Her voice sounded a little breathy when she confessed, 'I plucked my eyebrows.'

'I didn't notice your eyebrows.'

'And put on some lip gloss.'

His thumb brushed her bottom lip, then he dropped his hand to his side. 'Now, that I noticed.' He sat and leaned his back against the tree, and she felt the acute absence of his touch. He brought his feet close to his behind and hung his wrist over his knee. The thin branch of a lignum vitae tree brushed his cheek, and he pushed away the thick green leaves and tiny purple flowers. 'There's a lot about you that I notice.'

'Like what?'

The vine hit his cheek again, and he pulled the fish knife from his boot and hacked it off. Then his eyes met hers once more as he returned the knife to his boot. He slid his gaze from the top of her head, paused a moment to examine the buttons closing her dress, then continued down her legs to her toes.

'That first night, I thought your toes were as sexy as hell.' He took a hold of her ankle and set her foot on the ground before him. 'I couldn't see shit for shinola, but I noticed your red polish.' He glanced up at her, then loosely wound the lignum vitae around her ankle as if she were a Polynesian dancer. The tips of his fingers brushed her bare skin, and she felt it at the back of her knee. 'And when I was tying you up with your skirt, I noticed your pink panties.' He smiled and pulled off a few leaves as he twined the thin branch around itself. 'I have a real fond memory of that.'

Lola did her best to suppress her reaction to his touch and to the sight of him, Max Zamora, snake eater, tying purple flowers around her ankle. But no matter how unwanted or confusing, the sudden butterflies in her stomach and the answering flutter next to her heart refused to go away or be ignored. 'Funny, but my memories of that night aren't so fond.'

He laughed. 'Go figure.'

'Do you want to know what I thought about you that first night?'

'Honey, I think that flare gun pointed at my chest said it all.' He wrapped his hand around her lower calf and tugged.

Before she knew how it happened, she was on her back and he was over her, his hands planted on the ground on each side of her head. 'And despite you having tried to kill me, I want you more than I've ever wanted any other woman.' He lowered his face to hers. 'But I think you know that,' he said right before he kissed her.

The touch of his naked mouth on hers instantly sent a ripple of desire across her skin. His lips gently pressed and coaxed. His tongue lightly caressed, and she let go and gave in to her hunger. Or perhaps, as with most of her dealings with Max, she really didn't have a choice. He eased onto his side next to her and took his time exploring her mouth. Her lips parted further, and the kiss deepened into a lush fondling of mouths and tongues. He tasted of dark passion and the promise of explosive, curl-your-toes, head-banging-against-the-headboard sex.

The languid kiss seduced and teased until her every thought narrowed and focused on the liquid warmth of his mouth. Heat flushed her breasts and stomach and pooled between her thighs. She ran her hand up the taut flesh of his arms, over his shoulder, to the side of his neck. She slipped her fingers through his short fine hair and he groaned into her mouth.

Max pulled back from the kiss and looked up into her face. His harsh breath caressed her cheek as his blue eyes burned into her. The way Max stared at her, all dark intensity, made her feel beautiful and desired and alive with anticipation.

His gaze drifted past her mouth and chin to the front of her dress. A smile of appreciation curved the corners of his lips, and she looked down at herself, at the buttons lying open, exposing the tops of her breasts and her Cleavage Clicker bra. His quick smooth hands had been busy again, and she grasped the front of her dress.

He grabbed her wrist. 'Just let me look at you,' he said, his voice rough. He buried his face in the side of her neck and whispered, 'Please, Lola.' His lips brushed her skin, and then he opened his mouth and sucked the hollow of her throat.

He let go of her wrist and brushed his fingertips along the scalloped edge of her bra. 'You're so beautiful. So soft,' he said, and not being a man given to patience, he slid his hand beneath the lace cup and palmed her bare breast. 'Everywhere,' he added, and took a deep shuddering breath as her nipple puckered to a hard, painful point against his palm. One of his knees parted hers and she brought his mouth back to hers. His tongue swept into her mouth, hot and wet and hungry. And without giving herself time to think better of it, she curled into him. He brought his knee between her thighs, and the feel of him against the thin layer of her lacy panties made her ache for more intimate contact. Of hot flesh to flesh. For his blatant erection pressing into her hip. The kiss turned ravenous, feeding, and so wonderful, it tore a drugged moan from her chest.

Max pulled back and looked into her face. His chest rose and fell, and he slid his gaze to his big hand on her breast. 'Lola, if you're going to stop me, do it now.'

She hadn't really given a thought to stopping him, and she didn't now. 'I saw some condoms on the yacht,' she said as she slid her palm over each defined muscle of his chest and arm, down his belly, to his fly. He sucked in his breath as she flattened her palm against his rigid erection.

'Too small,' he said as he exhaled. 'Are you on birth control?'

She'd had an IUD for five years and it had never failed her. 'Yes,' she answered.

'Thank you, God.' Lust burned hot and vibrant in his eyes as he peeled back the cup of her bra and exposed her to his greedy gaze. He stared at her for several long seconds, then lowered his face to her breast and gave her nipple an open-mouthed kiss. His tongue licked and stroked and instantly drove her wild. With each hot pull of his mouth, the tension built between her legs.

Lola's hand moved to his button fly and she tugged at it, but his hand on her wrist stopped her. He lifted his head, and a breeze blew across her heated skin and wet nipple. He stilled completely, then his gaze flew to the right.

'Max?'

He placed a finger to his lips.

Over the sound of her pounding heart and her shallow breathing, Lola heard it, too. In the distance, male voices rose in the still humid air. She reached for the front of her dress as Max rose to his knees. She knelt beside him and listened. From the other side of the blue hole, the voices blended together in a tangle of Spanish. Relief swelled within her like a balloon as she hurried to button her dress. She and Max and Baby were going home. Finally.

Through the tall grasses and brush, Lola watched three dark-skinned men move around the edge of the water toward them. She glanced across her shoulder at Max, and her hands stilled. Gone was the smoldering desire in his eyes. As if a curtain had fallen, his gaze was narrowed, intent, watchful. Then he turned and looked at her, his eyes flat and cold. Alarm ran up her spine to the base of her skull. She recognized the hard set to his jaw and the lines compressing his mouth. She'd seen it through the darkness that first night on the *Dora Mae*.

Max pointed to her pashmina and her dog and made a circling motion toward the tree. She didn't think to question him. Not now. She gathered her wrap, then on her hands and knees moved toward Baby. She picked him up from the duffel bag and crawled through the brush Max pulled aside for her. Through the foliage, he handed her the duffel and her purse. She fastened the last buttons on her dress with one hand and held Baby with the other.

Above the pounding in her ears, the voices drifted closer. Other than what she'd learned here and there growing up, Lola knew very little Spanish. She recognized not a word. The brush parted once more, and Max crawled through. For such a big man, he moved without a sound.

The voices grew closer, and Lola estimated they stood on the spot where she'd earlier bathed her feet. Max knelt on one knee beside her and slipped the fish knife from the top of his boot. At the sight of the long thin blade, her muscles froze.

Baby's ears perked up, and as she reached to wrap a hand around his muzzle, he barked and launched himself from her arms. Before she could call him back or dive after him, Max was on top of her, pinning her to the ground, his hand over her mouth. 'Let him go,' Max whispered right next to her ear.

She shook her head as Baby's excited barking filled the widening space between her and her dog. The voices stopped, and panic gripped Lola's stomach, just as it had the day she'd thought she'd lost him to the Atlantic Ocean.

'Do you want to die?' he whispered, his hard gaze pinning

her before he turned his attention to what was taking place by the blue hole.

She stopped struggling. No, she didn't want to die, but she didn't want to just sit back and let someone hurt Baby, either.

The dog's barking became more agitated, the way it did when he barked so hard his back legs lifted off the ground. She'd always worried that his Napoleon complex would someday be his Waterloo, and today it just might happen. Laughter joined the commotion and then a distressed yip.

Lola could not control the whimper that came from the base of her throat. She pulled air into her lungs through her nose, and everything blurred. Baby was just a dog, but he was her dog and she loved him. She knew that he could be a pain in the backside, but he was *her* pain in the backside, and he needed her.

Max felt the moisture of Lola's tears against his fingertips and looked down into her wide shimmering eyes. And he did it again. He opened his mouth and made a promise he wasn't sure he could keep. In fact, he was quite sure he couldn't keep it, but that didn't stop him from whispering next to her ear, 'I'll get your dog back for you. But you have to be quiet or we won't live long enough to get him back.'

She nodded, and the weight of her trust pressed in on him. What was he doing? Risking his life for a little yapper? For a little rat with a huge chip on his shoulder?

Max took his hand from her mouth and motioned for her to stay down. Of course, she didn't. She knelt beside him and peered through the thick brush. A pair of boots moved toward them and stopped less than three feet away. Right on the spot where he'd laid Lola on the ground and kissed her breast.

Where he'd been so consumed with her that he'd failed to hear the men until they were practically on top of him.

The men spoke Latin-American Spanish, and the others referred to the man in front of Max as *teniente*, but he wasn't a lieutenant in the Colombian military. In fact, Max doubted he had any military experience at all. Around the tree, grasses were bent, and on close inspection, it was obvious that the area had recently been disturbed. Max had quickly swept the area with a broken tree limb, but he'd had little time to do a thorough job. The *teniente* didn't seem to notice.

He issued orders to search the area and find the owners of the *perro*. He was so close, Max could see the seams of the guy's fatigues and the K-Bar knife stuck in the top of his boot. He noticed the slight protrusion beneath his pant leg, which Max would bet his ass concealed an ankle holster. The holster would just naturally contain a 9mm semi-automatic. In the man's hands, Max already knew he held an M-60. These boys were armed to the teeth and looking for trouble.

They were looking for drug drops, and if discovered, Max would immediately be shot. Unless these were members of the Cosella cartel. He didn't have to wonder what they'd do to him if that were the case. He'd already had a taste. Even though he doubted these men could positively identify him, his body still bore the telling bruises he'd received at the hands of José Cosella. But no matter what they would do to him, Lola would fare much worse. The thought of what she would suffer tightened his fist around the knife handle. If either of them stood a chance, he would have to take care of the man in front of him without alerting the others.

The boots moved on, and Max allowed himself to breathe. Without making a sound, he reached out a hand and parted the brush enough to see. Two men stood by the water. One held Baby by the collar, and the dog writhed in the air. The men laughed, and Max looked at Lola, the print of his hand still visible across her mouth. Her eyes were narrowed, promising murder. Damn, if she had an assault weapon, he would have been tempted to lay odds on her.

Max returned his gaze to the three men and watched them search the brush and tall grasses. They moved away from the blue hole and headed back down the hill. Max returned the knife to his boot, and he pulled his black T-shirt over his head. He ordered Lola to stay put and was surprised when she actually did. Keeping to the shadows, he followed the three men as they moved back toward the beach. A fourth man sat on the edge of a small inflatable that had been pulled up on the sand, two oars stuck out of the sides.

One of the men held up Lola's dog and they passed him around as if he were some sort of prize. Baby barked and snapped while they all laughed and talked at once. Max hoped like hell Lola stayed where he'd left her and couldn't see what was happening with her dog. He wouldn't put it past her to charge down the hill like the wrath of God.

Max lifted his gaze to the *Dora Mae*, which seemed to list even farther to port. He tried to recall if he or Lola had left anything aboard that could be tied to them. He didn't think they had. Anchored next to the *Dora Mae* was a forty-foot open-hulled speedboat. Known within law enforcement and in the drug business simply as a 'go-fast' boat because of its speed, its sole purpose was to retrieve water-tight drums of narcotics and outrun drug interdiction. The Coast Guard also called them powdercrafts for obvious reasons.

Typical of go-fast boats, this one had no identifying markings of any kind and was painted the same color as the waves. The craft's three 250-horsepower engines should have made enough noise to wake the dead. Yet he hadn't heard them. He'd been face down in Lola's cleavage and nothing had existed beyond her. Nothing beyond her rich brown eyes looking up at him with desire. Nothing beyond the touch of her satiny skin and the taste of her mouth. She captured his attention to the exclusion of all else, and that was dangerous. Real dangerous. Max had never been so careless. It wouldn't happen again. He couldn't afford to let it happen again. Their lives depended on it.

Over the sound of surf and the dog's continuous yapping, Max could hear very little, but what little he was able to gather confirmed his worse suspicions. They were members of the Cosella cartel, searching for drug drops scattered by the storm.

Sticking to the shadows, he moved a bit closer. He watched and listened, and it wasn't hard to determine that these four men weren't a very organized bunch. More like four guys screwing off when the big boss wasn't around to watch them.

All four jumped into the inflatable raft and rowed to the yacht, taking Baby with them. They held him over the side as he squirmed and yelped, and Max decided right then and there that if given the chance, he would make them pay. He wasn't a big fan of dogs, especially yippers, but any man who got off on torturing something weaker deserved to suffer as well.

Exactly if and when Max would have time or opportunity to

rescue the dog, he didn't know. He turned from the scene, and after a ten-minute climb back up the hill, he found Lola where he'd left her, with her bare feet planted by her butt, her arms around her knees.

'Where's Baby?'

'I couldn't get him yet,' he told her instead of telling her the bad news, that he didn't think he could get him without someone getting killed. 'I doubt they'll hurt him. You are a different matter.'

'How do you know? How do you know they aren't nice people? Maybe they'll take us to Miami.'

She'd been crying. Even with her eyes all swollen, she still looked like a sensuous treat, and he had to remind himself not to let his mind wander in that direction. He held out his hand, pulled her to her feet, and got serious. 'Do you remember I told you that someone might be looking for me?'

She brushed the dirt and leaves from her behind. 'Drug people?'

'Yep.'

Her gaze shot to his. 'Drug people have my dog?'

'For now.'

Max picked up the duffel bag and handed Lola her purse. 'Do you have a plan?'

Not yet. 'I'm working on it.'

Without a word, she followed him, and within five minutes they were at the cliffs overlooking the beach. He wondered what she'd do when she found out he might not be able to save her mutt. That his life and her life were too big a price to pay. He wondered if she'd ever forgive him. He wondered why he cared one way or the other.

It wasn't as if everything that had happened was completely his fault, and it wasn't as if he had any deep affection for that pain-in-the-ass dog. Once he returned home, he doubted he would ever see either of them. Lola would go off and live her life, completely free of him. And he would live his life free of her. Once they were back in the States, he doubted she'd give him more than a passing thought.

He held aside a branch and let her pass in front of him. So, why should he risk his life for a dog? Why should he care what she thought of him? He shouldn't, but he did, and the bitch of it was, he didn't know why. If he knew, then he could do something about it. He could stop it. Kill it. Cut its head off.

The branch swung back into place, and he told himself he cared about her because he felt responsible for her. It was just too damn bad he couldn't make himself believe it completely.

They found a shaded spot under a Caribbean pine at the edge of the cliff. Winds and storms had twisted the branches that grew away from the ocean and toward the ground. The thick needles provided perfect cover and padded the hard earth. They peered over the side of the cliff and watched the beach below, taking turns with the binoculars he'd shoved in the duffel before leaving the *Dora Mae* that morning. They watched the men unload booze and fishing chairs from the yacht, then the four jumped into the go-fast boat, but much to Max's surprise, they didn't leave. Instead they off-loaded a big boom box and a red cooler before rowing back to the beach. They set up chairs, cranked up the music, and prepared to party.

'Do you see Baby?'

Max searched the area until he found the dog tied to a chair with a piece of rope. 'I see him.' If he were by himself, he would have chosen a position near the action and waited for an opportunity to act, like when one of them walked into the trees to take a leak. But with Lola, he didn't dare move closer.

'Max?'

He lowered the binoculars and looked at her. 'What?'

'Are you a good secret agent?'

'I'm not a secret agent. You're thinking of the CIA. The agency I work for doesn't exist.'

'Well, whatever you are, are you good at it?'

'The government thinks so. Why?'

'Because,' she said as she took the binoculars from him and stared down at the beach, 'I think we can maybe knock all those guys out, or wait until they pass out, get Baby, and steal their boat.'

He'd already thought of that, except his plan didn't include knocking anyone out. 'I'm one step ahead of you.'

'So, what's our plan?'

'Our plan is that you stay here, and I'll take care of the rest.'

'I want to do something.'

'No.'

'Max . . .'

'Lola, I can't work if I have to worry about you.' He took the binoculars back. 'I know what I'm doing. You're going to have to trust me.'

'The last guy who told me to trust him put my naked pictures on the Internet.'

'Well, I'm not that guy.'

She ran her hand up his arm and patted his shoulder. Just a friendly touch, an innocent gesture, that sent pure fire to his groin, like she'd reached in his pants and touched something else. Damn.

'I know,' she said, 'so what's *your* plan?'

'First off,' he answered, and gave his attention to the men on the beach, 'I can't do a thing until it is completely dark. That will also give them a chance to drink a bit more.'

'What if they leave?'

'They won't. They'll probably pass out where they are or crawl onto the *Dora Mae* to sleep it off.'

'What then?'

He lifted one shoulder. 'Won't know for sure until I get down there. We have at least an hour to kill.'

The men on the beach cranked the boom box, and the longer they drank, the louder it got. Their choice of music consisted of salsa, Latino, and, of all things, Guns N' Roses. Just before sunset, they lined up empty bottles on the beach and sprayed them with automatic weapons fire. Baby wisely dove beneath the chair as the men shot up the sand. The palm trees and Caribbean pine were next, then the cliffs. Max and Lola hit the ground on their stomachs. Max covered her with his body as bullets strafed the limbs several feet above their heads. While Axl Rose belted out, 'Welcome to the jungle,' shredded needles and bark chips fell onto Max's back.

'Fucking idiots,' he swore.

'Max?'

'Yeah?'

She turned her head and looked at him, her mouth a breath away from his. Through the shadows of the pine, the orange and gold fingers of the setting sun touched her face and settled in the strands of her hair. She started to shake and he held her tighter. 'I don't like being shot at,' she said.

'It's not my favorite.'

'I don't want to be afraid any more. I've been afraid for so long now.' Moisture welled up in her eyes and a tear slipped from the corner. Her breath hitched as she battled to hold it all in. 'And I'm scared.' She lost the battle and a deep sob racked her chest. 'I'm tired of being scared. I just don't think I can take any more.'

'You've held up better than some men I know.'

'I hate to cry. I don't want to cry.'

'It's okay to cry,' he told her as he gently rolled her onto her back and looked into her watery eyes. He held himself up on one elbow and added, 'If I were a girl, I'd be crying, too.'

'But a guy like you would never cry, right?'

He glanced down at the party on the beach. The boom box changed CDs and the kind of music you'd hear in a border cantina rode the breeze. He'd seen grown men, war-hardened soldiers cry, but Max had only cried once. The night his father had died, he'd sat in the old man's house, alone, and cried like a baby.

'Guys like you don't get scared.'

He placed his hand on the side of her face and brushed the tears from the cool silk of her cheek. She was wrong. The thought of failing her, of anyone hurting her, scared the hell out of him. 'Right,' he finally answered. 'Guys like me aren't afraid of anything.'

Lola stared up into Max's face. The heat of his chest seemed to be the only thing letting her know she was still alive. Her fingers and toes felt numb as if she were standing in snow, and she was afraid that if she let it, she would become frozen with fear. For the past three days, she'd lived with it, battling it back and barely keeping it at bay. She wasn't sure she could do it any more. 'I want to feel safe again, Max.'

She'd been accidentally kidnapped, threatened, tied up, almost drowned trying to save her dog, barely lived through a storm. Baby had been stolen and now drug runners were shooting at her. Add the unfortunate accident with the flare gun, the near-rescue of the night before, her constant worry, and she'd had it.

The first night aboard the *Dora Mae*, she'd felt she was going to die, and she'd fought to live. Last night during the storm, she'd known the same fear, and now she had to face this latest threat to her life.

She raised her hands to the sides of Max's head and brought his face to her. In the past few days, the only time she'd come close to feeling safe was within the arms of the man who'd put her life in danger. The strength of those same big arms was the only thing making her feel alive now. 'Max,' she whispered.

He didn't have to ask her what she wanted; he knew. His mouth took hers, and she clung to him as he fed her the warmth of his kiss. It spread across her flesh like an accelerating flame and battled back her fear. He possessed her with his lips and tongue and she was able to concentrate on him. On the texture and taste of him. The scent of him filling her head.

She ran her hands over his neck and shoulders, touching as much of him as she could reach. She slid her palm under his shirt and warmed her hands on his powerful chest. He was so solid and alive. So potently male, his strong heart pounding beneath her hand making her senses alive and buzzing. She wanted more. Much more.

She moved her mouth to the side of his throat. 'Make love to me, Max,' she said on a heavy breath.

His hand found her bare thigh and slipped beneath the hem of her dress. The touch of his warm palm and the anticipation of more pooled between her legs. 'This isn't a good time.' His voice sounded as thick as the blood pumping through her veins.

She couldn't have heard him right. 'What?'

'This isn't a good time.'

She had heard him right, but she couldn't believe what he was saying. This was Max, the guy with the quick fingers who could undress a woman before she knew it. Max, the man who'd called her a tease no more than twenty-four hours ago.

She looked up into the shadows caressing his face. 'When

would be a good time for you? In a few hours when we might very well be dead?'

'Lola, I'll do my best to see that you get home, whole and in—'

'I know,' she interrupted, 'but you can't guarantee it.' She plucked the button at the waistband of his jeans. 'Everything we are, and everything that we'll ever be, might die tonight, Max. On an uncharted island in the middle of the Atlantic.' All of her hopes and dreams for her business, and having a family of her own someday, would die with her. There would be no more somedays for her. Her mother and father would never know what happened to her, and they would have to live the rest of their lives wondering if she was dead or alive. She knew them well enough to know that they would never give up hope. They would search for her the rest of their lives. 'No matter how much you might want to, you can't promise we'll be alive tomorrow.' All five buttons popped from their holes, and she slipped her hand inside. Through the clinging cotton of his boxer briefs, she found him fully erect. She pressed her palm against the incredible heat of him. Fire ran up the inside of her wrist, danced up her pulse, and shot straight to her heart. This was what she needed from him now. 'Give me something to think about besides how afraid I am.'

His nostrils flared and through the orange fingers of the setting sun his eyes dilated, and still he hesitated. 'You owe it to me,' she added, and couldn't believe he was forcing her to use strongarm tactics. 'It's your fault I'm here, now make it up to me.'

His hand slid farther up her thigh to the elastic edge of her panties and a smile curved one corner of his mouth. 'That's a persuasive argument.'

'I can't believe we're arguing at all.' She shoved her hand farther down his pants and softly took the weight of his testicles in the palm of her hand.

He sucked in his breath. 'You're not a screamer, are you?'

Not tonight she wasn't. 'I'll control myself.'

That seemed to be what he needed to hear, and he cupped her between her legs. 'Jesus,' he groaned, 'you're already wet.' His fingers slid beneath the crotch of her panties, and he parted and touched her slick flesh. She whispered his name, then turned her face into his shoulder. The tips of his fingers brushed her where she was most sensitive, and she bit the hard muscle at the top of his arm.

'Lola.'

'Hmm?' She kissed the spot she'd bitten.

'Nothing. Just Lola.' With each stroke of his fingers, he fed her intense desire and shut out everything but her need to feel him inside of her.

She pushed her hand beneath his underwear and closed her fist around his shaft. The air whooshed from his lungs, and she moved her hand up and down the long, hard length of him, feeling the tight silkiness of his skin and the incredible heat. She raised her lips to receive his kiss and took the plump head of his penis in her hand. She squeezed and a low groan sounded deep in his chest. His mouth opened wide over hers, and she tasted his passion, hot and vibrant on his tongue. Dimly, she heard the music from the beach, but nothing existed beyond Max. Beyond the scent of him, the smooth texture of his hard flesh, and the length of him.

Max rose on his knees and removed her panties. He moved between her legs and hooked his thumbs beneath the waistband of his jeans and underwear. Slowly, he pushed them down his thighs, revealing first the black hair that grew thicker low on his belly. Then his erection jutted free, huge and powerful. He took himself into his hand as his heated gaze moved over her. Within the shadows of the pine tree, the Caribbean sun set around him, bathing slices of him in gold. 'Unbutton your dress, Lola,' he said, his voice raw. 'I want to see you. All of you.'

The air around her was charged with longing as she worked each button until the dress lay open. She raised her arms to pull him close, but he planted his hands by her hips and lowered his face to her belly. He kissed her navel and stomach, and buried his face in her cleavage. His rough cheeks chafed her breasts as his wet mouth placed more kisses there. His smooth erection brushed the inside of her thigh and sent a shudder throughout her body.

With unsteady hands, she brought his face to hers. Their gazes met and held as he began his entry. He pushed the broad head of his hot penis inside of her, then his hips rocked back and forth. A slow and easy rhythm, giving her time to stretch and adjust before he grasped her thighs, and with one final thrust, he buried himself fully. Lola gasped and grabbed hold of his shoulders. He filled her completely, the heat of him burning her up inside. A moan she could not control poured from her throat and she wrapped one leg around his waist.

Max sucked in a breath and held it. Beneath her hands his muscles had turned to stone. 'Lola,' he whispered against her cheek. 'God, you feel incredible. So hot.' He pulled halfway out, then lunged forward. 'So good.'

Like the blast of a furnace, heat spread across Lola's skin. Down her legs to the soles of her feet. Up her belly and across her breasts and arms. Each thrust felt better than the last, leaving her greedy for more. Leaving her wanting. Wanting. Wanting more. More of him.

In and out, harder. Faster. She couldn't breathe. And still it went on. Stroking exquisite pleasure, and just when she thought she would combust, he placed a hand beneath her bottom, tilted her pelvis, and drove a little deeper.

'Max,' she whispered on a panted breath. 'Max. Don't stop.'

'I don't plan on it,' he managed as he hammered into her.

Below his T-shirt where their bellies touched, their skin stuck together. He wrapped his arm around her, and she felt completely consumed by him. With his taking of her, surrounding her, and filling her. Driving her toward orgasm with each thrust of his hips and stroke of his velvet penis. Her entire world was focused on the place he touched inside of her and how good he made it all feel. Her mind reeled and she may have spoken out loud, but she wasn't quite sure. She closed her eyes, and he placed his hands on the sides of her face. 'Lola, open your eyes and look at me.'

She managed his request, but barely. Her whole world was focused on where his body joined hers and the intense rush of sensation that had taken over and was forcing her to meet each plunge of his hips.

'I want you to look at me. I want to see your eyes when I make you come,' he said, then he got his wish as the first wave of orgasm took hold and pulled her into its fury. Her body arched and she clung to him as his body drove her into the vortex of hot, mind-numbing pleasure. She opened her mouth, and he kissed her, swallowing her long moan, taking everything she had, then demanding more. Within the shelter of the Caribbean pine, he swore and praised God in the same ragged whisper. On and on, until he tangled his fingers in her hair and a groan rumbled deep within his chest. His hips pumped faster and harder, then he drove into her one last time.

In the aftermath, their labored breathing filled the air. She wasn't certain how long they lay together, Max supporting most of his weight on his forearms, while his body covered hers. 'Are you okay?' he finally asked.

She ran her fingers through the sides of his hair and chuckled softly. 'I think so.'

'Jesus, I don't think I've ever come that hard. You're an incredible fu—' He caught himself. 'Lay. No.' He shook his head. 'I meant to say you're an incredible lady.'

Lola laughed without making a sound. Max's slip was one of the nicest compliments any man had ever given her. 'I've always wanted to be an incredible lay.'

'Well, you are that.'

Above the sounds of their breathing, salsa music penetrated their haven and the real world intruded. Max kissed her forehead and muttered something she didn't quite catch. Then, with her heart still thudding heavy in her chest and her skin still sensitive from his touch, he slid from her body and rose to his knees. The last fingers of light glistened on his wet sex before he pulled up his boxer briefs. He looked out through the branches, then returned his gaze to her.

'You deserve better than this, Lola. If I had my way, we'd do a little skinny-dipping, then go at it again, but real slow next time,' he said as he buttoned up his pants. 'But we don't have time, and we need to have a serious talk.'

Lola sat up and put her panties on. If she had her way, she'd lie around in Max's arms and bask in her afterglow. She didn't want to have a serious talk, but she knew they must. Tonight there would be no basking. No lying around. No skinny-dipping, then making love again.

'I don't know how long I'll be gone. It could be an hour, maybe longer. The main thing is, you've got to stay put right here. No matter what you see or hear.'

Meaning, no matter if he got into trouble, she wasn't to help him. She pulled her dress together, then buttoned it. 'I still think I should come with you.'

'No.' He placed his fingers beneath her chin and lifted her gaze to his. 'I can't protect you against four armed men.' His hand fell to his side. 'If anything happens to me, this is what I want you to do—'

She shook her head. 'Nothing will happen to you.'

'I want you to wait until those men are long gone,' he continued as if she hadn't spoken. 'Then start a fire on the beach. Get a really big one going, and throw all the plastic and rubber on it that you can find from the *Dora Mae*. Plastic and rubber give off a lot of black smoke which can be seen for miles.' He took the binoculars and stared down at the beach. 'Remember to keep the fire burning at night. If you soak the sand in some oil from the yacht, that will help.' He lowered the binoculars and handed them to her. 'Those birds' nests I told you I'd spotted are very dry and will make good kindling.'

'Max?'

'Yes.'

'Nothing will happen to you,' she repeated, as though, if she said it enough, she could make it true. She didn't even want to contemplate what could happen.

'I hope not.' He stood and pulled her to her feet. 'Promise me you won't move from this spot.'

'I promise.'

He placed his hand on the back of her head and gave her a quick kiss. 'When I come for you, be ready to move.'

'I will.' She placed her hand on his arm. 'Promise me you'll be careful.'

'Honey, I'm always careful.'

When he would have pulled away, her grasp tightened. 'Promise me you'll come back.'

He took her hand from his arm and kissed her palm. 'I'll do my best.'

There were only two real-life rules to any conflict, two principles of war, that Max followed. Win at all costs, and failure is not an option. Max had been in too many conflicts not to believe in these now more than ever.

He knelt by the creek that ran down the side of the hill and scooped up mud with two fingers. He smeared it across his forehead and around his eyes, down his cheeks and chin. On his arms and the backs of his hands.

The music coming from the beach stopped, and Max glanced through the foliage. Night had completely fallen, and he could see very little. Slightly below him to the left, he could just make out the glow of the campfire. Above the sound of the surf, the slurs and boasts of drunken men filled the cool breeze. Then a new CD kicked in with the sort of Latino music Max had been raised on – the kind of music that made him think of empty bottles and overflowing ashtrays.

He moved to the edge of the trees and became part of the inky black shadows. Three bad guys sat next to the fire swilling booze, while a fourth looked to be passed out in one of the fishing chairs. He didn't see Baby, but the rope that had been tied to him was still tied to the chair. Max crouched behind a palm tree and listened and watched and waited.

The three men by the fire were like most men who sat around getting shitfaced. They bitched about their wives and girlfriends, and they bitched about their jobs. About how hard it was to pick up drug drops and deliver them to waiting vessels on time, as if they were working for the freakin' UPS.

The longer he listened, the more they drank and the louder they got. They talked about the death of José Cosella and the bounty their boss had put on the head of the man who'd been responsible. Five hundred thousand pesos. Too bad no one had a clue who the gringo was or where he'd disappeared.

Max glanced up the hill to the point where Lola would be sitting. He envisioned her with her elbows resting on her knees, looking down at the beach through the binoculars. Her dress, a pool of blue in her lap, the moon touching her long legs and full lips. His gaze returned to the beach, but his thoughts weren't entirely on business. He raised his hand to his face and pushed his palm close to his nose. It was still there. Between his fingers. But just barely. The scent of Lola Carlyle. The scent of intoxicating sex. He breathed deep, and his body responded. Lust coiled in his groin and his dick hardened within his jeans. He closed his eyes and thought of kissing her there. There between her thighs, where she'd been wet and wanting. Wanting him.

If anyone had ever told him that he would someday have sex with Lola Carlyle, especially while drug runners partied below, he would have laughed his ass off. Max had always considered himself one lucky guy, he'd lived through too much not to believe it, but he wasn't that damn lucky.

Since the night he'd commandeered the *Dora Mae*, he'd thought of her beneath him naked. He'd thought of it in the context of living out every man's fantasy. Of Maximilian Zamora, son of an alcoholic Cuban immigrant, fucking a supermodel.

He closed his fist and lowered his hand. He'd been extremely shortsighted. Caught off guard, something that didn't happen often. There was no feeling of macho triumph. No urge to beat his chest or tell his buddies. Just the knowledge that he'd given in to his lust for her under extremely dangerous conditions. That he'd gone too far, and if given half the chance, he'd go there again. And again.

Max sat in the shadows for half an hour before he moved back through the trees and shrubs to a point where the island curved around and was out of sight of the beach. If there was one thing Max had always trusted in himself, it was his instincts, but lately his instincts were proving unreliable. They'd failed him during his operation in Nassau, and they'd failed him where Lola was concerned, too. Or perhaps his instincts weren't failing; maybe he just wasn't listening.

Tepid waves rushed over the toes of his boots as he bent to pull out the fish knife. In Lola's case, he figured the problem was the latter. He wanted her, and no matter how much he told himself that having her was likely to get him killed, he hadn't listened.

Now that he'd been with her, he knew without a doubt it had been a mistake, and he wasn't talking about the physical threat. Making love to Lola Carlyle wasn't as mind-blowing as he'd figured. As lustful as a thousand different fantasies. No, it was better. More. Being with her, looking down into her face as he buried himself in her warm, wet body, he'd gotten a glimpse of something bigger than lust. Something bigger than the desire pulling at his groin and urging him to plunge faster and deeper. To make her belong to him so completely, she wouldn't know where he began and she ended. He'd gotten a glimpse of what his life could be with her, and for those few moments, he'd given in to it. He'd let it crawl into his chest, steal his breath, and block his reason.

But it was just a glimpse. A fantasy, after all. In the real world, Max wasn't a forever kind of guy, and Lola wasn't the kind of girl who'd settle for someone like him. A man who couldn't guarantee he'd be around tomorrow.

Max waded into the surf and forced thoughts of Lola from his mind. She was a civilian, just like any other civilian. This was a job, like so many others he'd been given. Years of discipline allowed him to detach himself from everything but what needed to be done. Waves hit his chest as he stuck the fish knife between his teeth so he wouldn't lose it, then he kicked out and swam. Just the top of his head and his eyes broke the surface of the water as he made his way out five hundred feet. He made not a ripple or a splash as he turned and swam parallel to the shore.

From a distance, the white outline of the *Dora Mae* resembled an enormous beached whale, a sad and pathetic waste. The closer he swam, the more the yacht took its recognizable shape, but no less sad or pathetic. The go-fast lay twenty feet to the left of the yacht, yet it rode so low in the water, he wouldn't have seen it if he hadn't known where to look.

The open-hulled speedboat rocked within the gentle waves as Max silently hoisted himself over the side. He took the knife from his mouth and gave his eyes a moment to adjust to the light within the hull. Three plastic barrels were stowed starboard next to what looked like an army ammunition crate. He glanced toward the beach, counted all four bad guys, then lifted the lid.

Bingo. A cache of all kinds of goodies. Through the light of the moon, Max made out several MP4 machine guns, but no ammo. There were about a dozen sticks of dynamite and blasting caps, and the last thing he touched made him smile.

'Hello,' he whispered, and pulled out one of his all-time favorite weapons, a .50-caliber sniper rifle. Right after he'd completed SEAL training and received his BUD/S, he'd been sent to sniper school at Fort Bragg. For months he'd hidden within the North Carolina weeds, shooting the hell out of paper targets and dummy vehicles while chiggers feasted on his ankles and wrists. A few years later, he'd used his training in real combat during Desert Storm, taking out necessary targets and learning a whole lot about living and dying.

He'd been just a kid.

What those boys on the beach wanted with a weapon that was capable of blowing a big hole in a target from a mile and a half away was anyone's guess. Max took a quick inventory of what he had and what he didn't. He didn't have ammunition for the MP4s, and figured the men had used it all to shoot the hell out of the trees. He didn't have a detonation cord for the dynamite, but in the bottom of the crate he found five half-inch .50-caliber bullets.

After a quick check of the beach, he slipped over the side of the boat and, keeping the rifle and ammo above his head, swam to the *Dora Mae*. Except for patches of light filtering in through the windows, the inside of the yacht was as dark as a tomb. It didn't help that the interior had been ransacked and things were thrown everywhere. Glass crunched beneath his boots as he made his way to the stateroom. It took less than a minute to find what he was looking for. He shoved half a dozen condoms in his pocket, then opened several packs and stretched the thin latex over the rifle. He dumped the bullets in the last condom, tied it to his belt loop, then left the yacht once more.

Relief tugged at one corner of his mouth as he slipped into the ocean and headed again toward the go-fast. He was finally in familiar territory. Things were definitely looking up. Hell, all he had to do was snatch Baby Doll Carlyle from beneath the chair of a passed-out drug runner, get Lola and the dog aboard the powdercraft without the bad men on the beach suspecting anything, then haul ass out of the Bahamas.

Piece of cake.

Beyond the firelight on the beach, Lola could see very little. Her eyebrows ached, but she refused to lower the binoculars. Max had been gone at least an hour. He was out there somewhere, yet she hadn't caught a glimpse of him. A few times she thought she'd spotted him, but each time the sighting had turned out to be nothing more than waves. She lowered her gaze to the beach. She hadn't been able to spot Baby, either, even though she knew where he was.

The sound of mariachi music floated up to Lola, as loud and clear as if the actual band were playing on the beach. She wasn't a big fan of mariachi music, and from now on she was sure she would hate it. She had dirt in her hair, bug bites on her arms, and her only consolation was that no one was shooting at her. The only thing that gave her peace of mind was that no one was shooting at Max, either. Not yet, anyway.

Finally her arms gave out and she lowered the binoculars. She'd wrapped her pashmina around her legs, but the bugs on the island were nasty and seemed to bite right through the cashmere. She was tired and itchy, and so hungry she'd sell her soul for a pan of macaroni and cheese or a king-sized Snickers.

She slapped at a mosquito having dinner on her neck. If Max didn't hurry, she doubted she'd be able to walk from loss of blood.

Just thinking of him brought a smile to her face. It wasn't logical. It didn't make sense, but she supposed Stockholm syndrome didn't make sense. In the whole mixed-up mess, he was the only constant. The only thing that was stable. Real.

He'd certainly seemed very real when he'd made love to her. The touch of his hands and his mouth on her, the incredible feeling of his body joined with hers. Of all the men she'd known, of the men she'd loved, she'd never felt as connected as she did with Max.

As if her thoughts conjured him out of air, he suddenly appeared next to her. In his arm, he held Baby, and Lola didn't think she'd ever seen anything so wonderful. She wanted to give Max a big smack on the mouth, then cover his entire body with kisses. The dog squirmed with excitement as Lola stood, but Max's hand on his muzzle kept him from barking.

'I need the duct tape,' Max said just loud enough to be heard. 'It's in the duffel bag.' When Lola found it, he told her to tear off a piece, then he wrapped it around the poor dog's mouth.

Although Lola knew it was necessary, she still felt bad for him. 'Can he breathe?'

'Yes, ma'am,' Max answered, the tone of his voice all business as he handed over the dog. 'He just can't bark.'

Even as Baby Doll scratched at the tape with his paw, his whole body shook with excitement. 'You don't know how close you came to living in Mexico,' she chastised as she squeezed him against her breasts.

'Colombia,' Max corrected. He knelt by the duffel and for the first time she noticed the rifle strapped to his back. A gray baseball cap stuck out of his back pocket. She wasn't sure, but it looked like some sort of rubber was stretched over the rifle's barrel.

'Are you going to kill those guys?' she asked.

'Do you have a problem with that?' He pulled out the two pieces of Styrofoam and stood.

Did she? Not if there was no other way. 'No,' she answered, and held Baby as Max once again taped the water wings to the side of her dog. 'Have you ever killed anyone before?'

He didn't answer and asked instead, 'Do you think you can swim without hyperventilating or making any noise?'

If it meant getting off the island, she could do anything. 'Yes.'

'Good, because our getting out of here depends on it.' Once again he knelt by the duffel. He pulled out the flashlight and a map, then he stuffed her pashmina inside. Next, he filled the bag and her purse with several big rocks.

'What are you doing?'

'These are going in the blue hole. I want nothing left behind that could identify us.'

'My toothbrush is in there. I'll need it.'

'You'll have a new one by morning.'

What he didn't say was that she might also be dead by morning. 'I'll need my wallet. It's Fendi.' His exasperated grunt told her what he thought of that. 'Okay, but I'll need my American Express.'

He pulled out the cash she had in her wallet, but no credit card. With her free hand, she stuffed the money in her bra.

In one fluid motion, Max stood and shoved the flashlight and map beneath one arm. Then he reached into his back pocket and pulled out something square. Moonlight shone off silver foil, and Lola thought it looked a lot like one of those chocolate mints, the kind room service left on her pillow when she called for turn-down service.

'Is that a mint?'

'Condom.'

For several silent moments she stared at him through the darkness. He had to be kidding. 'I thought you said those were too small for you.'

He looked up and their eyes locked. 'They're not for me.' For a brief second she thought she saw a corner of his mouth tilt up, but she wasn't sure. 'Take this,' he instructed as he thrust the flashlight toward her. Once she held it in her free hand, he ripped open the condom, stretched the latex, then rolled it up the flashlight. When he was through, he tied the end to his belt loop. 'I want you to follow right behind me without making a sound.' He rolled up the map and slipped a condom around that, too. 'You and I, and your mutt, are going to swim to that boat out there, slip aboard, and haul ass out of here.' He tied the map to his belt loop too. 'When I tell you to do something, I want you to do it. Don't think about it first. Just do it. Right now, I just want you to say, "Okay, Max."'

She wasn't in the military. She wasn't used to taking orders. But she trusted him with her and Baby's lives. 'Okay, Max.'

He placed his hands on his hips and looked her up and down. 'You're going to stick out like a shiny beacon.'

'What do I do?'

'I'll take care of it in a minute. Right now we need to go over the op plan.'

'Op plan?'

'Operation plan,' he explained. 'Once we're on board the boat, I'll take up a position in the rear, and when I tell you, I want you to start the engines.'

'*Me?*'

'Have you ever driven a boat?'

'No, but I drove a motorcycle once.'

He wiped his hand across the stubble on his jaw. 'It's easier than driving a motorcycle. Just turn the key and push the throttle forward.'

'Do I have to put it in gear?'

'You don't have to worry about that. It's ready to go.'

'Okay. Turn the key, then push the throttle forward,' she repeated as her stomach twisted into knots. 'If I pull it back, is that reverse?'

'Yes, and don't even think about doing that.'

Her stomach twisted a bit more. She could do this. No sweat. 'Anything else?'

'Yes, keep your head down.' He adjusted the rifle on his back. 'Ready?'

Not really. 'Yes, Max.'

'Then let's rock and roll.'

She suddenly felt sick. This was it. They would either make it off the island or die. She followed him to the blue hole and stood on the large rocks as he slid the duffel and her Louis Vuitton bag beneath the water. Everything she possessed disappeared in the blue hole. She held Baby tight as the three of them moved down the hill toward the beach. Just as she'd agreed, she followed Max. She stuck her hand in the back pocket of his jeans, as she'd thought of doing earlier that day, and neither of them made a sound.

They knelt beside the stream he'd helped her across on their way up the hill. He handed her the baseball cap, and as she stuffed her hair beneath it, he dragged his fingers through the mud, then smeared it on his face and arms. She was next, and she closed her eyes as he spread the cold wet dirt over her cheeks.

'Think of it as a facial,' he whispered.

She opened her eyes and looked into his face close to hers. '*That* mud is clean,' she whispered back.

One brow lifted the dirt on his forehead and his silent laughter touched her cheek. 'Clean mud? That's a new one.'

The mariachi music stopped and Max glanced over his shoulder toward the beach. The muffled voices of three men rose above the sound of the surf, their slurs not quite as loud as before. Max dug into the mud, and with quick impersonal hands rubbed it on her arms and legs. Baby attempted to jump from her grasp, but she held him closer. Then Max rose and she followed him through the trees and brush. Again she was impressed with how silently he moved for such a big guy. They kept to the deepest shadows, Max sometimes blending in so well, she had to hold on to the back of his shirt so she wouldn't lose him. Sometimes she reached beneath the rifle strapped to his back and touched him just to reassure herself that he was still Max. Still strong and warm and alive. And each time she did, she felt a bit stronger herself.

He led her to a part of the beach away from the drunken men, and together they walked out into the ocean. The waves rushed over her ankles, then her knees and thighs, washing away the mud, which had started to itch. She walked out until just her shoulders were above the water, then she and Baby paddled against the current, making little progress.

The third time Max came back for her, he reached beneath the water for her hand and placed it on the barrel of his rifle. She grabbed Baby with her other hand, and without a word, Max towed them. Lola kicked her feet, careful not to make a sound. She had the feeling that even if she didn't help, he could have managed.

Salt water filled her mouth and splashed into her eyes. One shoe fell off her foot, and the muscles in her arms and legs burned. It seemed as if they'd been swimming for an hour when they finally came upon the open boat. Max cut the anchor rope, then took Baby from her and set him in the bottom. He grabbed the side with one hand, grabbed her butt with the other, and shoved her over the gunwale. She slid to the bottom like an exhausted fish and stared up at the night sky. Tired and afraid and so winded she could hardly catch her breath. Max passed the rifle over, and it hit her shoulder. The boat rocked as he hoisted himself over the side and landed smack on top of her. The air whooshed from her lungs and his forehead knocked the visor on her hat. Immediately he lifted his weight from her, straddling her on his hands and knees.

'Remember,' he whispered, 'on my signal, turn the key and push the throttle.'

Signal. What signal? Her throat was so dry, she couldn't catch her breath. All she could do was weakly shake her head.

'Lola.' He flipped up the bill of her hat. 'Are you hyperventilating again?'

She covered her mouth with her hand and nodded. Good Lord, of all the times to hyperventilate! Lying in the bottom of a drug runners' boat, while the drunken drug runners themselves partied and shot up the beach with machine guns. She had to turn the key and push the throttle. This was *not* a good time to pass out! A distressed little squeak escaped from her lips and from behind her fingers.

'Come on, honey,' he whispered, and rubbed her arms. 'Relax. You can do this. Just relax. Slow deep breaths through your nose.'

Lola concentrated on the dark outline of his face so close to her. The sound of his calm voice and the scent of seawater on his skin. She felt Baby rest his head on her ankle, and she did her best to push away her fear.

'Feeling better?'

She pulled a slow breath of air into the bottom of her lungs, then moved her hand to her chest. 'What's the signal?' she managed, fighting for a calm she didn't feel.

'I'll hold up my hand, and when I want you to turn the key and punch the throttle, I'll make a fist.'

'Okay, Max.'

'That's my girl. And remember, whatever you do, keep your head down,' he said, then gave her a quick kiss and crawled over her to the back of the boat.

Keep her head down. Turn the key. Push the throttle. She could do it. Lola rolled onto her stomach and crawled past two big plastic barrels and some sort of crate. She made her way around a small bench seat to the helm. By touch, she found the steering wheel, the key in the ignition, and the throttle.

She raised her head just enough to see over the top of the

seat and felt her brow shoot up her muddy forehead. Max's black outline knelt in the back, propping the barrel of the rifle on one of the three engines. Beyond him, the campfire glowed orange. The three men stood around it, their machine guns leaning against the rubber raft about ten feet from their reach. Their low voices and drunken laughter squeezed the back of her neck; the clammy night air weighed down on her skin like a wet towel. One of the men separated himself from the others and moved to the drunk passed out in the chair. He kicked the man's foot, then reached down and gave a tug on the rope. The end flew out from beneath the chair, and he looked down at his feet. Slowly, he bent to pick it up, then stared as if he couldn't believe what he was seeing. Or rather what he wasn't seeing.

His voice carried over the water as he turned back to the men and held the end of the rope high in the air. '*Perro?*' he said.

Lola lowered her gaze a fraction to the black outline of Max's back, willing him to hurry. Baby jumped up on the seat, and without taking her eyes from the beach, she set him back on the floor. One of the men looked out toward the boat, and Lola held her breath. He walked to the edge of the water, and the voices on the beach rose, becoming agitated.

'Come on, Max,' she whispered against the back of the seat. Then, as if he'd heard her, he raised his hand, glanced over his shoulder at her, and closed his fist.

She spun around on the seat, and with shaking hands, found the ignition. *Turn key, throttle forward* raced through her mind, and that's exactly what she did.

Nothing happened. She tried again, and this time the engine sputtered and died.

'Shit! Shit! Shit!' she whispered. The voices on the beach rose, and she tried again.

Nothing. She glanced over her shoulder and saw the men running toward the raft.

Over the chaos rose Max's calm voice, 'Time to go, honey,' he said.

She turned the key; the engine sputtered and died. The next time she tried, it started with a low rumble and she thrust the throttle as far as it would go. The boat shot forward across the water and her hat flew off her head. She grabbed hold of the steering wheel and held on for dear life. The boat bounded over the waves as the night erupted in a steady *brrrap brrrap* of machine gun fire. Lola kept her head down and hoped Max was doing the same. She couldn't see where they were going, but she supposed it didn't matter, since once away from the beach, the night was so pitch-black she wouldn't be able to see anything anyway.

Then suddenly an explosion, like the boom of thunder at ground zero, lit up the sky. Lola looked behind her as a huge fireball blew the *Dora Mae* into the black night. Two more explosions followed, sending burning pieces flying left and right. Against the fire and destruction of the yacht, Max rose. He stood with his feet spread apart and lifted his fists in the air as if he were the heavyweight champion of the world.

Max had spent a lot of his professional life cold and wet. It wasn't his favorite way to pass an evening, but he was used to it. Lola was not. He found a blanket in the front of the boat and handed it to her.

'Take off your wet clothes,' he advised, and took control of the steering wheel.

The fiery glow from the island faded as Max cut the flashlight and map from his belt loops. Equipped with the latest gadgets and goodies, the boat was everything a drug runner would need in order to find floating barrels of dope in the Atlantic. He sat beside Lola on the bench seat and shone the light next to her face. Her fingers trembled, and she had trouble grasping the buttons. Her lips were blue, and she held her shaking dog close to her chest.

Keeping one hand on the wheel, he brushed her fingers aside and helped her out of the dress. He tossed it in the bottom of the boat. Then he managed to peel the tape from Baby's muzzle. The dog let out a series of fierce barks as Max dropped the blanket over both Lola and her mutt.

'Hang in there just a bit longer,' he told her, and turned his attention to the Global Positioning System. He flipped on the boat's running lights and unfolded the map. A grease pencil and a ledger were clipped to the helm, and he used the pencil to mark their coordinates. He wanted to make sure the Coast Guard would know where to find the island and the four stranded drug runners. He didn't think the explosion of the *Dora Mae* had killed anyone, just rained a little fire down on them and singed their hair.

Some might have considered blowing up that yacht a bit excessive. Max wasn't one of them. Even though he doubted the four men were capable of dislodging the *Dora Mae* and making her operable, he wasn't willing to leave them any options. And he wasn't taking any chances that he or Lola had left anything behind that could be traced directly back to them. The *Dora Mae* had had to die. And damn, but there was very little in this world that could compare to a good explosion.

He turned on the radio and listened for any sort of traffic. He wasn't surprised when he didn't hear anything. But just because he didn't hear other vessels didn't mean they weren't out there. He tuned the radio to the Coast Guard channel and reached for the microphone. 'What's your middle name?' he asked, unwilling to announce to the Coast Guard or anyone else that he and Lola were in a stolen go-fast.

Lola's teeth chattered when she answered, 'Faith.'

'Coast Guard Florida Keys Group, Coast Guard Florida Keys Group, this is the vessel *Faith*. Copy? Over.' He waited a half minute before he repeated. Still, nothing. By the light of the LCD screen, he read their position and determined the storm had blown them eighty nautical miles southeast of the Florida Keys. Sixty miles south of their previous position aboard the *Dora Mae*.

'Where are we?' Lola asked between her tightly clamped teeth. 'Are we close to Florida?'

'About ninety miles,' he answered, too tired to calculate precisely the difference between miles and nautical miles. When he finally got home, he planned to sleep for at least three days.

'Do you want some of my – my blanket?'

'No, it shouldn't be long now.' The three engines on the boat would have allowed them to travel at speeds more than fifty knots, but without much protection from the wind, Max kept it at twenty-six. The sky overhead was perfectly clear and crammed with stars.

'Ma-Max?'

'Yes.' He looked over at her. At her reaching a hand from beneath the blanket to pick the mud from her forehead. At the strands of her hair bouncing about her face and catching the moon's pale reflection. The golden light of the helm touched her lips and poured into her mouth like honey when she spoke.

'I really thought we – we were going to die,' she said just over the sound of the engines.

'I told you I'd make sure you got home.'

'I know.'

Baby stuck his head from the hole in the blanket, looked around, then ducked back inside where it was safe and warm against Lola's breasts and belly.

That lucky dog didn't know how good he had it. Max knew, and he wished he didn't. Even now, with the cold and the wind biting his toes and cheeks, the memory of her smooth skin warmed the pit of his belly. It would have been so much better if they parted without him knowing how good it felt to make love to her. It would have been better if he could spend his life, like every other man in the world, wondering what it was like to hold her face in his hands while kissing her mouth.

Now that he knew, it was going to be a hell of a lot harder to let it go. To let her go. Now that he knew that beneath her sweet, cover-model curves resided a woman of courage and determination. The kind of courage and grit he admired.

As the boat sped toward the Florida coast, with each mile he put behind him, the closer they got to the moment he would hand her over to the Coast Guard. His responsibility over, he knew he should start putting distance between himself and her. She did not belong to him, but when she laid her head on his shoulder, he couldn't quite bring himself to push her away. He kept one hand on the wheel, and with his other he raised the microphone to his mouth.

'Coast Guard Florida Keys Group, Coast Guard Florida Keys Group, this is the vessel *Faith*. Copy? Over.' Still nothing.

'Max, when we're rescued, please don't leave me.'

He couldn't promise her that.

'Max?' She leaned her head back and looked up at him.

For the first time, he didn't make a promise he knew he couldn't keep. He was saved an explanation by the crackle of the radio, then the smooth flat voice of a coastie.

'*Faith*, Coast Guard. Roger, Skipper; please state your traffic, over.'

Max paused and looked down into Lola Carlyle's beautiful face. Then he raised the microphone and took the first step toward home and his life away from her.

Lola arrived at the Florida Lower Keys Medical Center sometime around two in the morning. It was the first time in days that she knew the exact hour. She was assigned a private room so she could be observed through the night. Her arms and legs felt too heavy to lift, and she wondered why she didn't feel like jumping up and down. She'd waited for this moment since Saturday night. She'd been through hell, fought to survive, and all she felt was numb. This time, more than just the tips of her fingers and toes tingled with little feeling.

Overwhelming lethargy had started soon after she and Max had sped from the island, and it had only gotten worse with each passing hour. She'd figured it probably had something to do with her adrenaline rush eating up the last bit of her energy. That, and she'd only had one decent meal in the last several days.

She wasn't sure how long they'd been aboard the drug runners' boat, but once she and Max and Baby had boarded the Coast Guard cutter, she'd been examined by the onboard EMT, and he'd determined that she suffered from dehydration, mild hypothermia, and exhaustion. The exhaustion part she could have diagnosed herself. That one was a no-brainer, but the hypothermia and dehydration surprised her. Especially the dehydration, since her bra and panties were still wet from her swim in the ocean.

While she'd been given an IV and forced to lie flat on her back in the sick bay, Max had been somewhere on the bridge, chatting it up with the commanding officer. She'd been alone, but at least she'd still had Baby with her then.

By the time they reached the Key West Coast Guard Station, she'd felt worse instead of better. She was so exhausted she couldn't think straight. An ambulance had been waiting for her, and she'd been placed on a gurney, still wearing the blanket Max had given her.

Someone had taken Baby from her arms, and she argued to keep him with her, but to no avail. She'd been assured that he would receive food and water and excellent medical attention at the local animal shelter.

Max could have done something to keep Baby with her. He could have intimidated them with just a scowl, but he was nowhere to be seen. Lola was horribly weak and disoriented, and as she'd watched everything being done to and around her, she couldn't quite connect the events.

Her gaze fell on military and medical personnel, but nothing was in the least familiar. She looked past the bright lights shining down and bouncing around the station. She controlled nothing that was happening to her, and she looked for Max. Sure that if she could just find him, he would make everything okay. But she didn't see him anywhere.

Finally, as Lola was being loaded into the ambulance, she caught a last glimpse of Max. Standing on the edge of a pool of light, he lifted his hand in an abbreviated wave before he climbed into a waiting car. Tinted windows swallowed him up and then he was gone. Unexpected panic knotted her stomach, and she reminded herself that she was okay now. She was safe, and she didn't have to depend on Max. She didn't need him any more.

So, why did it feel as if she did? Even now, as she lay in a warm hospital bed snug as a bug, why did she think she needed him so badly?

'How do you feel?' a nurse in a mauve and turquoise splattered smock asked as she took Lola's pulse.

Confused, she thought. 'Tired.' She scratched at her neck. 'And eaten alive.'

'I'll get you some calamine,' the nurse told her as she let go of her wrist.

Shortly after Lola's arrival at the medical center, her family had been notified and she'd been told her parents were on their way to Florida. 'I can go when my parents get here, right?'

'You'll have to ask the doctor about that.' She wrote something down on Lola's chart. 'The kitchen is closed, but we keep some snacks in the refrigerator down the hall. If you're hungry, we have pudding and juices and sodas.'

The confusion and the hunger eating her stomach reminded her that all she'd eaten that day was some cheese and crackers. Her hands and feet were cold and she felt hollow, as if she were collapsing. These sensations were not new to her, they were old and familiar, but for the first time in a long time, she heard the familiar urging loud and clear. The seductive voice that told her if she didn't eat tonight, she'd lose three more pounds by tomorrow. 'I'm actually starving, so I'll take anything you've got.'

'I'll see what I can scrounge up for you.' The nurse smiled and turned for the door.

'Is there anyone waiting to see me?' Lola asked, stopping her.

The nurse stuck her head out and looked up and down the hall. 'No. A sheriff was here earlier, but it looks like he left.'

Lola knew about the sheriff. He wanted to ask her questions about the past several days, but she'd put him off until morning. At first he'd been persistent, but he'd finally relented. She figured it must have been because she looked as bad as she felt, but frankly, she didn't care why. She really was tired, but more than her exhaustion, she wanted to talk to Max before she said anything. 'Have you seen a tall man with black hair and a black eye?'

'No. I think I'd remember someone like that,' the nurse said, and her white rubber clogs squeaked on the linoleum as she left the room.

Lola scratched at an insect bite on her throat, then she picked at the tape covering the IV needle in the back of her hand. The nurse brought her some vegetable soup, a piece of bread, pudding, and a Coke. When she was through eating, she pushed aside the tray table and thought about Max. She wondered where he'd been taken and when she would see him again. She didn't have a doubt that he would come to see her before he left the state. They'd been through too much together for him to leave without speaking with her. He'd saved her life and they'd made love. And yes, she knew it wasn't love for either of them, but it had been an intimate connection that she would never regret. Or forget, especially since he'd been the only man she'd ever had to practically beg for sex. Well, if not beg, she'd certainly had to *convince* him, for goodness' sake.

Lola tried to stay awake, sure he would come to her soon, but exhaustion overtook her. As she slept, she dreamed she went to the animal shelter to spring Baby and both of them got trapped inside. In her dream, she pounded on the door and called for Max, but he never arrived.

The sound of a familiar, soft southern voice woke her from her dream. 'Lola Faith?'

Her lids fluttered open and she looked toward the end of her hospital bed. She looked into her father's sunken bloodshot eyes. They were red and watery, as if he hadn't slept for days. His usually ruddy cheeks were pale, the worry lines on his forehead more pronounced.

Beside him stood her mother, a silk scarf covering her usually perfect bubble of blond hair. One side of the bubble was flat and fuzzy bangs stuck out from her forehead. Bags pulled at the bottoms of her eyes, and her lips were colorless.

Lola burst into tears, and not teeny, wimpy tears, either. Big, painful sobs – like the time she'd been eight years old and her daddy had accidentally left her at the Texaco. She'd been scared to death when she'd discovered he was gone, and overwhelmed with relief when he'd returned for her ten minutes later. She felt the same way now, at age thirty, only seeing how much suffering she'd caused them made it worse. They both looked like they'd aged ten years since she'd seen them a week ago.

Her mother rushed to the side of her bed and wiped Lola's

tears from her cheeks. 'You're going to be just fine now. Your mama and daddy have come to take you home.'

'They took Baby away from me,' she cried. 'An-and put him in the shelter.'

'We'll get your Baby back.' Her daddy patted her knee though the hospital bedding. 'Then you're going to come home to stay with us for a few days.'

Lola had a million and one things to do. She had a business to run. Yes, she had competent people who could run it in her absence, but Lola Wear, Inc. belonged to her. She wanted to speak with sales and marketing and get the early numbers on the new catalog. They were gearing up for a trade show in three months and she wanted to see the preliminary sketches for their booth. But as she looked at her parents and saw the strain on their faces, she figured they needed to pamper her in order to reassure themselves that she was okay. And perhaps she needed that, too. 'Will you make your special macaroni and cheese with the cut-up weenies?'

The corner of her mother's mouth trembled when she smiled. 'And I'll make you a Karo nut pie.'

Through her tears, Lola smiled, too. Her mother was one of the few people she knew who called pecan pie Karo nut pie. For the first time since she'd left, she finally felt like she was home again, but there was one thing that kept her from truly enjoying her return. One thing missing.

Max. She didn't have a clue where he was or why he hadn't contacted her.

'We've all been sick with worry,' her mother said. 'The Carlyle family reunion is this weekend, remember? I know everyone will be thrilled to see you.'

Lola felt a sudden ache just behind her eyebrows. She'd survived a storm at sea and drug runners, only to face the horrors of Aunt Wynonna's green pea casserole. And this time she would have to face the horrors alone, because Max had gone MIA.

At the naval air station in Key West, Max was provided a secure phone line to Washington. The fact that General Winter answered was Max's first inkling of the trouble he was in. The second was the Pavehawk helicopter that picked him up immediately and flew him from the air station to the Pentagon.

At the Pentagon, security showed him to an office on the fourth floor. In the daylight, he knew it had a great view of the Potomac and the Jefferson Memorial. The view of the brilliantly lit monument wasn't too bad at night either.

Usually Max met the general in a small planning room in the dark recesses of the basement. This was only the second time Max had been invited into this office. Given that and the lateness of the hour, he knew he was in trouble and prepared himself for a royal ass-chewing.

General Richard Winter sat behind his big mahogany desk, a computer monitor on one corner, a bronze eagle on the other. Max stood before the general at rigid attention. For a half hour, while his tired bones fused, he explained what had taken place since he'd left for Nassau the previous Saturday. Well, maybe not *everything*. He'd left out a few personal details concerning his behavior with Lola.

The general listened, then launched into a tirade. General Winter was as bald as a bowling ball, had big bushy eyebrows, and wore bifocals. He was the only man Max had ever met who could go on an apoplectic tear without blinking. It was uncanny and designed to inspire fear in men.

'This was supposed to be by the book, Max. Your directive was clear!'

'When the information I'm given is fucked up, there is no book. And as far as I'm concerned, there is only one directive. Get the job done and get the hell out, sir. I did not fail. The intel I was given failed me.'

Whether the general agreed, Max would never know. He continued to blister Max's ears, though, calling him every name in the book. A few he liked so much he repeated them again and again. His clear favorites were *shit-for-brains* and *asshole*. When he was finished, he expected Max to cower, as most men did when faced with such verbal intimidation. He should have known better.

'That's what I like about you, General Winter, sir,' Max said through a smile. 'You take the time for sweet talk before you screw with me.'

From behind the lenses of his bifocals, the general finally blinked. 'At ease, Zamora,' he ordered, and Max sat across the desk in an uncomfortable chair – which he figured was the general's intent. 'This is not a joking matter,' he continued, but his voice had lowered a few decibels. 'You commandeered a yacht with a civilian on board.'

'I explained that my vision was unclear, and I thought I was the only one aboard.'

'The fact remains that you shanghaied a famous underwear model and have been out of communication for four days. Stranded in the Atlantic, you say.'

'Yes, sir.'

'You've created a goddamn incident the government will be hard-pressed to deny.'

'How is that, sir?' he asked, even though he could guess.

'The minute Miss Carlyle was confirmed missing, her disappearance was reported by every news media in the country and half of Europe.'

Yep, that had been his guess.

'Now they're all going to want her story. She'll probably be invited to appear on the goddamn Letterman show.' The general leaned forward and stared at Max. 'You've spent time with her. What approach do we use to keep her quiet?'

'She's a smart woman. She knows about the Cosellas, and I'll remind her that she doesn't want to be tied to anything that happened in the Bahamas. I'll talk to her.'

'Negative, Max.'

'She'll listen to me,' he said with a lot more certainty than he felt. Because the fact was, now that she'd had some time away from him to think, he wasn't certain that she wouldn't want to press charges against him.

'I want you to stay away from Ms Carlyle and completely out of this, Max. The bureau is handling the situation.' General Winter stood. Subject closed. Meeting over. 'I believe you have something for me?'

Max stood and reached behind him. From the small of his back, he pulled out the map and the ledger he found on the powderboat and tossed the map on the desk. 'You'll find four of André Cosella's drug runners at those coordinates.'

'Dead?'

'I don't believe so.' Next, he tossed the ledger on the desk. He'd taken a good look at it while still aboard the go-fast.

It hadn't taken him long to figure out what he had and what it meant. The ledger recorded dates, times, position of drug drops, descriptions and quantities, and the names of the rendezvous vessels. It was all written down in plain Spanish, and he'd chosen to pacify the general with this information instead of handing it over to the Coast Guard.

After the public relations the military had suffered recently, this was a plum opportunity to redeem itself to the American people. If they didn't screw it up – which was always a possibility when dealing with pencil-pushers. 'I think you'll find that interesting, sir.'

General Winter glanced through the bound leather book, then looked up. 'This is the reason I put up with you, Max,' he said as he hit a button on his intercom. 'You have more lives than a damn cat and more luck than the Irish. Now get out of here and get yourself checked out.'

Max refused the general's order of medical attention and was escorted from the room by security personnel. He rode an elevator to the VIP parking lot, where a black Cadillac waited for him. Once inside the backseat of the car, he leaned his head back and finally relaxed for the first time since he'd sat in the galley of the *Dora Mae*, eating red snapper with Lola. He didn't let himself relax completely, though, fearing he'd fall asleep if he did. The lights of D.C. sped past the windows, and the sound of the tires on wet pavement filled the interior of the car, letting him know that it had rained. The sights and sounds were familiar ones and reminded him he was home. Almost.

After a short fifteen-minute drive, the Cadillac pulled up in front of Max's two-hundred-year-old townhouse in Alexandria. Now he was home. Finally. Max stepped from the car and tapped on the roof. The Caddie sped away, its tires splashing in inky puddles of water. The lights on the outside of the townhouse shone as they'd been programmed, but four days' worth of the *Journal* were flung on his porch. Since he hadn't anticipated being gone more than a day, he hadn't suspended service.

He didn't have a key. He didn't need one. When he'd purchased the townhouse three years ago, he'd designed and installed his own security system.

An exterior and interior keypad controlled the motion detectors, the exterior lights, and the locks on the doors. Max walked up the steps to the front door, flipped open the keypad, and punched in his code. He picked up the soggy newspapers and moved through the dark house to the kitchen. Beneath the sink, he pulled out the rubber garbage pail and dumped the papers into the empty trash bag.

Pale moon, and light from the back porch, poured in through the window above the sink, lighting patches of forties-red countertops, cabbage-rose wallpaper, and his chrome coffee-maker. Except for the security system and the new pipes he'd had installed in the two bathrooms, he hadn't quite gotten around to remodeling the townhouse like he'd always planned.

Without turning on the lights, he walked up the stairs to his bedroom on the second level. The hardwood floors creaked beneath his weight, and he sat on the edge of his mattress to unlace his boots. He'd been awake for forty-eight hours, and unbidden, memories of Lola rose in his head. Images of her bathing on the swimming platform of the *Dora Mae*. Kissing her on the aft deck. Holding her in his arms as the storm threatened to swamp the yacht. Touching and kissing her bare breasts, then making love to her as the sun set over an uncharted tropical island somewhere in the Atlantic. Hot memories and images flowed through him and he was too tired to fight them.

He took off his clothes and stood completely naked. Light from outside crept in around the shade covering the window. It striped the floor and lit up an edge of the dresser. Max stepped over the heap of clothes and reached for a battered St Christopher medallion hanging from one corner of the mirror. He raised his arms and placed the gold medallion around his neck. It had belonged to his father, and the cool metal was familiar against his chest.

The crisp bedsheets brushed his skin as he slid between them, and he wondered if Lola slept well wherever she happened to be. The last he'd seen of her, she'd looked pale and exhausted, and he imagined she'd been kept for observation in the hospital.

He thought of calling Key West to check on her condition. Then he thought better of it. It would be best to make a clean break. To stay out of her life. Not because General Winter had told him to, but because even as the responsibility of Lola and her dog had weighed him down and choked the air from his throat, he'd come to crave it. There was something about the warmth of her eyes. The way she'd looked at him. The way she'd shared her life and her body. Something that expanded his chest. A place deep inside he hadn't known for certain existed within his soul. Something reckless that made him ditch his better judgment and make love to her while ignoring the danger of that wild rash act. Something that consumed reason and caution and made him crave it all over again.

He'd saved her from drowning, and he'd saved her from drug runners. He hadn't been so lucky. He hadn't been able to save himself from her.

It was definitely best for both of them if he stayed away. She did not belong in his life, and he certainly didn't fit into hers.

One of the good things that came out of Lola's disappearance was all the press it generated. The same day the news of her disappearance was reported, her Lola Undercover line of delicately embroidered merry widows and silk nighties with cut-out roses and matching thongs had sold out and were now on back order. During those four days, catalog sales had topped projections by sixty-three per cent.

Business was thriving. Life was good, and even the *Enquirer* was taking a break from calling her a heavyweight. Now the cut line read, *Buxom Lola Finally Found*. She'd take buxom over heavyweight or Large Lola any day.

The *Enquirer* had generated a story about her supposed elopement with a strange man she'd met in the Crystal Palace Casino. Another tabloid speculated that she'd been in hiding because of a plastic surgery blunder, but Lola's favorite was a report that she'd been abducted by aliens and was living in a small wilderness town in the Northwest.

All of the speculation had given her more press than she could have bought, and they'd had to increase production of the Cleavage Clicker to meet demand.

The Lola Wear, Inc. offices were spread out over a ten-thousand-foot space in one of five old renovated tobacco warehouses in downtown Durham. The once-crumbling district had been transformed into an upscale eclectic blend of retail business, offices, and apartments. Lola had chosen to lease the space not only because it fit her needs, but because it was a part of her history. She had a connection here. A lot of her relatives had worked in the same warehouse, cranking out Chesterfields until the layoffs of the late seventies. Sometimes, on especially humid days, Lola could almost smell the sweet scent of tobacco leaves.

Anxious to get back to her life, she'd returned to her home and to her work the Friday after she'd been plucked from the Atlantic. But by two in the afternoon, she wasn't so sure she should have come in. It had taken the entire morning and part of the afternoon for Lola to be brought up to speed on what had taken place since she'd last checked in the Saturday before. Now she was so tired she just wanted to curl up and take a nap.

Instead, she shut the door to her office, letting everyone know that she wanted some time to herself. Every few minutes someone had popped his or her head in her office with a flimsy excuse or question. She knew they were just reassuring themselves that she was truly alive and back at work. It was sweet, but a bit overwhelming.

She was planning to launch a new line of no-wire seamless bras and panties this spring, and she had the sketches of promotional booths for the spring trade show in Madison Square Garden to look over. The line of microfiber lingerie had been created by the lead designer, Gina, and had huge market potential. The high-tech fabric breathed and moved with the body and had only one drawback. The bras could only support up to a C cup, although the company that held the patent on the material claimed support up to a D. Lola herself had tested the validity of the claim and had been less than satisfied. Lola Wear, Inc. would have to add an underwire in all seamless bras over a C cup.

She sat behind her desk in her brushed leather chair and slipped off her red Manolo Blahnik pumps. She spread her toes in the thick area rug and studied the sketches. But the more she looked at them, the more she got the feeling that something was wrong. Something slightly off that she couldn't quite put her finger on.

Her eyes blurred and she rubbed her temples. She had a headache, and she'd started her period that morning and had cramps. Maybe that was her problem. Whatever the cause, it felt so strange to be in her office once again, almost as if her real life was back on the *Dora Mae*, and that her life here wasn't real. When the facts were the complete opposite. This was her life. This was real. Floating aboard a disabled yacht, surviving a storm at sea, and escaping in a drug runners' boat – that was not her life. The horrible tangle of emotions she had for Max, the terrible feeling that she could not survive without him, was still there, right there on the peripheral of her consciousness, like a flash of light she couldn't quite catch, or a snatch of conversation she couldn't quite hear.

Yet there were times when she awoke and wondered if she'd dreamed of her time with Max. Without him beside her, there was nothing to let her know that the time she'd spent with him was real. Nothing but the twisted branch of lignum vitae still circling her ankle. The purple flowers gone, only a few leaves remained to remind her of the afternoon he'd put it there.

Most of the time she felt confused and suspended in air. Waiting. Waiting to hear from him, and every time the telephone rang, and it wasn't him, she was left crushed and disappointed.

She glanced about her office, at everything she'd chosen in it. Everything from the lavender-and-blue-striped drapes to the English primroses planted in miniature teapots placed at exact angles on the whitewashed sideboard and on the corner of her Louis XIII desk.

She'd chosen the ceiling fan that gently circulated the air about the room and the cream damask Queen Anne chairs. The colors and patterns blended and worked to create a soft feminine space. Everything was exactly as she'd left it, yet everything was different.

Her legs were a nice golden brown from her time searching for rescue vessels aboard the *Dora Mae*, and she hadn't been able to bring herself to wear panty hose, something in the past she'd always viewed as just plain tacky. Her clothes felt different, too. Her red sleeveless dress fit her looser than normal about the hips, and she couldn't stand to wear shoes. But it wasn't her lack of panty hose or the shoes or that she'd lost weight. It was something else.

A light tap rapped against Lola's door just before her office manager, Rose McGraw, peeked around the corner.

'Do you have a minute?'

Lola dropped her hands. 'Of course.'

'I need to get your okay for these purchases,' she said, and placed a manila folder on the desk.

Lola opened the folder and glanced over the list of office supplies. Her first question to herself was, *Why is Rose bothering me with this?* The answer came almost before she finished the question. *Because you like to control all aspects of your business, everything from strategies and goals to paper clips.* She closed the folder before she'd even begun to look it over. She'd hired good competent people, and the business she'd started herself didn't need her so much any more. It had taken getting stranded on the *Dora Mae* to see that she didn't need to control everything.

'This looks fine,' she said. There had been a time when buying supplies had been tight, but those days were long past. She didn't need to hold so tight any more. 'You're a competent woman. That's why I hired you. You don't need me to okay printer ink and copying paper.'

A comical mix of confusion and relief washed across Rose's face. 'Are you sure you don't want to look it over?'

'I'm sure.'

'Are you feeling okay?' Rose asked.

'Yes, thank you.'

'You've been through quite an ordeal.'

Rose didn't know the half of it. No one did. No one knew the real truth. No one but her and Max. The first few days she'd stayed at her parents', she'd confided a bit to them. She told them that Max had been with her on the *Dora Mae*, but she hadn't told them everything. She hadn't mentioned that he'd kidnapped her. She'd left out a lot of the details because they were worried enough without knowing she'd almost died three times in the space of those few days.

The story she'd given to the press had only been a light version of the truth. The day she'd been released from the hospital, she'd stood before reporters and told them she'd been stranded on a tour boat in the Atlantic. Nothing more.

'I'm fine,' she answered Rose, but she wasn't sure that was true, or rather it was true, only a different truth from what she was used to. Which made no sense and meant she'd obviously lost her mind. This time Lola managed a more genuine smile. 'Thank you.'

The heels of Rose's pumps echoed on the hardwood floor as she left the room. She shut the door behind her, and Lola put her elbows on the desk and held her face in her hands.

Even before her release from the hospital in Key West, she'd been visited by two very official-looking gentlemen who'd impressed upon her the need for secrecy. They'd appealed to her patriotism and self-preservation. They could have saved themselves the trip and a lot of breath. She wasn't an idiot. She didn't need the FBI or CIA or anyone to tell her that her life might depend on her keeping the details of where she'd been, what she'd seen, and whom she'd seen it with to herself. She knew she couldn't talk about it to anyone. No one but Max, but she couldn't talk to him because she didn't know how to reach him, and he hadn't contacted her.

Lola blew out a deep breath and reached for her desk calendar. Before she'd left for the Bahamas, she'd written out her schedule for the next four months. The days were filled with meetings and lunches. Some of them important, some of them trivial. None of them life-or-death.

She looked up. Maybe that was it. Maybe her life just felt anticlimactic now. Now that she was no longer in danger and had no need of a big strong man to save her, perhaps her life just felt dull.

At ten past three, Lola grabbed her shoes and matching red clutch and headed for her three-thirty appointment at her favorite day spa/beauty salon. Once there, she got a deep muscle massage and a herbal wrap, her eyebrows plucked, fingernails cut and buffed to a shine, and she had little white and yellow daisies painted on her pink polished toenails.

When her nails were finished, she looked at herself in the mirror and ordered her hair cut – short. She chose highlights the color of butter to be woven throughout, and when she was through, loose blond curls touched the back of her neck and the tops of her ears. The cut made her eyes look huge and dramatic. She ran her fingers through the soft curls and smiled. For some reason, she felt like herself, whoever that was.

The second she drove her BMW into her garage, Baby let out a series of yaps from inside the condo. He jumped up and down when she walked in and followed at her heels as she set several sacks of groceries and a bouquet of peach tulips and white roses on the kitchen counter. Today, Baby was dressed in his BAD TO THE T-BONE tank, and she took him into her arms and scratched between his ears. 'What do you think of the hair?' she asked. He licked her cheek and wiggled with excitement. 'You're such a stylin' dog, I knew you'd like it.'

The telephone rang, and it wasn't until she recognized her mother's voice once more reminding her of the Carlyle family reunion that she realized she'd been hoping it was Max – again. But it wasn't, and her disappointment blossomed into anger.

Her anger stayed with her during the five-minute conversation, and when she finally hung up, she stepped out of her red shoes and carefully slid the lignum vitae off the back of her heel. She wanted nothing more than to forget Max Zamora, and she placed the twisted branch on top of her refrigerator.

She fed Baby his special low-fat food and set his special Wedgwood plate on the hardwood floors she'd had installed shortly after she'd signed the mortgage.

She'd purchased the condo a year ago, paying a little over half a million for it, and all because she and Baby had fallen in love with the backyard. It resembled a small English garden, with a fountain of a nymph on a clamshell, and had plenty of space for the doghouse/castle she'd had built for Baby.

She'd been less impressed with the interior and had it gutted and redecorated with the same vibrant shades of lavender, pink, and green that were found outside. Like her office downtown, it was feminine, a bit fussy, but cozy.

On her way upstairs to change out of her red dress, the front doorbell rang and she retraced her steps. She expected to see her daddy standing there, relief softening his worried brown eyes as he saw for himself that his thirty-year-old little girl really was all right.

She swung the door open and froze, a half-formed welcome for her overprotective father on her lips. It wasn't who she expected, or rather it was who she'd expected days ago. At the sight of Max standing on her welcome mat, funny little butterflies fluttered about in her stomach and just beneath her heart.

His familiar face stared back at her, only clean-shaven and the cut on his forehead was now just a thin red line. The masculine lines of his jaw and cheekbones were more perfect than she remembered, perhaps because the bruises had disappeared and the swelling was gone. But his mouth was just the same. Wide and perfect.

A pair of black Ray-Bans covered his eyes, but she didn't need to see them to know they were the color of the Caribbean. And she didn't need to see them to know he slid his gaze down her body. She felt it clear to the soles of her feet. It touched her here, lingered there, the warmth of it pooling everywhere. He wore a white dress shirt tucked into a pair of chinos. The sleeves of his shirt were rolled up his forearms, and he'd strapped on a silver wristwatch.

In one hand, he held a thin box about the length of a pencil wrapped up in pink paper and ribbon. The last time she'd seen him, he'd given her a brief wave before getting into a car and speeding away.

One corner of his mouth lifted. 'I like your toes,' he said.

Lola didn't know whether to laugh or cry. Throw her arms around him and kiss him all over his handsome face or punch him on the jaw. He hadn't even bothered to call since they'd been back. She'd expected better, especially since they'd made love. Then again, she'd had to cajole him into it, and if that wasn't galling enough, she wasn't certain she wouldn't do it again.

Years of practiced restraint and generations of southern pose and breeding came to her rescue. She leaned a shoulder into the doorjamb, folded her arms beneath her breasts, and raised a brow. 'Are you lost?' she inquired, as cool as a frosty glass of Coca-Cola.

The other side of his mouth slid up. 'No, ma'am. I don't get lost, just a little blown off course occasionally.'

From the rear of the house, Baby darted through the living room and entry, barking as if he were on the hot trail of a cat. He ran between Lola's feet, through the door, and hopped around on his back legs in front of Max.

Lola straightened as Max bent down and picked up her dog with his free hand.

'Hey, B. D.,' he said, and held him up for inspection. 'What in the hell are you wearing?'

'His silk tank.'

'Uh-huh.' He turned him to the side. 'Except for that sissy shirt, he looks pretty good. Any problems since he's been back?'

Lola chose to ignore the disparaging fashion commentary. 'His vet said he has a slight bladder infection and his immune system is a little weak, but he'll be okay as soon as he finishes all his medication.'

Max glanced up from Baby. 'What about you? How are you, Lola?'

Now, there was a question. Her heart beat a little too hard in her chest, and she suddenly felt a little short of breath. She spread her arms wide as if she were perfectly fine. 'I went into the office today.'

'I like your hair.'

'Thank you.' She brushed several loose curls behind her ears and looked behind him at the black Jeep parked by her curb. 'Is that yours?'

He glanced over his shoulder. 'Yeah.'

'I figured you for a guy who'd drive a Hummer.'

His quiet laughter filled the space between them as Baby yapped and licked Max's chin. 'Hey, now, mutt,' he said, and once again held Baby up and away from his face. 'Settle down before you have an accident.'

'He's just excited to see you.'

Max set the dog on the porch, then slowly rose to his full height. He looked down at her through the dark lenses of his sunglasses. 'And what about you, Lolita? Are you excited to see me?'

The sound of her name on his lips cut through her like sunshine on a foggy day, but she didn't know if she'd go so far as to say she was excited. She was too upset with him to be excited. She tilted her head and drawled, 'I'm likely to go mad and bite myself.'

'Can't have that,' he said through a smile. 'Maybe you should invite me inside, just so I can make sure you don't hurt yourself.'

Well, since he was here anyway. She took a step back. 'Come on in.' As she moved to the kitchen, she heard him shut the front door and follow. Baby raced ahead to his dinner, and Lola took a bottle of red wine from one of the grocery bags she'd set on the counter.

'I saw you on television Wednesday,' Max told her as he entered the kitchen.

She shook her head and reached for two glasses. 'I looked horrible.'

'You could never look horrible.'

He was being kind and they both knew it, but when she glanced up at him, he looked serious. He'd taken off his sunglasses and those gorgeous blue eyes of his looked back at her as if he meant every word. 'Wine?'

'No, thank you.'

'That's right. You're a beer drinker.'

'Yes, like your daddy's branch water cousins.' He handed her the thin box he held in his hand. 'I didn't know if you'd want to see me, so I thought I might have to bribe you with this.'

She took the present and shook it. 'Why would you have to bribe me?'

'After everything, I didn't know if you'd be out for my blood.'

She tore away the paper and ribbon and couldn't help her smile. A ridiculous little glow lit up her chest and went a long way to cool her anger. Unlike gifts from other men in her past, it wasn't expensive or lavish. 'Thank you,' she said. 'No man has ever given me a toothbrush before.'

'It's an Oral-B, just like your old one.'

'Yes, I see that.'

'I figured I owed you.'

'Yes, you do. I'll cherish it always.' She set the toothbrush next to the groceries on the counter, then pulled a Waterford vase from the glass-fronted cupboard. 'You know, I probably shouldn't want to see you,' she said as she filled the vase with water. 'But Baby and I still suffer the lingering effects of Stockholm syndrome.'

'Stockholm syndrome? Don't you have to be kidnapped to suffer from Stockholm syndrome?'

She turned off the water and looked over at him, at the light from the ceiling shining in his hair. At him standing in her kitchen filling up her senses with the sight of him and the barely detectable scent of his cologne. She'd been wrong about the bruises. Blue still smudged one corner of his eye. 'Are we going to debate that again?'

Max shook his head and leaned a shoulder into the refrigerator. 'So, how long do you and your dog think you'll be suffering?'

She placed the vase on the counter, then began to arrange the flowers she'd bought at the market. It was so strange having him here, in her condo, talking to her in her own kitchen instead of the galley of the *Dora Mae*. Yet at the same time, it didn't feel strange at all. As if she'd known him all of her life. Further proof that maybe she really was going crazy. 'I can't speak for Baby, and I'm not sure about myself.'

'Through dinner?'

She looked up from a peach tulip. 'Are you buying?'

'Of course. I thought we'd grab a steak and talk about your plans to get your naked photos off the Internet.'

She'd already put her new plan into motion. 'I called a private detective, and I meet with him Monday.'

'Hire me instead.'

He couldn't have surprised her more if he'd told her she should hire him to fly her to the moon. 'Are you offering to help me?'

'Yes.'

'You'd do that for me?'

'Sure.'

If there was anyone who could shut down Sam's site and get those photographs back, she was sure it was Max. Mad Max. The man who ate cobras and rescued drowning dogs. Saved her from drug runners and blew up yachts. Max the hero. She felt her burden lighten and an accompanying little tug at her heart. 'How much?'

'For you, I'll work extremely cheap.'

'How cheap?'

'We'll talk about it over dinner.' He took the tulip from her, touched the end of her nose with the soft petals, then stuck it in the vase. 'I'm starving and I think better after I eat.'

One of the last things Lola felt like doing was putting her shoes back on. 'I really don't feel like going out, but I'll let you cook me dinner here.'

He hooked the top of the sack with his finger and looked inside. 'What ya got in there?'

'A few vegetables. Milk, chicken, hamburger, and some other stuff.'

'A king-sized Snickers,' he said as he pulled out the candy bar.

'Of course.'

He dropped it back into the sack. 'Do you have rice to go with that chicken?'

She pointed to a cupboard above her. The bottom shelf was filled with food staples, the top two shelves with some of the foreign cookbooks she never used. 'Up there.'

Max moved behind her and reached over her head, his

chest brushing her back as he opened the cupboard and pulled out a bright red box. The touch was nothing, just a slight brushing of fabric, but it sent goose bumps up her back.

'Minute Rice?' he said just above the top of her head. 'I can't make arroz con pollo with Minute Rice.'

Lola placed her hands flat on the counter. It would have been the easiest thing in the world to lean back into the solid comfort of his chest. To have him wrap his arms around her and melt into him. To close her eyes and let him take her mind off everything. To once again feel the warmth and strength of being with him.

'What's arroz con pollo?' she asked.

'Chicken, rice, spices, a little tomato sauce, a little beer and peppers.'

Before she could give in to the urge, he put the box back in the cupboard and moved to the end of the counter, putting distance between them. It felt to Lola as if he were trying to put more than physical distance between them. It was as if he were purposely keeping a professional arm's length, and she got that strange feeling again. The feeling of being suspended in air and waiting. 'Can you barbecue?'

'Yeah, I can do that.' He took a package of chicken out of the grocery bag. 'Lola?'

She frowned and stuck a rose in the vase. 'Yes?'

'You never really answered my question.'

She thought she'd answered them all and looked up. 'Which one?'

'How are you doing?' His gaze poured over her face and hair. 'Really?'

'I'm okay.' She turned her attention back to the flowers and selected a beautiful closed tulip. 'Everything is a bit weird, but I'll get back into the swing of things. It was just my first day back to the office, so I wasn't—'

'I'm not asking about your work.' He placed his fingers beneath her chin and brought her gaze back to his. 'I'm asking about *you*.'

His light touch raised the hair at the back of her skull and little tingles tickled the hollow of her throat. She set the tulip down on the counter and looked into his familiar blue eyes. Into the face of the only person who might understand – even what she herself did not understand.

'I don't know how to feel. I know that I'm supposed to be glad I'm home, and I *am* glad. But at the same time, I feel like something has changed and I don't know what it is. My house, my job, my *life*, all look the same, but they . . . I don't know. It all *feels* different. Disorienting. Weird.'

His brows lowered, he dipped his head a little, and peered into her eyes. 'Are you having any sort of flashbacks or difficulty sleeping?'

'No.'

'Any bad dreams?'

'I dreamed I couldn't get Baby out of the animal shelter.'

'Hmm. How about dreams of death or dying?'

She shook her head. 'No.'

'Jumpy?'

'No.'

'Afraid?'

'Not since I've been back.' She shrugged. 'I'm just having trouble concentrating.'

He placed his hands on the tops of her bare arms. 'It sounds like you might be a little shell-shocked. It's not uncommon with people who have gone through something traumatic. Maybe you should see somebody.'

'A psychiatrist?'

'Yeah.'

No, she didn't want to talk to a doctor. She'd been through therapy before. Several years of it, and it had helped her then, but this didn't feel like anything she needed a professional to help her through. She only wanted to talk to Max. Just the touch of his warm palms on her arms made her feel better. Just as it had the night of the storm and the night they'd made love.

'Have you ever seen a psychiatrist?'

He laughed. 'No, I'm afraid of what he'd find.'

'Like maybe you're as crazy as a bullbat?'

'Definitely.' He slid his hands down her arms to her elbows, and again she had to fight the urge to lean into him. 'Have you been eating?'

She'd been having a bit of trouble with that. She'd been having to remind herself to eat, but she'd been there before and knew the routine. It was nothing she couldn't handle. Nothing she couldn't conquer, and nothing she wanted to talk about. 'Why all the questions?'

'I need to know you're okay.' He dropped his hands to his sides, taking the warmth of his touch with him. 'In my life, I've done some things I'm not especially proud of, but I've never screwed up the life of an innocent woman. I did that with you, and I'm sorry.' He looked into her eyes as if he could read her mind. 'I want to make sure you're going to be all right, and I want to help you get those photographs off the Internet. I owe you that much.'

He made it sound as if the only reason he'd come was because he felt responsible for her. As if he were here because he felt he owed some unpaid debt. As if she were just another job he needed to finish before he checked her off his list and eased his conscience. 'You don't owe me anything. I can hire someone to help me with Sam. And you didn't have to drive all the way down here from Alexandria just to make sure I'm okay. You could have called to do that.'

'I'm on my way to Charlotte.'

'Oh.' She'd been a stop on his way to somewhere else, and she was embarrassed at how horribly that hurt.

'I would have come anyway.'

'Why?'

'You and I have been . . . a . . . we . . .' He struggled for the right words, just as he had the afternoon on the *Dora Mae* when he'd tried to clean up his language for her. 'I thought we were getting along better. More friendly, anyway.'

Yes, she'd say making love was *more* friendly. She wondered what he was really getting at. If he was getting at anything at all. With Max, it was hard to tell. 'Are you trying to say you want to be friends?'

He folded his arms across his chest and rested his weight on one foot. 'Friends is good,' he said, although he didn't look particularly happy about the prospect. 'We can do that.'

The man who'd stood on her welcome mat, looking at her as if he were sizing her up for his next meal, had not come for friendship. But the man in front of her now reminded her of the Max who'd told her she could walk around naked and he wouldn't feel a thing. 'Have you ever had a woman friend?'

'No.'

'Are you sure you can handle just being friends with me?'

'Sure.'

She stuck a tulip into the vase and looked at him out of the corner of her eye. 'Because I remember several times when you kissed me and, before I knew it, your sneaky hands had unbuttoned my clothes.'

'I can keep my hands to myself,' he assured her. 'Can you?'

'Not a problem.'

He tilted his head to one side and studied her beneath lowered brows. 'You sure about that?'

'Positive.'

' 'Cause I remember you sticking your hand down my pants and grabbing my balls.'

Lola's mouth fell open and Max smiled. She'd forgotten he could be so rude. 'Well, that's only because I thought I was going to die. Since I don't plan to ever be in that situation again, your . . . your . . . body is safe.' She tilted her chin up. 'Yes, I think we can be just friends,' she finished. But could they? How did she really feel about Max? Confused, mostly. And how did he feel about her? She didn't have a clue.

'I've never had a man friend before. Well, not a friend who wasn't gay anyway, so this could be interesting.' She put the rest of the flowers in the vase and wondered if she and Max could be friends after everything they'd been through. Just friends? Perhaps, but she had her doubts. She didn't know if she could really be friends with a man who had sexually knocked her socks off.

'Okay,' she said, 'why don't you put the chicken on the barbecue in the backyard, and I'll go change?' She moved past him but stopped in the doorway. 'Do we call each other buddy now?'

'No, you call me Max, and I'll call you Lola.'

Smoke bellowed from the electric grill as Max lifted the lid and flipped the chicken. He brushed barbecue sauce on the breasts and thighs and eyed Baby's doghouse, or rather his dog castle. It sat in a covered part of the garden, surrounded by pink and purple plants heavy with blooming flowers, and looked like something fairies would live in. It was light blue and lavender and had little flags on the corner towers. It was about three-by-four feet and had a drawbridge for a door. Next to the inside of the condo, it was about the sissiest thing he'd ever seen.

On the drive south, Max had wondered what Lola's home would look like, and he hadn't been far off. Fluffy pastels the color of cotton candy, doily-covered pillows on the dark purple leather sofa, and lace curtains. White carpeting and flowers on the wallpaper. It was the kind of stuff that could suck out testosterone and shrink a guy's nuts if he wasn't careful.

Max looked down at the dog by his feet and pointed to the castle with a pair of tongs. 'Doesn't that make you feel like a little fairy?'

Baby barked and his eyebrow twitched.

'If you're not careful, you'll be wearing pink toenail polish and little pink bows on your ears.'

'Baby is secure in his masculinity,' Lola said as she walked through the French doors and out onto the brick patio.

Max shook his head and flipped a chicken leg. 'Sugar, your dog has had all of his juice sucked out of him. Probably the reason he has such a big chip on his shoulder.' He glanced over at Lola, but further comment died on his tongue. She moved toward him with a glass of wine in one hand, a bottle of Samuel Adams in the other. She wore a pair of loose-fitting jean shorts that hung low on her hips, and a white T-shirt. But not just any T-shirt. It was so tight it fit her like shrink-wrap, and across her big breasts, in neon green, were the words EAT ME IN ST LOUIS.

'Nice shirt.'

She looked down at herself and smiled. 'A friend of mine opened a restaurant in St Louis a few years ago, and this is what he named it,' she said, and handed Max the beer. 'Charming, isn't it?'

'A boyfriend?'

'No, Chuck is gay. I did a little free advertising for him at the time, and he catered a party for me. The restaurant went out of business, but I still have my EAT ME shirt. It's one of my favorites, but of course, I don't dare wear it anywhere.'

Of course not. Just in front of him. Just to make his eyes ache and his brain seize. Just to make him wonder what she'd do if he tossed her on the ground and took her up on the invitation.

'How's the chicken?' she asked.

Max tore his gaze from her shirt and looked at the grill. This friends thing was not going to work out. He took a big swig of beer before he answered. 'About ten minutes more.'

'I'm almost done with the salad. Do you want to eat inside or out here?'

His grip tightened around the bottle and he wondered if she was torturing him on purpose. 'Outside.'

She smiled up at him, all innocent, as if she didn't know the chaos she created just by breathing. 'I'll set the table out here, then.'

Max watched her walk into the condo, his gaze moving down her back, over her butt, and down her long legs. Coming here was a mistake. He'd known it even as he'd loaded his Jeep that afternoon.

Turning his attention back to the grill, he flipped a thigh. He'd used the trip to Charlotte as an excuse to see her, plain and simple. He didn't have to be anywhere until Monday morning, and in fact, he had a round-trip airline ticket stuck in his suitcase. He'd booked the flight several weeks ago in anticipation of his business in Charlotte. There had been no need for him to make the long drive – except to see Lola. He'd had to see for himself that she was all right. Not knowing had been driving him crazy and keeping him up at night.

Baby dropped a squeaky toy at Max's foot, and he picked it up and tossed it for the dog. It landed in some phlox, and Baby dove into the bushes and disappeared. He glanced about the backyard, at the ivy growing up the high fences and the profusion of roses. At the little bench seat beneath a magnolia, and he asked himself what he was doing here.

She'd been right. He could have called and determined that she was all right. Just as he could have called one of a dozen guys he knew who could take care of her problem with her ex-fiancé. He did not have to involve himself. This was her life, her home, her world, and he did not fit. He would never fit. He was Max Zamora. Black operative, existing within a world he understood. Living the only life he knew. The only life he'd ever wanted.

But even if he had ever wanted more from life, he knew it

was not in the cards for him. Lola was not for him. She was a fantasy, and how long would the fantasy last? Until his beeper went off and he'd have to leave in the middle of the night? Would she be satisfied with a kiss good-bye and no explanation?

No. She wouldn't. No woman would. And how could he begin to imagine a life with her, when the chances were extremely good he would make her a widow before she turned forty? Max was not a fool; he'd been lucky, but in his profession a man's days were numbered. He was not afraid of dying, but he was of leaving someone behind. How could he expect any woman to settle for that kind of life? Especially a woman like Lola who could do so much better.

Lola moved through the French doors and set a white platter next to the grill. 'Max, there's something I've wanted to talk to you about since the night we fled the island,' she said as she moved to the table sitting in the corner of the patio. 'But so much was going on, I didn't get the chance.'

'What's that?' He took a drink of his beer and watched her shorts slide up the backs of her legs as she spread a red-checked tablecloth.

'Did you blow up the *Dora Mae*?'

'Yep.'

'How?' She moved to the other side of the table and looked up at him. 'It was dark and I know you had some sort of rifle. Did you shoot the fuel tanks?'

'No. I'd loaded some dynamite with blasting caps and shoved them inside one of those condoms aboard the yacht, then I taped it in the *O* of *Dora*. When we were far enough away, I shot it with a .50-caliber round. The second explosion was the fuel tanks going up.'

She smiled and tiny creases appeared in the corners of her eyes. 'My hands were shaking so badly, I could hardly hold on to the steering wheel. And it was so dark, how did you manage something like that?'

'Practice,' he said. 'Years of practice.'

She shook her head and threaded matching cloth napkins through little rings that looked like watermelons. 'Well, you are one coolheaded guy. When those engines wouldn't start and those bullets started hitting the water, the blood drained from my head and I about passed out.'

'You looked like you were going to pass out.' He put the chicken on the platter and closed the lid to the barbecue. 'You did great, though.'

'No.' She shook her head and set flatware beside two red plates. 'I was so scared I was numb, but you . . . you weren't scared at all.'

She was wrong. He'd been afraid. He'd been more afraid than he'd ever been in his life. Not for himself, but for her. He moved to the table and set the platter in the center beside two lit candles that looked just like pears. 'I've learned how to deal with fear,' he told her. 'I don't let it interfere with what I need to do.'

'Well, I don't ever want to learn how to deal with fear, because I don't ever want to be shipwrecked and shot at ever again.' Lola walked into the house and returned in less than a minute with salad and a basket of sliced French bread. 'Once we got to the base that night, where did you go?'

Max held out her chair for her as she sat. 'The naval station right next door to the Coast Guard base. Within an hour I was on my way to D.C.'

'Oh.' A little wrinkle appeared on her forehead as she placed a barbecued thigh on her plate. 'I tried to wait up for you.'

He sat next to her and spooned salad into bowls that resembled hollowed-out heads of lettuce. He handed one to her, then spread his napkin in his lap. 'I'm sorry,' he said, just as he had all the other times, with all the other women whom he'd disappointed over the years.

'No, I don't want you to be sorry.' She chose a piece of bread, then handed him the basket. 'You never said you would come and see me, so there is nothing for you to feel sorry about,' she said, but he didn't believe her, not really. She took a big bite of salad and washed it down with her wine. 'What sort of business do you have in Charlotte? Is there some hostage situation that the rest of us don't know about? A spy conference?'

'Nothing that exciting, I'm afraid. Duke Power has hired me to come and check out their security.'

'Why? Is there a terrorist threat?'

'No. They've hired me because that's what I do. I'm a security consultant.'

She stared at him. 'You mean you have a *real* job?'

'I have a real job and a real company.' He reached into his back pocket and pulled out his wallet. 'Here,' he said, and handed her his business card.

As she ate a piece of bread, she studied the card. 'Z Security. Are you the Z?'

'Yes, ma'am.' He dug into his chicken. 'That's me.'

'You have a real job, yet you do all that secret agent stuff on the side? Why?'

'Why, what?'

'Why would any man in his right mind risk his life when he has another job? His own business.' She set the card on the table. 'Why would you choose to get shot at and beat up when you don't have to? Is it the money?'

'No, but the money is very good.'

'Are you insane, then?'

He wiped his mouth with his napkin. 'Probably.'

'Because I don't think normal people like to get shot at, Max.'

'I don't like to get shot at, Lola,' he said, and reached for his beer. 'But it comes with the job.'

'But that's just it, you have a real job. You don't have to be involved with drug lords or blow up yachts.'

'I know I don't have to.' He stabbed another piece of chicken and put it on his plate. He'd had different versions of this conversation before. With other females. Although Lola was the only woman who knew what he did for the government, the only one who knew the dark side of what he did, it always came back to the same basic thing. Why couldn't he just settle down and live a normal life in the suburbs and raise two children and drive a minivan? He had no answer other than the truth. He just wasn't that kind of guy.

He glanced up and caught her staring at him. The sun had begun to set, and light from the candles flickered across the table and onto her plate and hands. A light breeze tousled her new blond curls, and her brows were lowered. 'What?'

'You like it, then. You like the fear biting the back of your neck and stealing your breath. And not knowing if you're going to live another day.'

238

'I like what I do, yes,' he answered.

'No wonder you don't get romantically involved with anyone. I imagine it would be very hard to have a serious relationship with a woman when you have to leave in the middle of the night to save the world. Especially when you don't know when or *if* you'll return home again.' She shook her head and took a big bite of her chicken.

He reached for his beer and watched her over the bottle as he took a drink. He wondered if she was being sarcastic, but she didn't look like it. 'Relationships are hard in my line of work, yes,' he said, which was an understatement. Relationships were impossible.

She nodded. 'Mine, too. It's hard when I don't know if a man wants to be with *me* for me, or just wants to be *seen* with me.' She sat back, her eyes wide. 'Wow, that sounded really conceited, didn't it?'

He laughed as candlelight flickered across her lips. 'Yeah, it did, but I imagine it's true.'

'It's just that if a person gains any sort of notoriety, for any reason, there are people who want to use you to get their face in the media. To get attention. They don't like you, they just want to be seen with you.' She ran her fingers through the top of her hair and combed it back off her forehead. 'Remember John Wayne Bobbitt? His wife cuts off his penis, and all of a sudden he's famous, or infamous, rather, and surrounded by strippers and porno queens. And you know those girls wouldn't have paid him one lick of attention if he hadn't been on all the talk shows getting his fifteen minutes of fame.'

She folded her arms beneath her breasts and was filled with

such indignation, he had to laugh. 'Maybe John Wayne has a good personality. Maybe he's a great guy.'

The corners of her mouth turned downward. 'Max,' she said as if she were talking to someone with half a brain, 'he'd made his wife so mad, she took a knife and . . .' She paused to make a slicing motion with her hand. 'Lopped off his penis.'

'Damn.' He sucked in air between his teeth. 'Can we talk about something else?'

'Oh, sorry,' she said, but she didn't look sorry at all. The corners of her mouth turned up and she flashed him a white smile. 'I guess I got carried away. My other friends and I talk about stuff like that.' She sat forward and took a bite of her salad. 'What do you and your friends talk about?'

Nothing that he would share with her. 'Sports.'

'That's boring. I bet you talk about women.'

He thought it wise not to comment, and instead concentrated on his meal.

'Come on. You can tell me. We're friends, remember?'

He shook his head and swallowed. 'Forget it. If I told you, we wouldn't be friends.'

'That bad, huh?' Instead of letting it go, she dug in like a tick. 'I'll tell you what women talk about if you tell me what men talk about.'

Growing up, there had never been a female influence in Max's home. His father had had several off-and-on relationships, but never anything permanent enough to have an effect on him. The single women Max had known seemed to talk mostly about their work and past relationships, while his friend's wives talked about the agonies of childbirth. And while Max was mildly curious to know what women talked about when men weren't around, he figured this conversation would likely blow up right in his face. 'When was the last time you spoke to your ex-fiancé?' he asked, changing the subject.

She crossed her arms beneath her breasts. 'Let's see. The last time I spoke with him was when I offered him money for those photographs. The last time I saw him was in court a few months ago. He showed up wearing an Armani suit and Gucci shoes. I'm sure he paid for his suit and shoes from the money he's making off me, and I just wanted to wrap my hands around his neck and choke him.'

Max wanted to choke him, too. To pick him up by the throat until his feet dangled off the ground, but not so much because of the suit or shoes or Internet site. No, but because Lola had loved him. Jealousy, thick and potent, churned in his gut. Max had never been jealous over a woman, and he didn't like it. 'Didn't he have money before the Internet site?'

'When I was with him, he did. But he'd invested heavily in tech stocks, and when the market went south, so did his money. Which is the main reason for the site. Sam loves money.' She shrugged. 'And he hates me.'

'Why does he hate you?'

'Because I broke off the engagement three months before the wedding. He couldn't handle it. I think mostly because I was an accessory to him.'

He pushed his empty plate aside. 'Is that why you broke off the engagement?'

'No, I didn't see that part of the relationship until I was out of it. I broke it off because when I decided to get out of modeling, he wasn't supportive of my decision. In fact, he tried

to sabotage my recovery. He wanted the thin bulimic Lola.'
She spread her arms. 'That's not who I am any more.'

Maybe not, but she looked good to him. So good, he had to
concentrate on his next question. 'Where does Sam live?'

'He used to live in Manhattan, but when he lost his money,
he was forced to move. The last I knew, he was living in
Baltimore and working for himself. Now he makes a living day
trading, and running *lolarevealed.com*.' She finished her
chicken and pushed her plate aside. Candlelight flickered
across her face and the front of her shirt. 'So, what's the plan?'

'I don't know yet,' he answered. Roses and magnolia
scented the night breeze, and Max once again wondered what
he was doing sitting in Lola Carlyle's backyard, listening to the
sound of her voice, while her dog jumped and snapped at
fireflies. Usually, on Friday and Saturday night, he played pool
or darts with his buddies in dark bars where the beer was cold
and the bullshit thick. Where you could throw peanut shells
on the floor and fistfights broke out on a routine basis. 'I'll have
to make some inquiries. Find out exactly where he lives and if
he still works out of his home. His schedule. Where he goes
and what he does.'

'He's fanatical about baseball. If he is still in Baltimore,
then I'm sure he has season tickets to the Orioles.'

'I'll make sure.'

'Are we going to spy on him?'

'We?'

'Yes, I'm part of the plan.'

'No, you're not.'

She leaned forward and grabbed his hand. 'Max, I want to
help get him.'

He pulled his hand from hers and closed his fist over the lingering warmth of her touch. What was it about her that made him say yes even as he meant to tell her no? It was more than her beautiful face and body, although sometimes it was hard to get past the packaging to see what lay beneath. But he had seen it many times.

The last night they'd been together, he recognized it for what it was. Lola was a warrior. She was a warrior with big breasts, a nice ass, and soft lips that begged to be kissed, but she was a warrior at heart. She wasn't very good at it, but deep down where it counted, she was a fighter just like Max. 'You have to do exactly as I tell you, Lola. No letting your emotions get involved. The minute you do, we're caught.'

'I won't.' Through the darkness and the flickering candle, she smiled.

'All I want to hear from you is, "Yes Max." '

She frowned but agreed. 'Okay. When do we get started?'

'When I get back from Charlotte.'

'What time do you have to leave tonight?'

'I don't have to meet with the Duke people until Monday morning. I'm going to grab a room somewhere here and head out tomorrow.'

'It's only about a two-and-a-half-hour drive. What are you going to do until Monday morning?'

'Research the area,' he lied. When he'd thrown his suitcase in the Jeep, he hadn't had a plan, just some vague idea of seeing Lola, maybe spending some time with her, making sure she was going to be okay. And yes, he'd hoped to end up naked, face down in her cleavage.

'You could stay here. I have a guest bedroom.'

Okay, so there was probably no hope of rolling around naked in her bed, but that hadn't been the only reason for his trip. He could keep his hands and all other parts to himself. He would behave, but he knew there wasn't a chance in hell that he would actually sleep. 'That sounds great.'

'Good. I haven't had a friend sleep over in years. It'll be fun.'

He reached for his beer and grumbled, 'Depends on your definition of fun.'

'What?'

'Nothing.'

Lola rose and collected the dishes. She moved behind Max's chair, and when he would have stood, she placed a restraining hand on his shoulder. 'I'll get this,' she said, and leaned over him. Her stomach brushed his back, and if he turned his head, his nose would be buried in the side of her breast.

'Let's do something really fun tonight.'

Oh, yeah. He could think of several fun things to do. The first began with eating off her EAT ME shirt. 'Like what?'

'Let's pop popcorn and watch *Pride and Prejudice*. I have the A&E video. It's six hours long, but I'll fast-forward to the good parts.' She patted his shoulder. 'And tomorrow is my family reunion on my daddy's side. I wasn't going to go, but now that you're here, we can go together.' She gave him a little squeeze. 'You're going to love it.'

He closed his eyes. Jesus, she was torturing him on purpose. She was getting back at him for tying her up last week and threatening to drop-kick her dog off the *Dora Mae*.

The Carlyle family reunion was always held on the first Saturday in September, on account of the first Saturday also being the anniversary of the day the Yankees had ridden through North Carolina and burned down the original Carlyle 'place.'

Never mind that the 'place' had been nothing more than a shack, that the original Carlyles slept with their chickens, and that the war had ended in 1865. Carlyle men had fought and died in the War of Northern Aggression, and their genetic memory lived on in the souls of the current generation.

This year the reunion was being held at Lola's parents', much to her mother's dismay. The Carlyle woodpile had its share of bubbas and bubbettes, and Lola's mother didn't especially care for hell-raisers and beer drinkers in her own backyard. She was a little fearful of that particular breed of men. Those who were devoted to hunting and NASCAR, driving around with Lynyrd Skynyrd cranked on their cheap stereos while lobbing empties in the back of their pickups.

And she would never understand women who thought the sun rose and fell on bubba, who fixed Rotel dip and kept the kids quiet so he could enjoy his *Monday Night Football*. Those women whose hair could survive the wind whipping through bubba's truck windows. Although, if her mother was honest, she'd have to admit that her own 'do could outlast an Oklahoma twister.

The Carlyles' half-acre yard was shaded with old maples and towering oaks. Long tables were burdened under the weight of fried chicken and cornbread, ham and redeye gravy, Brunswick stew – minus the squirrel – and various homemade pickles and chutneys. A myriad of salads and casseroles took up one table, while three full tables were devoted strictly to cakes and pies.

As with all families, some relations had not traveled beyond their original countrified roots, while others held corporate jobs and lived in the most elusive neighborhoods in Chapel Hill. Rusted-out Chargers and pickups with Confederate flag stickers in the windows were parked next to shiny new Cadillacs and gleaming SUVs.

All of them had come wearing their best. The women in floral print dresses and skirts, Lola in a simple silk chiffon dress with a square neck and little cap sleeves. The men wore nice pants and dress shirts, but none of them looked as good as the man with his hand resting casually in the small of Lola's back. Max's tailored shirt was the same blue as his eyes and was tucked into a pair of charcoal pants. European cut, they were fuller around his big thighs and long legs and were cuffed at his hand-stitched loafers. Tall and dark and gorgeous, he looked good enough to eat with a spoon, and Lola thought she might like to sink her teeth into him.

Shortly after they arrived, she introduced Max to her

parents, and his gaze turned a bit bemused when her father shook his hand, slapped his shoulder, and thanked him for taking care of his 'little girl.' Her mother couldn't thank him enough for Lola's safe return, and within moments, everyone at the reunion knew that Max Zamora was the hero who'd saved her from certain death aboard the disabled yacht.

'You forgot a few little details about the night we met,' he whispered next to her ear as they headed across the lawn toward Lola's great-aunts, who were waving like the lunatics they were.

'You mean the part about you tying me up with my skirt?'

She felt his smile against her temple when he said, 'That and you shooting a flare gun at me.'

She didn't bother telling him that the flare gun had accidentally discharged. She figured it was best to keep him on his toes.

Lola introduced Max to her great-aunts Bunny and Boo, who sat at the genealogy table, puffing on Viceroys, drinking bourbon and branch, and handing out copies of the Carlyle family tree.

They'd stapled it together with a list of the previous year's dearly departed, along with stories the two had penned from their earliest recollections. In Boo's case, there wasn't much written on account of 'the sugarbetes.' What an insulin deficiency had to do with her memory, no one was quite sure, except that it always got her out of doing anything she didn't want to do.

'Aunts Bunny and Boo, I'd like you to meet my friend, Max Zamora.' She introduced him to the women who were both in their mid-eighties. 'Max, these two ladies are my great-aunts.'

'Ooh, a Latin lover,' Boo announced, because of course, since Lola had modeled lingerie, it stood to reason that she was loose as a slip knot and Max was just naturally her lover. 'Do you speak Spanish?'

'*Sí. Buenos tardes, señoras Bunny and Boo. Como esta usted?*' rolled perfectly off Max's tongue, and the two aunts gazed up at him as if he'd suddenly turned into Julio Iglesias.

Bunny belted back her bourbon. 'You're as handsome as a silver dollar,' she told him, her voice raw and gravelly from her three-pack-a-day habit. She flicked her Bic, fired up a smoke, and got down to business. 'Where are your people from?'

'Texas, mostly, ma'am,' he answered as his hand slid from the small of Lola's back to rest on her hip.

Everyone knew Texas was southern, but it wasn't quite as good as being a North Carolinian. Obviously it was good enough for Aunt Boo. 'I dated me a fella from Texas once,' she said. 'W. J. Poteet. I don't suppose you know the Poteets?'

'No, ma'am.'

'I remember W. J.,' Bunny joined in. 'Isn't he the one who liked silkies?'

'Yep. Couldn't abide no cotton undies. Ever since W. J., I only wear silkies, or I wear nothing at all.'

Lola felt her eyes widen and hoped the horror she felt didn't show on her face. Max simply laughed and gave her hip a gentle squeeze.

'You like silkies?' Boo asked him.

'Well, now—'

'We have to go,' Lola interrupted. 'Max hasn't met Natalie,' she added, referring to her sister.

'It was nice to meet you ladies,' he managed before Lola pulled him away.

'I think my aunts were coming on to you,' she said as they moved past a group of children whacking each other with badminton rackets.

'They're nice ladies.'

'They're crazy. Between them, they've been married eleven times. They have a weakness for tobacco, bourbon, and husbands. And not necessarily their own. It's a wonder they aren't dead of lung cancer, liver failure, or shot by jealous wives,' she said as she found Natalie and her husband standing beside one of the many picnic tables. Natalie held her youngest, two-year-old Ashlee, and Lola immediately took her in her arms.

'Hey, baby girl,' she cooed, and buried her nose in the toddler's neck where she smelled of baby lotion and of her little cotton dress. She glanced around the yard and began to wonder if she was the only cousin over twenty-five who'd never been married. She'd bet she was, and she wondered why. She was attractive, successful, and had all her teeth. Yet she was alone. It hadn't bothered her last year, or even last month. It did now.

She wanted more. More than her work and more than the faithful love of her dog. She wanted a man who loved her and a family of her own. She was thirty, but this wasn't her biological alarm clock signaling the hour. This was different. After the past week, this was knowing firsthand that her life could be taken from her and she hadn't lived it fully.

She glanced up at Max. At his profile and the fine lines in the corners of his blue eyes. Her stomach got all queasy like she was on a roller coaster, and her heart paused in anticipation of one of his smiles. She knew the feelings for what they were. She was falling for Max. She watched his mouth move as he spoke with her sister and Natalie's husband Jerry. He was obviously at ease and comfortable with her family. He told them about his security company, yet he said very little about himself. She was falling for a man who kept his secrets locked up tight.

'Do you want to hold the baby?' she asked him.

He looked at her as if she'd spoken a language he didn't understand. Then he shook his head. 'No.'

She was falling for a man who might not be capable of returning her feelings. A man who preferred to live on the edge, never knowing if the next day might be his last.

The cell phone clipped to his belt rang and he reached for it. 'Excuse me,' he said, and moved a few feet away to take the call.

She was falling in love with a man who answered calls from secret government agencies. Who disappeared, perhaps never to return. A man who preferred living a shadowed life.

'Did you get enough to eat?' Natalie asked, and Lola forced her attention to her sister. That was the thing with having had an eating disorder: the people who loved you watched to make sure you weren't skipping meals or heading off to the bathroom after gorging yourself. No matter that you'd been recovered for years. And she *was* recovered. She'd had a rocky week, but she hadn't let it suck her into the cycle of sickness again. That part of her life was over. 'We haven't eaten yet,' she said.

'Aunt Wynonna brought her pea casserole again this year.'

'Did you eat it?'

'You know how she gets. I had to, but if you don't look at it, it isn't too bad.'

Ashlee held her arms out for Natalie and Lola handed her over. 'I'm going to take your word for it.'

She glanced over her shoulder as Max moved behind her and wrapped his arm around her middle. He pulled her back against his chest, and she might have melted into him if he hadn't said next to her ear, 'I need to talk to you alone for a minute.'

Her lungs constricted, and she closed her eyes. This was it. He was leaving, and she might never see him again. Would she know if was killed? Would anyone think to contact her?

Max took her hand and they moved away from the others to stand behind an oak tree. Leafy shade cut across his forehead and nose while the sun caressed his mouth and chin.

'You have to go, don't you?' Lola began before he could speak. 'You have to go on one of your insane missions and get beat up and shot at.'

He stepped closer. 'I don't get beat up.'

Just shot at. 'You forget how you looked when I first saw you.'

'That was a rare exception.' He placed his hands on her bare shoulders. 'I don't usually get caught and tortured. That was really the only time.'

'Tortured?' She raised a hand to her chest and her voice caught in her throat. 'You were tortured?'

His mouth compressed before he said, 'Roughed up. I was just roughed up a bit.'

Before, when she thought he just got shot at and beaten,

had been bad enough. Now he was telling her he got tortured, too? The backs of her eyes stung, but she refused to give in to her tears. She would not cry for him. Would not cry for a man who took such stupid risks with his life. 'Why do you have to go get roughed up at all? Can't someone else go?'

'You don't understand.'

'Then make me understand,' she pleaded, because he was right. She didn't understand.

'It's what I do, Lola. It's who I am.' He took a deep breath, then continued. 'If I didn't, I don't know who I'd be any more.'

'You'd be someone who lived to see another day.'

'That's not living.'

She looked away from the pull of his blue eyes. What could she say to that? For some reason, he felt he needed to save the world, or at least a bit of it. Which might not be bad if he were Superman and bullets bounced off his chest. He seemed determined to get himself killed, and her problem was that it didn't seem to make a difference to her heart. Now who was insane?

'None of that matters right now. That was my cell phone, not my pager.' With a touch of his finger beneath her chin, he brought her gaze back to his. 'I had a guy I know track down your ex-fiancé. You're right. He lives in Baltimore. I've got his address. When I get back from Charlotte Wednesday, I'll check out the area.'

A light breeze carried the scent of his starched shirt and a hint of his cologne. He wasn't leaving to save the world. And while that knowledge brought a certain relief, she also knew that someday his cell phone would ring or his pager would go off, and he would leave. If he was killed in some foreign country, on some covert operation, would she ever know? Or would she just never see or hear from him again?

'Tonight, we'll brainstorm a plan to get those pictures back for you,' he said, and suddenly she felt small and petty. He was offering to help her. Putting himself at risk to take care of her problem with Sam. Including her when she knew he'd rather work alone, and she owed him more than her anger. Max was who he was. She could not ask him to change to please her; all she could do was protect her heart.

From several car lengths away, Max followed Lola's ex-fiancé to Camden Yards in downtown Baltimore. The Orioles were playing Toronto at seven o'clock in the first of three before they took it on the road. Max watched the man's car pull into Oriole Park, then he backtracked to the simple white house in the suburbs. He parked down the street beneath the shade of an oak, and he reached for his phone and dialed Lola's cell number.

She picked up on the third ring, and just the sound of her hello twisted his gut. 'Where are you?' he asked.

'At work,' she sighed. 'Where are you?'

'About a hundred feet from your ex's. He's at the Orioles game just as you suspected.' Max glanced at his watch. 'I'm going to wait until it gets dark before I venture over there and get a look at his security system. See what toys I'll need to bring day after tomorrow.'

'A gun?'

'I doubt I'll need a gun.'

'Oh,' she said, sounding disappointed as hell.

'Might bring a Taser,' he added to cheer her up.

'Can I zap him with it?'

'Hopefully we're going to be in and out before he returns home.'

'Dang. I kinda wanted to zap him.'

Max laughed. 'You're bloodthirsty. But I'll tell you what. If you're nice, I'll let you look at the weapon.' He lowered his voice and added, 'Maybe even touch it.'

Several moments of silence passed before she spoke again. 'Are we talking about your stun gun, Max?'

'I am.'

'Right,' she said, but she didn't sound convinced. 'So we're still on for Friday?'

'Yep, I'll pick you up at Ronald Reagan at six.' He quickly went over the plan they'd talked about over the weekend, but instead of trying to disguise her appearance to get her in and out of town before anyone could recognize her as they'd discussed, Max had revised the plan that morning. A disguise of any kind would automatically make her appear guilty, and when Sam noticed his hard drives were wiped out and the photographs missing, the first person he'd suspect would be Lola. Since Max would be Lola's alibi, the last thing he wanted was for either of them to seem as if they were hiding.

He figured the police would question Lola – him, too – but they would have no proof to tie either of them to anything. With no evidence, the case would get shoved in a file and just be one of a thousand other unsolved crimes in an area of the country that had its share of crime.

'Are you sure that's the wisest thing to do?' Lola asked after he'd relayed the latest.

'Yep. We're going to hide in plain sight. Let everyone know

you're in town.' He thought of that red dress she'd been wearing the other night when he'd driven to her house. He'd liked that dress. It had been classy and sexy at the same time. Then she'd changed into shorts and that T-shirt and he'd about lost his mind. 'Maybe act like we can't keep our hands off each other. That we're so hot for each other that when we leave a little bar I know, people will naturally assume we're headed straight for bed instead of breaking and entering into your ex-finacé's.'

'Hmm, are you sure that will work?'

'Yeah, I'm sure. So wear something memorable,' he added before he pushed the disconnect. He tossed his cell on the passenger seat and prepared to wait for the first shadows of dusk. He leaned his head back, closed his eyes, and tried to catch a few, but his thoughts of Lola made sleep impossible.

He'd ended up spending the weekend with her, and it seemed as if he'd spent a lot of it right there on her purple sofa, surrounded by all those doily pillows while Baby lay on the top of the couch by Max's head and licked Max's ear.

Lola hadn't made him sit through six hours of *Pride and Prejudice* as threatened, but she had popped in some boring-as-hell Kevin Costner flick about some guy building a boat. Max had fallen asleep, but Lola had woken him in time to catch a part of another movie. One about Mel Gibson reading women's minds and knowing what they really wanted. He'd kind of liked that one, although his favorite Mel movie would always be the first *Lethal Weapon*.

The Carlyle family reunion hadn't been the torture he'd envisioned. In fact, they'd all seemed to be real down-to-earth people, and for some reason they'd liked him. He supposed that had a lot to do with Lola herself, and her stretching the truth so far that he'd come off as a hero who'd saved her from all but certain death.

After they'd eaten at the reunion, he and Lola had returned to her condo and sketched out an op plan. Then he'd gone to bed. Alone. And for the second night, he'd gotten very little sleep. He'd left early the next morning for Charlotte and checked into a hotel just so he could catch some z's before meeting with the Duke people the following day.

He was obsessed with her. When he wasn't with Lola, she wasn't far from his thoughts. He'd been in Charlotte for two days, but it had seemed longer. As he'd met with the heads of the Duke Power Company, she'd played hell with his concentration. That had never happened to him before. He'd always been able to focus on the job before him.

But as he'd toured the Duke facilities, pointing out the weak links in their security, images of her popped into his head. The way she'd appeared in her backyard, the moonlight tangled up in her short hair. Simple things, too: the way she smiled when she walked toward him and held out her hands.

After he'd concluded his business in Charlotte, he'd planned a short stop off in Durham. It was on his way home, and he always had the excuse of going over the final details of their plan with Lola. But in the end he'd driven past every exit. He hadn't given in to his weakness to see her.

Oh, yes, he was definitely obsessed. And there was only one thing to do about it. As soon as he took care of her problem for her, as soon as he handed her those photographs, he had to stay away from her. No more excuses. No more playing hero just to insinuate himself in her life. He had to get out before his thoughts got any crazier, before he was in so deep, there was no way out for him. Before he did something desperate and gave up his life to be with her. Before he changed who he was to fit into her world. Before he changed so completely he didn't know who he was any more. Before he was nothing.

Yeah, once he put her on a plane back to Durham, he'd get back to his own life.

The hard beat of rock and roll poured through the Foggy Bottom, thumped against the walls, and pounded like a heartbeat through the soles of Lola's lavender python sandals. The air inside the Alexandria bar was thick with cigarette smoke and the smell of beer. In the back room, the lamp above the pool table shone down on the green felt like a tent of light as Lola slowly leaned over and hooked a finger over her cue stick. She glanced at the man at the opposite end, awash in smoke and shadow, light bathing the bottom half of him. His arms were folded across the front of his navy polo, muscles bulging. He held his own stick in one hand. The lamp provided just enough light to see that his brows were lowered in a scowl over his blue eyes.

Lola bit the corner of her mouth as butterflies fluttered about in her stomach. She lined up her shot and tried not to think of what she and Max had planned for later that night. Even though she would love to zap Sam with a stun gun, the last thing she needed or wanted was to get caught breaking into his house. Her nerves were frazzled, and Max's black mood made everything worse.

'Six ball in the corner pocket,' she said, even though she doubted anyone could hear her. The balls smacked together, and the six rolled neatly into the pocket by Max's right thigh. Lola rose, pursed her lips as if she were striking a pose for a lipstick ad, and blew across the end of her stick. Just as she'd suspected it would, Max's scowl turned a bit more grim. She picked up her chalk and moved toward him, peanut shells crunching beneath her four-inch heels. 'I told you I'm a shark,' she said as she came to stand beside him. 'Might as well pay up right now.'

'You need to stop bending over the table like that,' he said just loud enough for her to hear. 'Everyone is staring at you.'

'I thought that was our op plan,' she reminded him. 'To attract attention. Hide in plain sight. Remember?'

'We never discussed you flashing your breasts and butt.'

Lola glanced down at herself. At her dark purple bandeau top that showed a bit of cleavage and flirted with her navel and the waistband of her python miniskirt. Under her skirt she wore a purple thong so she wouldn't have a panty line, and beneath the bandeau, her purple bustier kept her breasts in proper order, but the boning dug into her ribs. She'd yet to create a bustier that was completely comfortable. 'You said I was supposed to make sure people noticed me. I think they've noticed.'

'You were supposed to come in and flip your hair like other fashion models.' He turned to her and let out an exasperated breath. 'And that's another thing. What's with the hair? It looks like you just got laid.'

She smiled and ran her fingers through the big loose curls she'd separated with pomade. 'I thought that was the point, too. To make people believe we're together. Am I the only one here who remembers the plan?'

'No, I remember. I just had no idea you'd get off the plane wearing nothing but a little snakeskin.'

'It's Dolce & Gabbana.'

'It looks like a purple python wrapped himself around your ass.' He shook his head. 'I never should have let you out of the car dressed like that.'

'Max,' she sighed, now as exasperated as he, 'you can't tell me what to wear. So don't ever try.'

He glanced behind her toward the bar. 'I'm going to have to bust some heads before we get out of here tonight, and I'm really not looking forward to that.'

Lola looked over her shoulder into the dark interior. At the glowing Miller sign and the string of chili pepper lights hung along the huge mirror behind the bar. Yes, people were staring, but no one looked as if he would approach the two of them. Not with Max glaring as if he were spoiling for a fight.

When she and Max had first entered the bar, several men had shouted out greetings, but he'd ignored them. 'You told me these people are your friends.'

'They are. I earned my BUD/S with some of these guys. That one sitting on the stool wearing a BAD DOG T-shirt is Scooter McLafferty. He was my swim buddy, and a big fan of your *Sports Illustrated* days. I'm sure he'd just love to meet you.'

'Well, are you going to introduce me to him?'

'Hell, no. Music's too loud.'

Lola rolled her eyes toward the ceiling and turned her attention back to the table. The music wasn't too loud. Max was just being contrary. 'Five ball in the side pocket,' she said, and lined up the shot. She took a deep breath, but it did little to calm her nerves. Being so near to Max, hearing his tenebrous growl, seeing his handsome face and blue eyes scowling at her, plus the contemplation of what they had planned for that evening, made her feel flushed and antsy and uncertain all at the same time.

'For the love of Christ,' he swore.

Lola jumped and missed the shot. 'You're not supposed to talk while someone is shooting,' she said as she rose. 'This plan isn't working. People are going to think we hate each other, and when it's time to go, they'll never believe that we're leaving because we can't keep our hands off each other.' She pointed a finger at his chest. 'And it's all your fault. You jerk!'

Max grabbed her wrist and brought the heel of her hand to his mouth. 'You're so beautiful you make me insane.'

Okay, so maybe he wasn't a jerk. 'Now everyone will think you're schizophrenic.'

He shook his head and his lips brushed across her pulse. 'Lovers' spat.'

Warm little tingles danced up her arm. 'We're not lovers.'

He pulled her forward and wrapped her arm around his neck. 'Not yet,' he said through a sudden smile so sensual and carnal and totally masculine, it tweaked her heart and hastened the rhythm. 'But we could be if you're really nice and talk real dirty to me.'

That wasn't going to happen. She didn't talk dirty, at least she didn't think so, and if they were ever going to make love again, which she wasn't sure would be a good idea, he would have to make the first move. Something he hadn't bothered to do since they'd left the island. 'Max, I don't talk dirty,' she told him.

'Yes, you do.'

'No, I was raised to believe that a lady never uses bad language.'

He laughed and grabbed his pool stick. 'Well, honey, I distinctly remember one time you forgot.'

Her hand fell to her side, and she watched him move to the other side of the table and line up his shot. He had to be talking about the one time they'd made love. She didn't remember using profanity, but she supposed it was entirely possible, since she'd been so frightened and hadn't been herself. And if she was completely truthful, Max had set her on fire that night. Now just thinking about it made her feel ready to combust all over again.

Max pointed at the pocket next to Lola's left hip, then took the shot. The eleven ball rolled neatly into the pocket and he looked up at her. As he lined up his next, a smile crooked his mouth and his blue eyes shone in anticipation of beating her.

Lola couldn't let that happen. If there was one person more competitive than Max, it was Lola. She placed her palms flat on the edge of the table and gazed over at him. Back in her modeling days, when she'd needed to seduce from the flat pages of magazines, she'd used certain tricks. One of them had been to think of the best lover she'd ever had. Now, years later, her old trick came back to her. Just like riding a bike, but she didn't have to think long or hard to come up with a candidate. He was staring right back at her. She thought of her hands on his bare body, touching him all over, her fingertips feeling the different textures of his flesh. She licked her lips and her mouth parted on a slight inhaled breath. Her lids lowered and Max missed his shot.

He moved toward her and she straightened. 'Nice shootin', Tex,' she said.

'I was a little distracted by your cleavage and that do-me-on-the-pool-table look you were giving me.'

She laughed and didn't try to deny it. 'It worked.'

'Yeah, too bad I don't have anything that works that good on you.'

He had no idea. Just the thought of him flustered her. 'Max, I'm sorry I called you a jerk.'

'Don't worry about it.' He slid his palm across her shoulder to the back of her neck. 'I was being a jerk.'

'True, but I shouldn't have said it. I'm just very nervous.'

'About later?'

'Yes.'

'It's not too late to call it off.'

'No. I want to do this. I need to.'

'I'll take care of you.' He leaned his cue stick against the table and pulled her closer. 'Nothing will happen.'

She believed him. He had a way of making her feel as if he could protect her from anything. As if by his sheer size and the force of his will, he could make sure nothing bad happened to her. In the past, men who'd wanted to protect her had also made the mistake of thinking she was too stupid to take care of herself. Not Max. He actually listened to what she had to say. During the engineering of tonight's op plan, he'd listened to her ideas and input, even if he'd decided to do the exact opposite. He'd *heard* her, and she was afraid she was falling desperately in love with him, and there was absolutely nothing she could do to stop it. It was like going down one of those dark tunnel slides. There was nothing to grab on to stop herself, and she didn't know what waited for her at the bottom.

No, that was wrong. She did know. Heartache, because she could not live his life or ask him to change for her. She looked into his eyes, which were so familiar to her now. 'I hate being afraid, Max,' she confessed, although at the moment she didn't know which she feared more: getting caught breaking into Sam's house or falling in love with Max.

One corner of his mouth pulled into a mock frown. 'Poor baby, let me give you something else to occupy that gorgeous head,' he said, and lowered his mouth to hers. One of his hands slid to her behind, the other to the back of her head. His fingers tangled in her hair, and he held her against his hard body.

Then, right there in the back pool room of the Foggy Bottom bar, the lamp lighting up the bottom half of them, Max Zamora made love to her mouth. He kissed her as if he couldn't get enough. As if he would eat her up if she let him. And she did let him. She let him cup her backside in his big hand, and she tilted her head to one side and sucked his tongue into her mouth. A low groan sounded deep in his throat and her pool cue dropped to the floor. She ran her hands over as much of him as she could reach, the muscles of his arms and shoulders and back. He was hard strength and edgy passion wrapped around a hidden core of sweetness that made him save dogs he didn't particularly like and wrap purple flowers around her ankle. The combination was intoxicating and irresistible, and she felt herself slide farther down the tunnel to the very brink.

The alarm on Max's watch beeped next to her ear and he pulled back, his lips moist, his eyes heavy. 'It's time to go to work.'

Her mouth felt swollen. Desire beat heavy between her thighs and her knees were weak.

'Are you ready?'

Was she ready to break into Sam's house? Not really, but there was only one answer to give. 'Yes, Max.'

On the forty-minute ride to Baltimore, Lola crawled into the backseat of Max's Jeep and opened her suitcase. She changed into black jeans, a turtleneck, and the pair of Jimmy Choo black ankle boots she'd bought just for the occasion. Max switched on the radio to an oldies station, and 'Sympathy for the Devil' filled the interior. As they sped north on Highway 95, Mick Jagger belted out, 'Pleased to meet you . . . hope you catch my name,' and Lola shoved a black ski hat on her head and covered her hair.

She glanced toward the front, into the rearview mirror and the black shadows of Max's face. The second they'd left the Foggy Bottom, it had been as if he'd turned something off inside himself. His touch had become impersonal. The tone of his voice, strictly business. Lola wasn't so lucky. He still bombarded her senses. The scent of him filled the vehicle, sliding into her lungs and warming her chest. As best she could, she pushed aside her emotions and desire, her fear of tonight and her future with Max, and concentrated on their plan.

She climbed into the front seat and snapped the belt across her lap. She could be a professional. As Max had told her the night he'd agreed to help her, failure was not an option. She would not let him down.

'Are those heels on your boots?' he asked as they took an off-ramp and headed toward the suburbs.

'Yes, but only three inches.'

The golden light from the dash lit up his chest and throat. He said something in Spanish, and she figured it was best not to ask him to translate.

'You told me to wear shoes that had no discernible tread,' she reminded him.

'I also told you to wear shoes you can run in.'

'I can run in these.'

He made a rude scoffing sound and neither of them spoke again until he pulled the Jeep to a side street and parked.

'Sam's house is a block over and down. All the property down that street abuts the woods,' Max said, and looked across at Lola. Within the dark interior, he could just make out the shape of her face and eyes. 'We're going to come in from the back.' He reached behind his seat on the floor and grabbed his rucksack. 'Stay right behind me, just like you did on that island. No talking until we're inside.' He pulled the keys out of the ignition and flipped off the interior lights. 'Once we get to the house, I'll cut the power to the alarm system. That will also cut the power to the rest of the house.'

'Without power, how will you erase the hard drives on Sam's computer?'

'He has a battery backup that will kick on for about half an hour. We'll be in and out in half that time.'

'How do you know all this? Have you already been in his house?'

'Of course. I don't work totally blind.' He opened his door and shut it behind him without a sound. Lola met him by the right front tire, and together they moved from the side of the road. Within seconds, they were swallowed up within lush Maryland woods.

It took a few moments for Max's eyes to fully adjust to the heavy darkness around him. Lola stumbled twice, then she slipped her hand into the back pocket of his Levi's. The warmth of her touch swept across his behind and spread fire to his groin. He wondered if she knew what she was doing to him. If she knew the torture she put him through. If she knew that the sight of her in the airport earlier, walking down the gangway toward him, had nearly sent him to his knees, begging her to let him love her.

He reached behind him and took her hand from his pocket. He held her palm to his and gave it a little squeeze. Removing her hand from his pants was just one more step he would take this night to remove her from his life. No more torture. No more jealousy, yet the prospect of a torture- and jealousy-free life gave him no comfort.

Within five minutes of leaving the Jeep, Max and Lola were in Sam's backyard. They both pulled on leather gloves, then checked the garage to make sure his car was gone. The garage was empty and they moved to the darkest side of the house and crouched by a basement window. Max took a pair of wire cutters from his rucksack and snipped the power. Light from what he knew to be the kitchen shut off, and he stuck the blade of his K-Bar knife between the window's frame and slid the lock free.

The window opened without a sound, and Max entered

first. He helped Lola through, then he took her gloved hand in his. The two of them moved through the pitch-black basement and up the stairs to the kitchen. Moonlight poured in through the back door as he led her to a room down the hall.

'Shut the drapes,' he whispered, and moved to the desk shoved against one wall. The soft hum of a computer filled the thick air and the backup power source blinked from beneath the desk. Once Lola had done as he'd asked, he pulled a flashlight from his rucksack and took a seat. He stuck the end of the flashlight between his teeth, shone the beam on the keyboard, and slid a diskette into the A-drive.

'Max,' Lola whispered as she knelt beside him. She placed her hand on his thigh and was so close, her breath touched his cheek. 'What is that?'

At the DOS prompt, he typed in *wipeout d:*, hit enter, then took the flashlight from his mouth. 'This is your ex-fiancé's worst nightmare. A nuclear bomb. This is the software the Department of Defense uses to erase data from their hard drives. Or, for that matter, the hard drives of any other government, terrorist, or badass little dictator.' He dug around in his sack and pulled out a pin light. 'Look around for those original photographs and negatives. I didn't see the pictures when I was in here the other night. Maybe you'll have better luck,' he said as he handed her the light. He was fairly certain Lola wouldn't find them, either, because Max was sure they were in the safe in the closet. 'And bring me any backup disks you can find.'

While Lola checked the file cabinet, Max erased everything on the remaining drives. As he verified each wipe, and overwrote them so completely there was nothing remaining that could be recovered, he watched her outline and couldn't decide which was sexier, that snakeskin she'd been wearing or her black turtleneck and jeans.

'I didn't find anything but this box of disks,' Lola said as she came to stand by his chair.

'Put them in the sack, then go out in the hall,' he told her as he removed the wipeout disk from the A drive.

'Why?'

'Because I'm going to blow the lock on the safe.' He rose and she grabbed his arm.

'I want to stay here with you.'

'Lola, please go to the hall. I'll join you in a minute.' He thought she might argue, but in the end she turned and the soft tap tap of her boots echoed off the walls as she left the room. Max grabbed his sack and moved to the closet. He swung the doors open and shone his light on a standard two-foot safe. The thing weighed about two hundred and seventy-five pounds and had a garden-variety combination lock.

If Max had more time, he would have listened with an electronic eavesdropping device as the tumblers fell into place one by one. But he didn't have time, and he carefully sprayed a thin line of explosive foam around the circumference of the lock. The sticky foam seeped behind the face of the dial, and he stuck a wad of Semtex explosive, about half the size of a Chiclet, beneath the six. Then he inserted a ten-second nonelectric firing device into the plastique and hauled himself out into the hall. The explosion was louder than he would have liked, but he doubted the neighbors heard anything.

'Come on,' he said to Lola, and didn't wait for the smoke to clear before he re-entered the room. The lock had been blown off, and the door swung easily open. Max shone his light on stacks of cash, boxes of disks, and several stuffed files. Once again he placed his flashlight between his teeth, then riffled through the files. 'Bingo,' he said around the flashlight, and handed Lola a pack of photographs, complete with negatives.

'Thank you, God,' she whispered.

'Max,' he reminded her as he shoved everything from the safe to the rucksack.

'What?'

He took the flashlight from his mouth and rose. 'Thank you, Max.'

'Yes, thank you, Max.'

He shoved the infamous photos in the sack, then zipped it closed. 'You're welcome,' he said, and dropped a kiss on her lips. 'Ready to go?'

'Oh, yeah.'

Again he took her hand, and together they left the same way they'd entered. He even shut the basement window behind them, and once they were in the woods behind Sam's house, he checked his watch.

Thirteen minutes.

They'd done the job with two minutes to spare.

It was over. Finished. Now there were no more excuses.

Lola didn't need him any longer. In twelve hours and forty-seven minutes, he'd put her on a plane back to North Carolina. He'd say good-bye for the last time. He should have felt relieved. A part of him did.

Mostly he just felt the weight of the inevitable, and for a man who liked to set his own rules, the inevitable always pissed him off.

15

'Max, what are we going to do with Sam's money?' Lola asked from the passenger seat of the Jeep. To be on the safe side in case they were stopped, he'd told her to change into the skirt and bandeau she'd worn earlier.

'What do you want to do with it?'

She looked over at him as she pulled off her half boots. 'Give it to charity,' she said, and tossed them in the back. 'Maybe we should shove it in a mail slot at some church.' She unzipped her jeans and they soon joined her boots. She cast a quick glance at Max's profile as she wiggled into her python skirt. Still all business, he kept his gaze on the road.

The hair on the backs of her arms tingled and her heart continued to pound in her chest. Stealing back those photographs had been one big adrenaline rush, and something she never wanted to experience again. Unlike Max, she was not cut out for black missions and undercover operations. For walking in the shadows and blowing up safes. She just wanted to breathe normally again.

A bead of perspiration rolled between her cleavage as she pulled her turtleneck over her head. 'How much was in the safe?' she asked, then drew her arms through the bandeau and adjusted it over her breasts. When he didn't answer, she looked up at him, and through the dark interior of the Jeep, he was finally looking back.

He gave her a quick once-over, starting at the top of her head and sliding to her breasts. But his gaze got stuck on her skirt riding up her thighs, perilously close to the crotch of her thong underwear.

'Not sure,' he answered as if he were distracted and trying to figure out the exact color of her panties. 'Maybe a thousand.'

'He probably made that money off my naked pictures,' she said as she gathered up her shirt. She raised herself to her knees on the seat and turned around. With her python-covered behind in the air, she reached around back and did her best to shove everything in her suitcase. After she'd zipped it closed, she turned back around and pulled down her skirt. Although there wasn't all that much to pull. She slid her feet into her sandals and lowered the visor to look at herself in the lit vanity mirror. 'I think some good should come out of the profit.' She finger-combed her hair and smoothed her eyebrows.

'Are you wearing thong underwear?'

'Yes, were you peeking?'

'Peeking? You make it sound as if you weren't doing your best to show me.'

She flipped the visor back up and looked at him. 'I wasn't trying to show you.' Of course, she hadn't been *not* trying to show him, either.

'You were practically waving them in my face.'

'You're twisted.'

'And you're a tease.'

Neither of them spoke again until after Max had stopped the Jeep in front of an old stone building with ivy growing up one side. Lola watched him pull his leather gloves back on, grab the cash from the rucksack, and run up to the door. He shoved the money through the mail slot, and it wasn't until they were back on the road that she asked him about it.

'What was that place?' She finally broke the silence.

'Light House Urban Ministry,' he answered, and tossed his gloves on the floor by her feet. 'They supply inner-city kids with school supplies and tutoring. They have a great mentoring program.'

He couldn't have surprised her more if he'd told her he was a priest. 'You're a mentor? What do you teach them to do, blow up their school?'

'Very funny, Lola.' He shook his head. 'I just send a little money now and then.'

Probably more than a little, she thought. On the heels of that thought came a question. 'Why don't you want children, Max?'

'Who says I don't?'

'You did, when we were on the *Dora Mae*.'

Street light slid across the lower half of his face as they moved through the city. 'I'd make a lousy father.'

'Why do you say that?'

He shrugged. 'I'm not home enough.'

Lots of fathers weren't home much. 'Weak excuse. What's the real reason?'

'The real reason?' He gave her a quick glance, then returned his gaze to the road. 'I don't want to disappoint a child, and I would. I grew up that way, waiting for promises that usually didn't come true. I used to wait for my dad to come home and take me fishing or to a movie or just to sit and watch the tube, but it never happened. He'd always make grand promises about the things he and I would go do someday, and the weird thing was, I'd always believe him. No matter how many times his promises fell through, and ninety-nine per cent of the time they did, I believed him anyway.'

Now she felt bad that she'd called him twisted and she reached over and laid her hand on his shoulder. 'I'm sorry, Max.'

'Don't be sorry. You asked and I told you. I have hundreds of stories just like it. Each one a bit more pathetic than the last.'

'I think you would make a wonderful father. The best kind. The kind that would make a child feel safe and secure.'

He looked at her hand, then ran his gaze up her arm to her face. 'Are you trying to tell me something?'

It took her a moment to understand what he wanted to know. 'No. No! I told you I have an IUD.'

'Have you had your period yet?'

Well, he certainly wasn't shy, and she pulled her hand away from his shoulder. 'Yes, a few days after I returned.'

'Thank you, Jesus!'

His relief was so obvious, so tangible, that it felt as if he'd slapped her. Right now a baby wasn't a good idea, but he didn't have to behave as if he'd just been given a reprieve. 'You don't have to act like it would be a fate worse than death.' She folded her arms beneath her breasts and looked out the window. At the lush woods and the other cars on the road. She'd been trying to make *him* feel better and he'd made her feel like a loser. 'I'm not that bad.'

'You're not bad at all.'

'Gee, thanks.'

The Jeep pulled into the drive of a brick townhouse, and Max reached above his head and hit the switch to open the garage door. The front of the townhouse was ablaze with light on the first and second floors as if someone were home.

'You still planning to fly out at noon tomorrow?' Max asked as the garage door shut behind them.

'Yep.'

He grabbed her suitcase and his rucksack from the backseat, and she followed him up a set of stairs and through the dark kitchen. Porch light poured through a window above the sink, and she got a vague impression of old wallpaper and worn linoleum before Max led her down a narrow hallway to the front parlor. The velvet maroon drapes were drawn closed and a single bulb burned from the hanging ceiling fixture of heavy pink glass. The wood floors appeared to have been recently refinished, but only half the walls had been stripped of the red and gold brocade paper. The newer blue-and-beige-striped furnishings and oak tables appeared totally out of place in the half-finished room.

'Make yourself comfortable,' Max said as he knelt in front of a woodstove that had been inserted in the original fireplace. Lola chose to kneel beside him as he lit the kindling. Within a few short minutes, he'd built a roaring fire, and together they fed the flames with everything they'd taken from Sam's house.

Max handed Lola the photographs that had caused her so much grief and embarrassment, and one by one, she tossed them in the stove. Each wisp of smoke curling from the pictures and negatives seemed to take ten pounds of weight off her shoulders, turning her burden to ash. She was free. Finally. Thanks to Max.

Max shut the door on the fire raging within the stove. No man had ever risked so much for her, and she wondered how she would ever make it up to him. 'You never did tell me how I can repay you for what you've done for me tonight.'

'Don't worry about it.' He stood and helped her to her feet. 'You don't owe me anything. After tonight, you can finally be rid of me.'

Be rid of him? The thought of never seeing Max pressed in on her chest, and only after his words ripped at her heart did she realize that somewhere between the time he'd kissed her at the Foggy Bottom and now, Lola had fallen completely in love with him. Or perhaps it hadn't happened tonight at all. Maybe she'd fallen in love with him the day she'd opened her front door and he'd been standing on her porch with a toothbrush in his hand.

Or perhaps it had happened even before that. On board the *Dora Mae* when he'd held her during the storm, or the night they'd sped toward Florida in a drug runners' boat and he'd made sure she'd been wrapped in the only blanket. Or maybe she'd fallen in love with him a little bit each of those times until it was so deep it cut clear to her soul.

He wanted them to go their separate ways, but she couldn't imagine not having him in her life. She opened her mouth to tell him what was in her heart, but her throat got clogged up.

Seeing her struggle, he asked, 'What is it, Lola?'

She shook her head as if she didn't know. But she did.

Standing beneath the glow of that tacky pink light fixture, she knew that falling in love wasn't supposed to hurt so much or be this scary. 'Max,' she began, and placed her hand on his chest, 'I don't want to get rid of you. Please, I thought we were friends.'

Air rushed from his lungs as if he'd been hit in the stomach. He looked down at her hand resting on his chest and whispered on a heavy breath, 'Friends? Jesus, are you torturing me on purpose?'

Lola looked up into his face, his black hair and brows. The deep furrow at the bow of his top lip and beautiful mouth. 'Being with me is torture?'

'Yes,' he answered on a strangled groan. She took a step back, but he pulled her against his chest and said next to her ear, 'Being near you is the worst kind of torture. I'm obsessed with you. The smell of your hair and the touch of your skin. When you're near, I'm afraid of losing control.'

It wasn't a declaration of love, but it was so close it fed her hope and warmed her heart. 'I want you to lose control.'

His fingers brushed her bare back above her bandeau. 'Honey, that is one thing you don't want.'

'You're wrong.' She kissed the side of his throat. 'I want you to lose control and take me with you.'

'I don't want to hurt you.' He placed his palm against her cheek and pulled back far enough to gaze into her face. 'I'm afraid that once won't be enough. That I won't be able to stop loving you until one of us is dead.'

She grasped his wrist and kissed the heel of his hand. Then she bit him. 'That sounds good to me, Max,' she whispered.

He took her jaw between his fingers, tilted her face up,

and lowered his mouth to hers. He pressed kiss upon hot kiss on her lips, then his moist tongue invaded her mouth and spread fire through her blood and warmed the pit of her stomach. She combed her fingers through the sides of his hair and held the back of his head. Standing within the partially refurbished parlor of his home, Lola felt the instant he lost control. The kiss turned hotter, wetter, feeding. He kissed her as if she alone were responsible for the breath in his lungs. He released her jaw and his hands moved over her, up and down her body, touching as much of her as he could. Her arms, waist, and back, above and below her bandeau. Her behind and hips. Grasping her through her skirt and finally working the side zipper until it slid down her legs to her feet.

A deep groan rumbled from his chest and he tore his mouth from hers. Their heated gazes locked, their tangled rasping breaths the only sound in the stillness.

His fists grasped the bottom edge of her top and he pulled it over her head. 'This is what you want?' he asked, and dropped it at her feet.

'Yes.' She dug the end of his shirt from his pants and pulled it over his head. His shirt joined hers on the floor and she slid her hands up his bare chest, sliding her fingers through the fine hair. She brushed aside the cool gold chain around his neck, and she placed her open mouth on the side of his throat and sucked. Hard.

'Then you better hang on tight,' he said as he bent at the knees and shoved his shoulder in her stomach. He rose and upended her as if she weighed nothing. 'This could get rough.'

'Max, what are you doing?'

'Taking you to bed before I completely lose it and toss you on the hard floor.'

'I can walk,' she protested as he carried her from the room. First one sandal then the other dropped from her feet.

'Not for much longer.' Then he followed that audacious boast with a kiss on one bare cheek.

She placed her hands in the small of his bare back as he carried her up a set of narrow stairs, past several closed doors, to a room at the back of the townhouse. He kicked the door closed behind them and moonlight poured from the big arched window onto a wrought-iron bed covered in a plaid quilt. He set her on her feet, and she stood before him wearing nothing but her purple bustier bra and thong underwear.

For an endless moment he said nothing. He just looked at her, his gaze going all sleepy with lust as he tossed his wallet and a black pager on the bedside table. Then he unlaced his boots and dropped them on the floor. 'It's a good thing I didn't know what you were wearing beneath your clothes at that bar.' He pushed his pants to his feet, then he shoved them aside with his socks. 'I had a hard enough time keeping my hands from diving down that top and giving Scooter a pleasant memory.'

She looked down at the satin bows on the front of her bustier. 'Do you like this?'

'Yes.' When she glanced back up, he was completely naked and moving toward her. 'I like it, and I like you,' he said, and she shivered as he pulled her against his warm body, his penis hot against her bare belly.

His fingers sank in her hair, angling her head back, and he kissed her mouth, her throat, then her mouth again. In between burning kisses, he murmured the things he wanted to do to her. Things that, if she hadn't wanted him so badly, would have brought a blush to her cheek. Sexually explicit words that left Lola arching her body against his. He shoved his bare thigh between hers and brought her crotch into hard contact with his rigid erection.

'Max,' she whispered as he moved against her, sensation collecting and pooling right there where the tiny barrier of silk was the only thing keeping his hot flesh from hers. His clever fingers worked the hooks on the front of her bustier. One by one he opened them until her breasts popped free. Before the bustier hit the floor, his hands were on her. Touching, possessing, rolling her nipple beneath his palm. His mouth fed her hungry passionate kisses, and he grasped the back of her thigh and urged her leg around his waist. His smooth erection stabbed at the minuscule crotch of her thong, now slick with her desire for him. He slid both hands down her sides to her behind and cupped her bare cheeks, pulling her tight against his body and smashing her breasts against his chest.

With his hands on her behind, he carried her to the bed and fell with her in the center. Max landed on top, pinning her with his weight and desire. He planted two hands by her shoulders and looked down at her, his gaze ravenous with his loss of control. His thin gold medallion swung between them and bumped her chin. She raked her short nails up the corrugated muscles of his belly and sternum, through the short hair on his chest, to his dark flat nipples. His breath left his lungs in a heavy whoosh when she brushed her thumbs across them. 'You have a beautiful body, Max.' She pushed his chest until she had him on his back, staring down into his face. Into his blue eyes, narrowed with passion. His strong jaw was clenched, and his mouth was moist from her kisses. 'Looking at you makes me go all hot and hungry.' She leaned down and her breasts brushed his chest as she licked his earlobe. 'It makes me want to nibble all your parts.'

In a flash, he reversed their position until she was once again on the bottom looking up at him. 'Tonight, I nibble your parts.' He kissed her eyelids, her nose, and her jaw. 'Starting right here.' He kissed the sensitive skin in the hollow of her throat and worked his way down. He slid his hot open mouth down the top of her breast, and he licked the tip with his soft tongue. From deep within his chest, she heard his low groan of need and arousal. He sucked one of her hard pink nipples before he palmed the sides of her breasts and pressed his lips to her cleavage. Then he moved to place wet kisses down her stomach, past her navel, to low on her belly. He reached for the waistband of her thong, pulled it down her legs, and tossed it on the floor.

He made himself comfortable between her thighs, then gave her a big, moist kiss just above her pubic hair. Hot little tingles spread outward across her flesh as if she'd been zapped with a white-hot current. His touch seemed different from the last time they'd made love. More personal. More possessive. She felt it deeper in her heart and in her soul. It swelled within her chest like a balloon, and she felt as if she might float away.

'Max,' she gasped, 'you're killing me.'

'Not yet.' He moved his lips to the inside of her thigh and shoved his hands beneath her behind. He lifted her to his gaze and simply looked at her. She didn't think anyone without a doctor's license had seen so much, and just when his up-close-and-personal scrutiny was beginning to embarrass her, he glanced up into her eyes and drew her to his lips. The immediate suction of his warm mouth stole her breath and she grasped the bedding in her fists.

He kissed between her thighs as he'd kissed the rest of her body, with passion and heat, drawing mindless sounds of pleasure from her throat and from his. She closed her eyes as feverish desire pulsed and beat just below her skin, out of control and curling her toes. Max might not know a lot about romance or relationships. He might not be quite as charming as he thought he was, but he knew a thing or two about how to please a woman.

He caressed her with his tongue, pressing into her slick flesh and drawing her into his mouth for a delicious kiss that nearly sent her over the edge. Repeatedly, he coaxed her to the point of orgasm, only to back off and place his open mouth on the inside of her thigh. Each time he took her higher, further, and just when she was about to come apart, he stopped.

When she opened her eyes, he was above her, reaching for his wallet on the bedside table. As if he'd had plenty of practice he tore open the condom and placed it over the head of his penis. He rolled it down the long shaft to the base, then he looked at her, fire and need and greed in his eyes, and she held up her arms for him. Placing one elbow by her shoulders, he kissed her mouth as he entered her body, plunging so fully, he pushed her up the bed. Again and again he delved into her, hard and deep, and she arched up to meet each thrust of his pumping hips. Her choppy breath matched his, over and over, until climax grabbed her in its hot grasp, and she couldn't breathe at all. Wave after fiery wave rushed across her flesh as the walls of her body gripped and pulsed and tore a raw groan from the depths of his chest.

He cursed in Spanish and English and praised her in the same tortured breath. She clung to him, holding him close as he plunged into her one last time. He collapsed on top of her, and she held him to her. Held him to her heart, which seemed to beat just to love him.

Only after their breathing had returned to normal did Max pull out of her body and leave to use the adjoining bathroom. When he returned, a rectangle of light flooded through the open bathroom doorway and lit up the end of the bed. Max pulled back the quilt and she joined him beneath the sheets. They lay face-to-face and she ran her hand over his wide shoulders and chest. She'd never loved a man the way she loved Max. It felt as if all the love and happiness that had taken place in her life up to that moment had only been a prelude to this. She would not think about tomorrow. She would not ruin what they shared tonight by worrying about an uncertain future.

'Max? Did you mean it when you said you're obsessed with me?'

He rolled onto his back and brought her with him. 'Is this a trick question? Where if I say yes, you accuse me of being a sick bastard, but if I say no, you get hurt and offended?'

She laughed 'No. I just always want us to be honest with each other.'

He lifted a brow. 'How honest?'

'Completely.'

He pushed a curl of her hair behind her ear. 'I've developed an obsession for the little throaty sounds you make when I'm loving you.'

'I make throaty sounds?'

'Yep, and I've a real fondness for the weight of your breasts in my hands.'

'Max?'

'Hmm?'

She wanted to ask him what he felt for *her*, not the throaty sounds and the weight of her breasts, but she didn't have the nerve. She brushed her fingers across the thin gold disk nested in his black chest hair. It was beat-up and she couldn't see the details very well. 'What is this?'

'A St Christopher. It was my father's. He gave it to me when I was eighteen.'

'Why eighteen?'

He grinned. 'He thought I needed protection from wild women.'

'I might not be Catholic, but I do know that St Christopher is the patron saint of travel.' She gently tugged on his chest hair. 'Not of boys who need protection from wild women.'

'Ouch. Jesus, I think you pulled some out.' He held up her hand in front of his face.

'Don't change the subject. Why did your father give it to you when you were eighteen?'

He kissed her knuckles. 'Besides the clothes on his back, when my father left Cuba, it was all he brought with him. He'd obviously arrived safely, so he considered it lucky. When I joined the Navy, he gave it to me.'

'And you've certainly been lucky.'

He laughed against the back of her hand and tiny lines appeared in the corners of his eyes. 'Very lucky.'

'I'm not talking about that kind of luck.'

'I am. Do you know what it's like for a guy like me to be here? With you?'

'No, but I know what it's like for a girl like me to be here with you.'

'Not the same. You're so beautiful, and you could—'

She placed her finger over Max's lips. 'I want you.' She placed her hand to the side of his face and looked into his eyes. She loved him so much, it hurt. It just kept swelling in her chest, getting bigger, until she could no longer hold it in. 'I love you, Max,' she said on a rush of air.

He stilled and looked at her for a long moment before he very clearly said, 'No, you don't.'

Although she hadn't known what she expected him to say, that wasn't it. 'I don't?'

'No. You're just caught up in the afterglow.'

Incredulous at his response, she raised onto one elbow and stared down at him. 'What?'

'It happens after mind-numbing sex. When you're spent and not thinking clearly.'

'Has it happened to you?'

'No.'

She sat up and held the sheet to her breasts. 'Let me see if I have this straight.' She paused for a moment to get her thoughts together because she didn't want to misunderstand him. Just in case he wasn't saying what it sounded like he was saying. 'You think I said I love you because I'm suffering some sort of mind-numbing *afterglow* from your superb lovemaking?'

He sat also and looked at her a bit warily, as if he feared she could go off on him at any second. 'I think that might have something to do with it,' he said as if he'd been here before.

'Does this happen to you a lot?'

'What?'

'Women falling in love with you because . . . because . . .' She paused and pointed toward his middle. 'Because you stun them with your wonder dick?' He was so delusional, and it was her curse that she loved him more than ever. It would be so much easier if she didn't.

He hadn't told her he loved her. Obsessed with her, yes. Loved her, no. Knowing how he truly felt angered her almost as much as it hurt. 'You know,' she said, and threw the covers aside, 'you're extremely insulting. I tell you I love you, and you say I'm confused. Like I'm stupid and don't know the difference between love and sex. I'm thirty years old; I know the difference, Max.' She moved to his closet and threw open the doors. She flipped on the light and told herself she wouldn't cry. She felt raw and her chest ached, but to her vast relief, she discovered she was too angry to cry. And feeling extremely foolish for having blurted out her feelings.

'The least you can do is say thank you,' she continued as she rifled through his things. 'That's what I've always done when I've been in your situation. When someone makes a fool of himself and tells me he loves me and I don't love him back.' She pulled a black silk robe from the hanger and threaded her arms through it. Lola had suffered a broken heart before, but never like this.

'And for your information,' she said as she turned around and tied the belt around her waist, 'I fell in love with you before your performance here tonight. I fell in love with you for a lot of reasons that have nothing to do with sex.'

He was sitting up in bed with his elbows on his raised knees, holding his head in his hands. 'I don't think you're stupid or a fool, Lola,' he said in a voice gone so low she almost didn't hear him.

'Forget it.' She turned to the closed door of the bathroom. 'Forget I said anything. I take it back.' Just as she pulled the door open, he was behind her, slamming it shut.

With one hand planted in front of her face, Max said next to her ear, 'You can't take it back now.'

'Yes, I can.'

'No.' He leaned his big body into her and shoved her up against the door. 'I heard you.' His hot breath brushed her temple. 'You love me, Lola. I won't let you take it back. You can't ever take it back.'

Something in his voice cooled her anger. A deep yearning. An unspoken plea. It was in the depths, if not his words. It was in the hand caressing her hip and sliding around to her stomach.

'Don't leave.' He leaned his forehead against the door next to hers. 'I'm a real bastard, I know, but don't leave, Lola.'

'I wasn't going anywhere. I was just going to get my suitcase.'

'Oh.' He eased away from her and she turned and looked up at him.

'Funny, though. When you thought I was leaving, you sure jumped off the bed fast.'

'Charley horse.'

'Sure. I think you care about me more than you want to

admit. I think it scares the heck out of you. I know it scares the heck out of me.'

'What scares you?'

She looked into his eyes and said, 'That I have fallen in love with you, and there is no future for us. That you burst into my life suddenly only a short time ago. That it's too fast, too soon, and you will leave the same way you came into my life. I'll turn around one day and you'll be gone.'

He shook his head and inhaled deeply through his nose. 'Listen, I don't know what's going to happen tomorrow or the day after or next week. I only know that when I'm not with you, I think about you. I've never wanted a woman the way I want you. And it's not just physical.' He placed his hands on the sides of her face. 'I love the smell of your skin and the tangle of your hair around my fingers. I love your courage and your tenacity.' He pressed his forehead into hers. 'I love being with you, and we're good together. And I think we're only going to get better.'

Yes, but for how long? she wanted to ask. The thought of him alone somewhere, getting beaten and shot at, ate a little hole in her heart, but what could she do about it? She couldn't stop him any more than she could stop loving him.

'I don't want to let you go,' he said just above a whisper. 'I've tried and I can't. The thought of it twists me in a knot.'

'So, don't let me go.'

'It's not that simple.'

'I know.' Then she spoke her biggest fear out loud. 'I've fallen in love with a man who puts himself at risk as if his life is meaningless. But your life means something to me, Max, and I don't know how long my heart can stand it.'

He closed his eyes and breathed deeply through his nose. When he opened them again, his gaze was filled with passion, and he lowered his mouth and kissed her because there was nothing left to say. He was a man who didn't make promises he didn't intend to keep. He tore at the black robe and seemed to touch her all over at once. He worshipped her with his hands and mouth and carried her back to his bed. He made love to her again. This time more desperate than the last, almost frantic, as though, if he kept her in bed, he could keep the world away.

And it worked. Within his arms, and tangled in the sheets that smelled of him, nothing else existed. By the sheer force of his will, he kept reality at bay.

But for how long?

16

Two days after Lola and Max broke into Sam's house, they were questioned separately by the Baltimore police. She'd been back home for less than twenty-four hours when she'd had to place a call to her lawyer and make plans to meet him at the police station in Durham. Max and his attorney had answered the same questions in Alexandria, and since there was no evidence tying either of them to the crime, both had been cleared.

Her problems with Sam were finally over. Taken care of just as Max had predicted. He was her hero, but loving Max was both the best and worst thing that had ever happened to her. And each day that passed, she fell more in love with him. They spent every weekend together, and each hour she lost herself a little more in the pleasure of being with him. The pleasure of his hot mouth and strong hands. The solid wall of his chest against her breasts. Wrapped up in the warmth of Max, she felt safe and protected, as if nothing terrible could ever happen as long as they were together. Each time Max kissed her good-bye, his arms held her a bit tighter than the time before. Closer, as if he were trying to absorb as much of her as possible.

He hadn't told her he loved her. Not yet. It had only been three weeks since she'd blurted out that she loved him, but she was fairly sure that he did love her. No man could look at a woman, and touch her the way Max did, and not be in love. Still, she longed to hear the actual words from his lips.

During the weekdays when they couldn't be together, he telephoned her every night and during the day while she was at work. Sometimes just to ask if she was designing edible underwear.

'Are you hungry, Max?' she would ask.

'Yes,' he always answered. 'I'm hungry for you.'

In a very short amount of time, she grew to live for and fear his calls. The sound of his voice brought a glow to her heart, even as she held her breath. With each call, she half expected that he'd phoned to tell her he was off to Bosnia, Afghanistan, or Iraq. Although, she supposed, he wouldn't tell her where he was headed, just that he was going away.

How Max lived his life was out of her hands. Out of her control. She wouldn't ask him to change for her. She could only hope and pray that he was in so much trouble from the Nassau fiasco that the government had taken away his decoder ring and had crossed his name out of their secret black book.

She knew he carried a pager at all times, and she hoped the government had lost his number. But deep down inside she knew it was only a matter of time before it beeped. There was no doubt in her mind that it would happen.

It just happened sooner than she was ready, over breakfast the weekend she and Baby had driven up to see him. He'd toasted her a muffin and made coffee and they were supposed to spend the day steaming the horrible wallpaper from his kitchen. She'd brought him a photograph of her and Baby, and she'd put it in a silver frame with engraved and enameled dog biscuits. She'd brought her camera so she could take pictures of him, too. So he'd have a picture of them all together. Her, him, and Baby. Like a real family.

She never got the chance. His pager went off during his second cup of coffee as he was feeding Baby a hunk of bran muffin. Across the kitchen table, their gazes met and she knew. This was it.

Wearing nothing but a pair of white boxer briefs, he rose from the table and walked to the office at the back of the townhouse. The second Lola heard the door shut, her stomach turned and she felt sick. Her head pounded and her heart raced. Her chest felt as if it were caving in, and her gaze flitted here and there around the kitchen. On his coffeemaker, blender, and the magnet bottle opener stuck to his refrigerator. On the wallpaper that would not get replaced.

When Max emerged once more, he carried a duffel bag and his rucksack in his hands. A grim line twisted one corner of his lips, confirming her worst nightmare. Even before he opened his mouth, she knew what he was going to say.

'I have to go, and I don't know when I'll be back.'

She picked up Baby, then rose to stand before him. 'When or if, you mean.'

'We'll talk when I return.'

She shook her head. Since the beginning, she'd wondered what she would do when this moment came, and now she knew. 'I can't do this, Max. I love you, but I can't live like this. I won't be waiting for you when you get back.'

'Don't do this, Lola. We can make this work.' He set the bags on the floor and moved toward her.

She put out her free hand and stopped him. 'No,' she said, even as her heart told her to throw her arms around his neck and hang on. To hang on and never let him go. 'I don't understand why you have to go,' she said, her voice surprisingly calm. 'Only that you *are* going. I won't ask you to stay, Max. I won't ask you to stay for me. I would never ask that of you. Besides, I know you wouldn't anyway. And that is something I don't understand. Maybe because I love you. Maybe because you really don't love me,' she said, facing the very real possibility that he didn't love her. That she wanted it so bad, she'd read more into his soulful kisses than he felt. Than he would ever feel. 'Maybe if I were a stronger person, I could watch you walk away, not knowing if you'll get beaten or tortured or shot. If you'll die in a Third World country, all alone. Without anyone to hold your hand.' Her voice caught and she shook her head. 'I'm not that strong, and I won't go through this time after time so that you can go off and feed whatever need you have that makes you risk your life for people you don't know and a government who had you arrested for a crime you didn't commit just so they could get rid of you.'

'Don't leave like this, Lola.' He ran his fingers through the sides of his hair. The agony in his gaze cut clear to her soul. 'We'll talk when I get back. Please stay.'

'Say something to make me stay.'

He took a breath and let it out slowly. His hands fell to his sides. 'I love you.'

Not fair. Those were the three words she'd been waiting to

hear. Now they shredded her heart and left her bleeding inside. She was almost sure he'd never said them to another woman before, but they weren't enough. She felt sorry for him. Sorrier for herself. Sorry for the life they would not have together. 'I deserve more. I deserve a man who loves me enough to want to grow old with me.'

'It's not that simple.'

'Yes, it is, Max.'

'No!' His hands at his sides clenched into fists. 'You're asking me to give up my life for you. You're asking me to turn myself into someone other than who I am.'

'I'm not asking you to do anything. I am telling you I love you too much to watch you kill yourself.'

'I'm not going to die, Lola.'

'Yes, you will. Maybe not this time, but you will. And I won't live my life wondering if today is the day.' She looked one last time into his beautiful blue eyes and forced herself to leave the room, leave Max standing in his kitchen, telling her he loved her, and begging her to stay. Walking away from him was the most difficult thing she'd ever done.

With her dog held to her chest, she walked upstairs into Max's bedroom and grabbed her Louis Vuitton overnight bag. As her breaking heart urged her to stay, to stay because living with him under any circumstances was better than living without him, she quickly dressed. She half expected to hear the sound of Max's footsteps coming up the stairs to tell her he'd changed his mind or to ask her again to stay with him. They never came.

Before she left, she glanced about his bedroom one last time. At the double bed with the plaid spread. On his dresser sat a single photograph of him and his father standing on a crumbling porch, an old rosary hanging off one side. Beside it, the picture she'd given him of her and Baby. It was sad and lonely, and she turned from the room and walked down the stairs. Max was in the parlor, looking out the front window onto the street.

With dry eyes, she gazed one last time at the back of his beloved head and the width of his strong shoulders. If he had turned and looked at her, she wasn't so sure she would have had the strength to walk out the door. 'Good-bye, Max,' she said.

But he didn't look at her, and with her knees quaking and her hands shaking, she walked out of his townhouse. She placed her bag and Baby into the passenger seat of her BMW, then climbed in and fired it up. Without a backward glance, she drove away. She didn't cry until she'd driven half a mile. She didn't fall apart until Fredericksburg.

She had to pull her car off the highway into the parking lot of a Best Western. As tears streamed down her cheeks, she placed her arms on the steering wheel and let go. Big sobs racked her chest and pinched her heart.

Until that moment, she'd never known that love could feel so bad. She'd been in love before, but not like this. Not the kind that felt as if she'd been ripped apart.

Lola didn't know how long she sat in her car before she realized that she couldn't make the four-hour drive home. Her head pounded and her eyes were scratchy yet watery at the same time. She pulled her dark sunglasses out of her purse and headed into the lobby of the Best Western. She and Baby checked into a room near the ice machine, and she turned on the television, hoping for a distraction. But nothing distracted her from the pain of losing Max. If she'd thought he'd still be at home, she might have called and told him she didn't mean it. That she'd changed her mind, that she'd take him under any circumstances for however long it lasted. But she knew he wasn't home, just as she knew that if she didn't get out now, this scene would play out again and again and again.

Baby whined and licked her face as if he, too, mourned the loss of Max. As if he, too, felt lost and empty inside. Lola lay on the bed and wrapped her arms around herself. The horrible emptiness ate a hole in her stomach and she reached for the telephone book, flipped to the yellow pages, and dialed.

'Delivery, please,' she sobbed into the receiver. 'I'd like a medium meat lover's pizza, an order of bread sticks, and a small order of chicken wings. Do you have diet Pepsi?'

Within thirty minutes, she sat at the small table by the closed curtains, gorging on fat, greasy comfort food. She'd eaten two pieces of pizza, three bread sticks, and half the wings when she pushed the food aside. It wasn't helping. Just making her feel worse. An old and familiar voice urged her to purge all that fattening food, but she tuned it out. Baby jumped up on the table and snitched some pepperoni. Lola didn't have the heart to scold him. She understood his pain.

There was nothing to make her feel better. Nothing to take away the pain and emptiness she felt clear to the depths of her soul.

The C-130 banked port and descended to thirty thousand feet. The interior lights shut off, pitching the craft into darkness. The pilot cracked the hatch, and from inside his wet suit, flight cover-alls, life vest, and fifty pounds of gear, Max felt the temperature plunge about a hundred degrees in less than five seconds. He took steady breaths through his oxygen mask and could sense his fog-proof combat goggles frosting over as the C-130's ramp lowered.

Three other men stood within the aircraft with Max. All of them former SEALs, all of them tethered to the bulkhead with yellow safety harnesses. Max had worked with two of the men before, and they both were seasoned warriors. The third, Max had only heard about by reputation. His name was Pete 'Boom-Boom' Jozwiak, and he was supposedly the best demolitions expert around. He was Max's swim buddy on this trip, and Max hoped like hell the kid was as good as his reputation. Five miles below, on an island south of Soledad, a group of anti-American terrorists were holed up with two nuclear warheads they'd appropriated from the former Soviet Union. The U.S. government wanted those warheads out of terrorist hands, yet in order to keep relations with the world on an even keel, they could not do anything overt. They had to retain deniability, and they figured the wisest choice was to send in black operatives. For five days, Max and the other men had met with the powers that be and had come up with a tactical operations plan that would make the warheads disappear. At least that was the objective, and as always, failure was not an option.

The four men pushed the rubber combat raft toward the end of the ramp. A parachute, communications package, and the team's assault gear were lashed to the assault raft, as were the engine and fuel that would take them to the island. Max checked the GPS on his chest to make sure it was working and waited for the green cargo bay lights to blink, indicating that they were over the area and it was time to go. He double-checked the Velcro closures on his assault vest and felt for the Heckler & Koch 9mm semiautomatic pistol strapped to his thigh.

The cargo lights blinked twice and the four men shoved the rubber craft and pushed it out of the C-130. Max unhitched the safety lines, moved to the end of the ramp, and rolled into the night sky. Within seconds, the cells of his parachute opened and he was hauled upward by his harness. Then everything evened out, and he flipped on his GPS, corrected his heading with the steering line, and sat back to enjoy the ride. Or at least he tried to. For the first time since he'd joined the Navy, he didn't feel the thrill of anticipation. The rush of adrenaline that let him know he was alive. For the first time, he wasn't exhilarated by jumping out of an aircraft or pushing his physical and mental capabilities past the limit of endurance. For the first time, the thought of Mission Impossible did not pump him up. For the first time, he just wanted to get the job done and get the hell home.

He rolled his head back and looked up at the stars. Normally, this was the part of the mission he enjoyed the most. The calm before the storm. Not this time. He was too angry to be calm, and he'd been angry since the day he'd told Lola he loved her, and she'd walked out the front door. No, anger was too mild a word. What he felt churned in his gut like acid and filled him with impotent rage. He'd always known that any involvement with her was going to cause him pain. He'd fought against loving her, but in the end, it had been like fighting not to breathe. After a time, it just proved impossible.

I won't ask you to stay, Max. I won't ask you to stay for me, she'd said. *I know you wouldn't anyway.*

In the end she'd done exactly what he'd always known she'd do. She'd wanted him to give up his government work for her. For a life in the suburbs. He'd been right about her, but being right brought him no comfort.

I won't go through this time after time so that you can go off and feed whatever need you have that makes you risk your life for people you don't know and a government who had you arrested for a crime you didn't commit just so they could get rid of you.

At the moment, his need to risk his life for an ungrateful government paled in comparison to his desire to hightail it to North Carolina and rip her heart out, just as she'd ripped out his. Jesus, she was evil. She'd waited until there wasn't a thought in his head that didn't revolve around her, then she'd walked out. She'd waited for him to fall in love with her before she'd plunged the knife deep in his chest. Then she'd waited for him to tell her he loved her to twist it for good measure. Evil and vicious.

Max checked his altimeter and tore off his oxygen mask. He sucked in a breath of fresh air, but it did nothing to clear his troubled mind.

I deserve more. I deserve a man who loves me enough to want to grow old with me.

He'd always thought she deserved more. Always thought she could do a hell of a lot better than him. Again he'd been right, but again it brought him no comfort. The thought of her with another man embedded the knife so deep, he didn't think he'd ever get it out again. Evil, vicious, and vindictive. If she'd wanted to get back at him for the *Dora Mae* fiasco, or anything since, she'd done a good job. Brilliant. The first time in his life he tells a woman he loves her, and she tells him it's not enough. Well, that would teach him to lead with any part of his body but his head.

Twenty-five feet above the surface of the water, he cut away his parachute. He wore enough hardware to drag him to the bottom, and he felt for the pull-tab that would inflate his CQC vest. Then he crossed his arms over his chest and prepared to plunge into the ocean.

For thirty-six years, he'd lived without Lola Carlyle. He would live without her for thirty-six more.

Lola stuck her pencil behind her ear, then massaged the back of her neck. Seated around the conference room table to her right were four members of sales and marketing, along with her lead designer, Gina. To her left sat her creative director, and together they were endeavoring to brainstorm a new name for the seamless line of Lola Wear, Inc.

Barely There was their thirteenth idea of the afternoon. And the thirteenth idea that failed to blow Lola's socks off.

'The new line is as comfortable as a second skin,' she said. 'Soft and smooth and very sexy. We want the advertisement to reflect that. We need something short and snappy. Something that says I'm comfortable but sexy.'

The faces around her looked as tired as she felt. They'd been at it for over three hours and no one was coming up with anything that distantly resembled anything brilliant.

'What if we use something with your name in it, Lola?

Something fun and sexy,' Gina said, and everyone threw out their ideas, no matter how off-the-wall.

'Sheer Lola.'

'Translucent Lola.'

'Sheer Lola, or Sheerly Lola, isn't bad,' she said, 'but I think we can come up with something better. One word, like ... oh ...'

'We could simply call the line Lolita,' someone threw out.

'Yes.'

'I kind of like that.'

'No!' Lola said with more force than she intended. Everyone looked at her and she took the pencil from behind her ear. 'Sorry, I don't like Lolita.' Max had called her Lolita. Just the sound of the name stabbed at her still-bleeding heart. It had been more than a week now since she'd walked out of Max's townhouse, and her heart had not even begun to recover. And it wouldn't, either, if she had to hear the name Lolita, see it in a catalog, or read it on a label.

The door to the conference room opened and Lola's assistant, Wanda, approached her.

'There's a gentleman here to see you,' she whispered in Lola's ear. 'He says he's not leaving until you speak with him.'

Lola figured the gentleman in question could be one of two men. Her ex-fiancé, Sam, whose numerous phone calls she'd been avoiding, or the graphic designer she was to meet shortly.

'Did he give you his name?'

'Sam.'

Her first thought was that he'd found out she'd been involved in the disappearance of those nude photographs. But if that were the case, the police would be here, not Sam. Her second thought was that he'd unearthed something new to use against her, and she figured she had two options: get the confrontation over or have security throw him out. She took a moment to review her choices and decided it was best to hear what he was up to, just in case he had more nasty surprises or something to use to blackmail her. She'd learned long ago not to put anything past Sam. 'Show him to my office,' she said as she stood and excused herself from the meeting.

He can't hurt me any more, she told herself, but apprehension twisted a knot in her stomach as she moved through the hall to her office. Just outside her door, she looked down at her white crocheted dress and pasted on the pleasant smile she'd perfected over the years. No way would Sam see her sweat. When she entered the room, he was waiting inside for her.

'Sam,' she said, leaving the door open just in case. 'What brings you to North Carolina?'

He didn't answer for several prolonged moments. He simply stared at her, his clothes a bit more rumpled than she remembered. Perhaps now that he was no longer making money off of her, he could no longer afford to send his shirts out to be starched. Maybe he'd had to put that crease in his own gabardine trousers. He'd let his blond hair grow past his collar, sort of shaggy and strategically unkempt. At one time she'd thought him handsome and exciting. She'd thought she'd loved him, but what she'd felt for him wasn't even close to what she felt for Max. What she would always feel for Max.

When Sam spoke, he hardly bothered to conceal the anger in his voice. 'You broke into my house,' he said.

'The police don't seem to think so.' She walked past him

and stood behind her desk. To the one place she always felt powerful and in control. When she'd first decided to start her business, he'd been one of the people who'd told her she was making a mistake. Now, surrounded by her success, she felt herself relax a bit. She could take whatever he threw at her. 'I'm sure you know I've been cleared of suspicion.'

'That doesn't mean you didn't hire someone to break into my house, destroy my property, and steal from me.'

She folded her arms beneath her breasts, waiting to learn if he had a bomb to drop on her again. 'Now, that would be sneaky and underhanded. Sort of like you digging up those photographs and creating that website. But I didn't break into your house,' she said, which she figured was a half-truth. Max had done the actual breaking, she'd just happily followed him. 'I have an alibi.'

'Yes, I heard. You were with your new boyfriend.'

Had Max ever been her boyfriend? No, he'd been much more than that. In a short period of time, he'd become her life.

She waited for Sam to say something else. For him to pull the rug out from beneath her. For him to get to the point of his visit, and when he didn't, she asked, 'Is that it?' The silence stretched on and she realized by the look on his face that he had nothing else. No more photographs. Nothing to use to hurt her.

He tried anyway and said the one thing that used to freak her out and send her over the top. 'Your boyfriend must like his women fat.'

Lola's smile turned genuine and she started to laugh. Sam had always wanted her thin and sick and insecure. Needy. She was no longer the person who cared what he thought, and without those naked photographs of her, he didn't even have the power to make her angry. She shook her head. 'He loves my body just the way it is.' She told him the truth. Her trouble with Max had never been about weight or appearance. With just a look, he'd always made her feel desired and beautiful. It had nothing to do with her being weak and needing a man to take care of her. It had everything to do with his need to get himself killed.

When Sam didn't speak, she lifted a brow. 'Did you drive all this way just to accuse me of breaking into your house and to call me names?'

'I just wanted you to know that you haven't fooled me. I know you were involved.'

'Now you've told me.' She pressed a button on her telephone. 'Wanda, call security, please. Our uninvited guest needs to be shown the door.'

'You're kicking me out?'

'Oh, yeah.' She released the button. 'And if you come here again, I'll file harassment charges against you.'

As she watched Sam leave, she felt truly free of him once and for all. If it were only that easy to get over her feelings for Max, she thought as she made her way back to the conference room. But she doubted she would ever fully recover from Max.

She'd just sat down when Wanda interrupted once again.

'There is another gentleman to see you. This one wouldn't give his name,' Wanda continued, 'but he said to tell you that if you don't meet him pronto, he'll commandeer your dog until you do.'

If it was possible, it felt as if her poor broken heart stopped and sped up all at the same time.

'Should I call security?'

As if security could stop Max Zamora.

'No.' She stood and closed the portfolio on the table. 'Let's all take a fifteen-minute break,' she suggested. Then, as she and Wanda walked toward the door once more, she looked at her assistant and said, 'Show Mr Zamora to my office.'

'I'm afraid he's already in your office.'

'Of course he is,' she muttered as she moved down the hall. Once again she paused before the closed door and took a deep breath. Dealing with Max would be a great deal more difficult than dealing with Sam. She placed a hand on her rolling stomach and moved inside. And there he stood. His back to her, as tall and imposing as ever.

He wore a blue broadcloth shirt tucked into a pair of khakis, and the blades of the ceiling fan didn't so much as stir one black hair. At the sound of the door, he turned and his eyes met hers across the room. 'Hello, Lola,' he said. No bruises marred his handsome face, and she let out a relieved breath as his warm gaze slid down her body, then back up again. 'What is that you're wearing? A doily?'

As always, the sound of his voice warmed her from the inside out. He was alive, but he looked tired. And so good she had to fight the urge to run across the room and throw herself in his big arms. She leaned her back against the closed door and held on to the brass knob. 'What are you doing here, Max?'

'Looking for you.'

She didn't want to talk to him, especially alone. She didn't trust him, but more, she didn't trust herself. She looked down at the toes of her sling-back sandals because she couldn't look into his eyes, afraid she'd beg him to love her any way he could. To take whatever he was willing to give, no matter that it tore her up inside. 'You shouldn't have come.'

'I love you.'

She closed her eyes and tried to shut his words out of her heart. 'It doesn't matter.'

'What do you mean, it doesn't matter?' Since she wouldn't come to him, he came to her. 'I have been through too *goddamn* much this past week for you to tell me it doesn't matter. I almost died, and for the first time, I actually gave a shit!' He grasped her shoulders and she looked up at him. The warmth of his palm seeped through the crocheted cotton of her dress and spread hot little tingles down her arms to her elbow. 'I gave a shit because I love you.' She tried to pull away, but his grasp tightened, and he forced her to look into his face. At the anguish in his eyes and the furrow creasing his forehead. 'When you walked out on me, I was so pissed off I could hardly see through the fog. I had a powerful anger burning toward you, but I thought I'd resigned myself to letting you go.' He shook his head. 'But I couldn't. No matter how hard I tried, no matter that when it was time to parachute out of a C-130, I couldn't concentrate on the mission ahead of me. Instead, all I could think about was you and how your leaving felt like a knife in my heart. Then I plunged into the ocean and my CQC vest wouldn't inflate. I fought like hell to get to the surface, but all the gear I was wearing weighed about fifty pounds and I was going nowhere but down instead of up.'

'Why are you telling me this?' she asked, trying and failing to keep the tears from her eyes.

'Because I want you to know. As I was being pulled down, I fought more than I've ever fought to live. I mean, I fought and kicked *hard*. I fought to get back to you. The vest finally inflated after about five seconds, but those five seconds felt like five lifetimes, and it scared the hell out of me. I didn't want to go, Lola. I didn't want to leave you. I want more from life than to end up as fish bait or cannon fodder. I want you.' He brushed the moisture from beneath her eyes and she felt her resolve softening. 'Remember when your parents told everyone at your family reunion that I'd saved you aboard the *Dora Mae*? Well, that's not true. You saved me, Lola. You saved me more than you'll ever know.'

'Okay,' she whispered, loving him and wanting him so much, no matter the pain. 'I'll try.'

'Try what?'

'Try to live your life,' she said, and leaned her head back against the door. This was what she'd been afraid of. Of looking into his face and wanting him no matter what. Of knowing that the pain of watching him live his life was better than the pain of living without him.

Max slid his hands to the sides of her face and stared into her brown eyes. He'd driven like hell to get to her, and before that, battled terrorists like a man possessed. Because he was possessed. A man possessed with the possibilities of a new life. A better life. 'No, Lola. You deserve more than that,' he said. 'I handed over my pager this morning. I don't work for the government any more.'

She simply looked at him. 'What?'

'I've decided I want to live long enough to take care of you for the rest of your life. Bring you soup when you're sick. Comb your gray hair when you get old and can't do it yourself.'

Typical of Lola, she said, 'I can take care of myself.'

'I know, but I want to take care of you. I want to make you happy and see your smiling face across my pillow every morning. I love you, and I think we can have a great life together.'

Her gaze searched his as if she were looking for more. Something he hadn't yet said. 'But Max, if we fight or you grow tired of me, you'll regret giving up something you've loved doing for a long time. You'll miss getting shot at.'

'No one misses getting shot at, honey.' He took her hand and kissed the backs of her fingers. 'I've found something more exciting than blowing things up, something sweeter than an adrenaline rush. Something that is truly worth fighting for.'

'What?'

'A beautiful woman who makes me laugh and feel more alive than I've ever felt in my life.' He swallowed past the lump in his throat and the burning in his chest. 'I've waited my whole life for you, even though I didn't know I was even waiting. You and I are different sides of the same coin, and you make me feel complete.'

'Max,' she cried, and wrapped her arms around his neck. 'I've missed you so much. I love you, even though I've tried very hard not to. You burst into my life, all macho and scary and beat to a bloody stump. You tied me up, kidnapped me, and I fell in love with you anyway.'

He pulled her tight against him, his heart pounding hard in his chest. He didn't know what he'd ever done to deserve Lola Carlyle. Nothing good, he was sure. The backs of his eyes stung, and he buried his nose in her sweet-smelling hair. 'Honey,' he said, 'I didn't kidnap you. You were commandeered. Just like I'm going to commandeer you for the rest of your life.'

She nodded her head and sobbed.

'Don't cry.' He pulled back and looked into her face. 'I love you, and I want to make you happy. I want to make babies with you.'

Her watery eyes widened. 'You want children?'

'Yeah, with you.' He placed both their palms on her flat belly. 'Three, and I was thinking we should have all girls, too, seeing how you have an excessive fondness for pastels.' With his free hand, he plucked at the shoulder of her dress. 'And doilies, but I think we should get married first.'

She bit the bottom of her lip and smiled. 'That's probably wise. I wouldn't want people saying I used the oldest trick in the book to trap you into marrying me.'

He lowered his mouth to hers and kissed her soft and slow, tasting her lips as he'd thought of doing since shortly after she'd stormed out of his townhouse. He'd missed her and wanted to drink her up in one gulp. 'Let's get out of here.'

'Mmm.' Her eyes were slightly out of focus and she nodded. 'Max, let's go home and tell Baby our good news. He'll be so happy.'

'Good God, I forgot about your dog. I guess he'll have to live with us.'

'Max, you know you love Baby.'

He thought about the little wuss. The dog definitely needed a male role model. 'Maybe he's not so bad.'

She smiled and opened the door behind her. 'Take me home.'

As he walked out into the North Carolina sunshine, Lola's hand in his, a smile curved one corner of his lips.

Not so long ago, he'd stood on the burned-out bridge of the *Dora Mae*, thinking himself cursed with a beautiful underwear model and her sissy little dog. He'd always believed Lola Carlyle would be the death of him.

'We never did get around to watching *Pride and Prejudice*,' she said, a teasing glint in her beautiful eyes.

Yeah, she would most definitely be the death of him, but what a way to go.

Pick up a *little black dress* – it's a girl thing.

IT MUST BE LOVE
Rachel Gibson
PB £4.99

Gabriel Breedlove is the sexiest suspect that undercover cop Joe Shanahan has ever had the pleasure of tailing. But when he's assigned to pose as her boyfriend things start to get complicated.

She thinks he's stalking her. He thinks she's a crook. Surely, it must be love?

978 0 7553 3746 0

ONE NIGHT STAND
Julie Cohen
PB £4.99

When popular novelist Estelle Connor finds herself pregnant after an uncharacteristic one-night stand, she enlists the help of sexy neighbour Hugh to help look for the father. But will she find what she really needs?

One of the freshest and funniest voices in romantic fiction

978 0 7553 3483 4

Pick up a *little black dress* – it's a girl thing.

TANGLED UP IN YOU
Rachel Gibson
PB £4.99

Sex, lies and tequila slammers

When Maddie Dupree arrives at Hennessy's bar looking for the truth about her past she doesn't want to be distracted by head-turning, heart-stopping owner Mick Hennessy. Especially as he doesn't know why she's really in town . . .

978 0 7553 3959 4

SPIRIT WILLING, FLESH WEAK
Julie Cohen
PB £4.99

Welcome to the world of Julie Cohen, one of the freshest, funniest voices in romantic fiction!

When fake psychic Rosie meets a gorgeous investigative journalist, she thinks she can trust him not to blow her cover – but is she right?

978 0 7553 3481 0

You can buy any of these other
Little Black Dress titles from your
bookshop or *direct from the publisher*.

FREE P&P AND UK DELIVERY
(Overseas and Ireland £3.50 per book)

The Accidental Virgin	Valerie Frankel	£4.99
Reality Check	A.M. Goldsher	£4.99
True Confessions	Rachel Gibson	£4.99
She Woke Up Married	Suzanne Macpherson	£4.99
This Is How It Happened	Jo Barrett	£4.99
The Art of French Kissing	Kristin Harmel	£4.99
One Night Stand	Julie Cohen	£4.99
The True Naomi Story	A.M. Goldsher	£4.99
Smart Vs Pretty	Valerie Frankel	£4.99
The Chalet Girl	Kate Lace	£4.99
True Love (and Other Lies)	Whitney Gaskell	£4.99
Forget About It	Caprice Crane	£4.99
It Must Be Love	Rachel Gibson	£4.99
Chinese Whispers	Marisa Mackle	£4.99
The Forever Summer	Suzanne Macpherson	£4.99
Wish You Were Here	Phillipa Ashley	£4.99
Falling Out of Fashion	Karen Yampolsky	£4.99
Tangled Up in You	Rachel Gibson	£4.99
Memoirs Are Made of This	Swan Adamson	£4.99
Lost for Words	Lorelei Mathias	£4.99
Confessions of an Air Hostess	Nina Killham	£4.99
The Unfortunate Miss Fortunes	Jennifer Crusie, Eileen Dreyer, Anne Stuart	£4.99

TO ORDER SIMPLY CALL THIS NUMBER

01235 400 414

or visit our website: www.headline.co.uk

Prices and availability subject to change without notice.